DEATH'S DOOR

RICK POLAD

**CALUMET
EDITIONS**
Minneapolis

**CALUMET
EDITIONS**

Minneapolis

Cover and interior design: Gary Lindberg

ISBN: 978-1-960250-45-2

DEATH'S DOOR

RICK POLAD

Door County's Dangerous Passage

The strait linking Lake Michigan and Green Bay, between the northern tip of the peninsula and Washington Island, is known as Death's Door. There are several stories about the origin of the name, but the fact is that the rough waters have claimed many ships over the years. Between 1837 and 1914 twenty-four vessels sank in those waters with another forty nearby. This was a factor in the decision to build a canal connecting Lake Michigan and Green Bay at the south end of the peninsula in 1881. A ship could cut about one hundred miles off of their trip and could avoid the dangerous waters of Death's Door.

Chapter 1
May 8

The drizzle started during the drive to the cemetery. Rosie and I were in the Lincoln behind the hearse, holding hands in the back seat. She had forced me to bring an umbrella, even though I was sure it wouldn't have the nerve to rain. On the way out, I had grabbed Mom's favorite. It was bright red. Rosie had given me a look, but it was exactly the statement I wanted to make. Her dress and my suit were black, as were the hearse and the Lincoln and most of the cars in the procession. That was enough somber.

Chapter 2

Six Days Prior, May 2

Lieutenant Stanley Powolski and I had played gin almost every Wednesday night for the last two years. This night it was raining, and we had decided to order pizza for delivery instead of going out. While we were playing we talked about the upcoming trial.

Six months ago, Stosh had been getting gas late at night at a Shell station ten minutes from his house. He was off duty. He was standing next to the pump and saw a young man walk around from the side of the building and enter the station. A minute later he heard a gunshot and saw the man run out of the building. The lieutenant yelled at the man to stop. The man did stop, long enough to point the gun at Stosh who already had his gun out and put a bullet into the man's leg, causing him to drop the gun and fall to the ground. Stosh grabbed handcuffs from his glove compartment, cuffed the man to the door of the station, and went to check on the clerk. There was only one person in the station, and he was lying in a pool of blood behind the counter. The cash register drawer was open. Stosh bent and checked for a pulse. The man was dead. Stosh used the station phone to call for help.

A patrol car arrived four minutes later and an ambulance two minutes after that. Fifteen minutes later the station apron was full of police cars. The man refused to talk. But he had a wad of bills in his pocket, a little over a hundred dollars, and his driver's license identified him as Montello Williams.

When he got back to the police station, Stosh called Robin Garth, the head of the gang unit, and asked him to come in. Montello Williams was the younger brother of Renald Williams, the leader of the Prophets, the largest gang in Chicago. Montello was charged with robbery and murder. Stosh was the only witness.

A week later the threats started.

***

I had just filled a four-card straight and was trying to decide which card to discard when the doorbell rang. Since it wasn't my doorbell, I kept my attention on the cards. I was still trying to decide when I heard Stosh say, "Yes? What can I do for you?" And then I heard the gunshots. I was surprised when Stosh didn't react and wondered if I had imagined it. I stopped wondering when he fell to the floor.

I knocked over my chair pushing away from the table and ran to the door and knelt next to Stosh. I quickly glanced out into the yard but didn't see anyone. Stosh was fighting to keep his eyes open. The red stain on the front of his shirt was the size of a quarter. I told him I was going to call 911 and to hang on. But as I was standing up, the neighbor from across the street ran up and said he would call. I opened Stosh's shirt and put pressure on the red spot that was growing bigger. His chest barely moved, but he was breathing. With my other hand, I felt his neck for a pulse and didn't find one.

"Hang on, Stosh. They're coming."

He looked at me, barely moving his lips.

"Don't try and talk." I could hear a faint siren. "They'll be here in a minute."

But he was still struggling to tell me something. I bent down with my ear next to his mouth and barely heard him whisper "she." He looked at me for another ten seconds before his eyes closed.

I had no idea what would happen next. But, unless there was a welcoming committee, Stosh was facing it alone. He had no idea I was there. I was holding him supported by my left arm, but I was alone too. It was then that I realized how lonely death was.

He was still taking sporadic shallow breaths, but there was no other sign of life. I wasn't aware of the paramedics driving up... I just knew they were there, removing my hand and calmly taking over. There must have been sirens, but I hadn't heard them since the first faint one. The room was filled with people, but it was like a dream. I was just watching in what seemed like slow motion.

Then most of them were gone, and Stosh wasn't in the doorway. Rosie was holding my hand, and Captain Perez was asking me questions. Two detectives were talking to the man from across the street. And then the only ones left were Rosie and the captain. I had lost track of time, but Rosie told me it was 9:20, more than an hour after it had happened.

Rosie told me the man across the street had heard the gunshots and seen someone running away, but didn't have a description other than the person was short, more than a head shorter than Stosh who was six foot, and wearing a dark sweatshirt with a hood. That put the person at not a lot more than five foot tall. That matched what I had noticed in the doorway, but most of the shooter had been blocked by Stosh. The neighbor hadn't noticed a car. Rosie told me there were policemen all over the neighborhood, and the homes were being canvassed. The captain asked me what had happened.

"We were playing cards. The doorbell rang, and Stosh went to answer it. I heard the shots, but it didn't register right away that they were shots. It was unbelievable. Then he fell to the floor, and I ran to him." I took a deep breath and tried to remember. I looked up at Rosie and shook my head. "All I remember is putting pressure on his chest. After that it's all a blur."

She squeezed my hand.

"How is he? Is he...?"

"He's still alive, Spencer. They're doing all they can."

I nodded.

The captain put his hand on my shoulder and told me to call him directly if I remembered anything else.

The quiet in the house was ominous. Rosie was calmly talking to me, but whatever she was saying didn't register. She drove me to the hospital, and we sat in the waiting room with the captain. Ten minutes later a doctor came out and told us Stosh was going into surgery, and it would be hours before they knew anything. He suggested we go home and get some sleep. At least he was still alive. None of us left.

We were talking about nothing when suddenly I stopped in mid-sentence. I looked at Rosie and said, "He said 'she.'"

"What?"

"He was lying on the floor trying to say something. I bent down and barely heard him whisper 'she.'"

"Are you sure?" asked the captain.

"Yes."

"Did you see the person?"

I shook my head. "I didn't. Stosh was blocking the doorway."

"That's all he said?"

"Yes."

"Okay. He could have been trying to say anything, but I'll get out the word that maybe it was a woman."

The captain left.

"What do you think he was trying to say, Spencer?" Rosie asked.

I thought for a minute and then wondered if I should say what I was thinking. I knew Rosie wouldn't think I was crazy.

"Sitting there holding him, I was thinking about death… about what happens. Maybe he was seeing Francine. Maybe she was waiting for him."

Rosie put her arms around me and didn't say anything. We'd never know. The last thought that I remember was that the Prophets didn't have any women in their gang. Francine seemed like a good explanation.

Rosie and I fell asleep on the couch in the waiting room. It was a little after three in the morning when I felt a touch on my shoulder.

"Spencer."

I stirred, opened my eyes, and saw the doctor and Captain Perez.
"Come with us," the captain said.
"Rosie?"
"She'll be okay here for a few minutes."

***

I returned twenty minutes later and woke her up with a gentle shake of her shoulder. I put my arms around her and let her cry. After ten minutes, I about had to carry her to the car. We went back to my place and fell asleep in each other's arms.

Chapter 3
May 8

T he priest was saying something about our souls and reuniting with our Heavenly Father. He had an altar boy holding his black umbrella. I was holding the red umbrella over Rosie and me and thinking about my folks and the funeral I had missed. I was all alone in the back country of Yellowstone when the ranger found me. That was a week after they died. I had felt all alone with Stosh too. No matter what, death was a lonely thing.

The rain was still a steady drizzle, but was a bit less under the large oak tree except for large plops on the umbrella when a leaf released its collection of water.

The service had been with a closed casket, and the procession to the cemetery consisted of only twenty-one cars. Normally a slain officer would have a procession of over a hundred cars from many departments and municipalities showing their respect, but Stosh had left instructions in his will that limited the number. The instruction wasn't specific, but the intent was clear. He believed police forces could best show their respect by doing their jobs.

There were about forty people around the gravesite. Chief Graff, Captain Perez, and I had spoken at the service. The only one scheduled to talk at the graveside was the priest, but Rosie wanted to speak. When the priest finished, we joined him in the Lord's Prayer, and he nodded to Rosie.

As she started toward the casket I started to follow her with the umbrella, but she shook her head and walked alone. She gently touched the casket with the fingers of her right hand, bowed her head, paused, and said, "Farewell, my friend. I love you."

I couldn't tell her tears from the raindrops. But I knew there were tears… just as many as anyone else's. We watched in silence as the casket was lowered into the ground, and I silently echoed her sentiment.

Stosh had also specified that he'd like everyone to get together for a party, but not for a month or so after the funeral. He didn't want it to be spoiled by the sorrow of the day.

Chapter 4
May 3

Several years ago, shortly after my folks died, Stosh had given me an envelope that he told me to open after he was gone. I had given that some thought and, curiosity getting the best of me, had opened it the night of the shooting. It held one piece of paper and a handwritten note that said to look in a fireproof case under his bed. It was late morning and I was hungry, but curiosity trumped lunch.

I passed two parked patrol cars a block up from Stosh's house. There was a patrol car and an unmarked car in front of the house, the front yard was cordoned off with yellow tape, and a crime scene placard was in the front window. I parked on the opposite side of the street and said hello to the two patrolmen, one of whom I knew.

"They still going over the house, Danny?"

"Yup. The team was all over the yard this morning, and we have officers up the block talking to neighbors."

"Anything?"

He shook his head. "Not that I know of. Whoever it was has disappeared. Do you have any ideas, Spencer?"

"Well, there's a gang leader that doesn't have to worry about the witness."

Danny looked angry. "I hope they still get the bastard."

"They still have the deposition, but it's always good to have a real person."

He nodded. "See you, Spencer."

"See you guys."

***

I had a brief chat with the evidence techs in the house. They hadn't found anything useful other than possible footprints in the garden next to the walk, but they weren't hopeful. I walked down the hall to the back bedroom, opened the door, and stood looking around the room. I knew Stosh hadn't slept in it since Francine had died four years ago. That added to the sadness.

I knelt, raised the bedspread, and peered under the bed. There were several boxes and one substantial container. There wasn't a key in the envelope so I wondered how I was going to get it open. I didn't have to wonder long… it wasn't locked. I placed it on the bed and sat next to it.

It contained five business-sized envelopes. One was fatter than the rest. I expected it to be full of hundred dollar bills. I opened that one first… it wasn't. It contained all the documents that were important to Stosh's life… his birth certificate, born in 1923 and his middle name was Gregory, his service discharge papers, the house mortgage papers, a copy of his driver's license, and Francine's birth and death certificates.

A second envelope was full of some type of foreign currency. My guess was Polish. I had no idea what the values were and assumed they were more sentimental than valuable.

The third had three letters from Francine. I took a deep breath and remembered how wonderful those two were together. It was as if they had been created for the sole purpose of spending their lives together, and there was no question that would happen. I didn't read the letters.

The contents of the next envelope took a bit of studying to figure out, and even after going over them several times I still wasn't sure.

There was a letter from the From Us to You Adoption Agency, in Green Bay, Wisconsin. It was dated March 8, 1975, and congratulated Stanley and Francine Powolski on the successful adoption of a baby girl named Janet. It listed several other details and ended with a paragraph saying that a Mrs. Peters would be in touch within the month to make arrangements. Stosh had never said anything about an adopted baby.

Also in the envelope was a canceled check, number 207, for six thousand dollars, made out to the agency and dated March 12, 1975. The check was clipped to three sheets of yellow-lined paper on which was written a list of check numbers and dates and amounts. The first check was number 212 and was dated June 1, 1975. There were nineteen checks, made out to Single Mother Outreach, dated every six months for ten years, with the last check dated January 1, 1985. All but four were for five hundred dollars. Those four were for varying amounts up to a thousand dollars. I went through it all several times and each time was just as confused as the first.

The Powolskis had evidently been trying to adopt a baby and had been successful at that, at least on paper. They had written checks for eight thousand dollars, but they had obviously never received the baby. That much was clear. The other checks were a mystery.

As I sat there thinking, I remembered the last envelope. Inside was one folded letter on letterhead from the From Us to You Adoption Agency. It was addressed to the Powolskis and basically thanked them for their generous offer. It didn't say what the generous offer was. It was dated May 6, 1975. I sat there for a few minutes trying to make sense of it all. I couldn't, but then none of the problems that landed on my desk made sense at first. It was only after shaking the trees that the pieces of the puzzles fit together. That took time and a starting point.

The obvious starting point would have been Stosh, but he was unavailable. The next candidate was the adoption agency. I asked one of the detectives if I could use the phone in the kitchen. He didn't see why not. I called the office, gave the name and address to Carol, and asked her to find out if they were still in business and whatever else she could discover. I also told her to see what she could find out about Single Mother Outreach and told her I'd be back in about an hour.

***

Watson looked up at me as I came in the back door. He had stopped growling at me after he moved in and learned who was paying for the food. My purchase of the office building had been finalized, and Carol and Billy had moved in a few months ago, giving Watson a new home. Comfortable in his office bed, and no longer being fed by me, Watson wasn't giving me any more than a look for a greeting. Billy was a different story. They were pals.

"Good morning, Spencer."

"Good morning, Carol."

She got up and met me in the hall with outstretched arms and gave me a hug. I returned it.

"That's a nice way to start the morning, but what did I do to deserve it?"

"I'm so sorry you lost your friend, Spencer. I can't imagine how you feel."

I put my arm around her shoulder and said, "Yes, you can. You lost your husband. Unfortunately, we both can imagine."

Her eyes filled with tears, and she looked up at me. "Thanks for everything you've done for me and Billy, Spencer. We're so lucky."

I smiled. "Not as lucky as I, Carol. You two have done so much for me. I love you both."

We hugged again, and then I pushed her away with a smile.

She asked if the police were getting anywhere with the shooting.

I shrugged. "Early yet. They've interviewed all the gang connections. Everyone has an alibi. Renald Williams, the leader of the Prophets, is saying his brother would get off anyway so why would they shoot anybody?"

"Yeah, why would a gang thug shoot anyone? Do you think they'll find him?"

"They usually do, especially with this many people working on it. Someone will make a mistake somewhere along the way."

"I hope so, Spencer."

"Me too."

"Are you going to do anything?"

I shrugged. "Not much to do that the cops aren't already doing. But I have some thoughts. In the meantime, anything on the agency?"

She handed me a sheet of paper with her notes. "Yes, they are still in business. They've been around for fifteen years and do exactly what their name implies. The lady I talked to, a Miss Meek, said they specialize in placing babies with couples who have had trouble with the system elsewhere. Evidently, they have some kind of magic that cuts through the red tape. She made it sound like they were my dream come true."

"Well, nothing wrong with that. What did you tell her?"

She sat at her desk and I sat on the corner. "Nothing specific. After hearing her pitch, I told her exactly what she was pitching. My husband and I were having trouble. We were on lists but weren't getting anywhere and really wanted a baby."

I sat down in front of her desk. "Good. What did she say?"

"She said we should come in for an interview. I told her I'd talk to my husband. She asked for my name, and I told her I didn't feel comfortable telling her until I talked to him. She said she understood and hoped to hear from me soon. She reassured me that I had called the right place to *solve my problem*."

"Interesting. Nice work. I wonder if they have an office in Chicago."

"I asked. They don't. Green Bay is it."

I shrugged. "Well, that's not all bad. It's only an hour from Aunt Rose's cherry pie. I've been looking for an excuse to head up to Door County."

"You don't need an excuse."

We both laughed.

"What about Single Mother Outreach?" I asked.

"They're also in Green Bay. I called and got an answering machine. I didn't leave a message. The address is a PO box."

"So why am I calling an adoption agency in Wisconsin?" she asked. "Or is this something else I'm better off not knowing about?"

I laughed again. "Not everything is so clandestine." I sat in the client's chair and explained the documents I had found in Stosh's bedroom.

She looked just as confused as I was. "That's all very odd, Spencer."

I agreed.

There was a screech of brakes and a crash, but not a very loud one. We both got up and walked to the window. A red Buick had run into the rear end of a cab. The cab driver was out and yelling. The driver of the Buick, a middle-aged woman, was bending over the bumper. I asked Carol to call the police and tell them it didn't look like anyone was hurt and walked out to referee, but it didn't get to the point of battle... the cab driver was satisfied with angry words. A squad car pulled up five minutes later, and they sorted it all out.

Carol handed me a cup of coffee when I came back into the office. "So, do we want a boy or a girl?"

I laughed and played along. "Let's throw darts for it. Even number, it's a boy... odd it's a girl."

She tilted her head sideways and looked at me out of the corner of her eye. "If you need a Mrs. Manning at some point, I'm available."

"Okay, if I ever need a wife for a day, I'll keep you in mind." I smiled and headed back to my office where I could feel helpless in peace and quiet. I had of course offered to help in any way I could. Captain Perez had thanked me and said he'd keep me informed. But there wasn't much to be informed about. They had to find a hole in the gang alibis or get someone to talk. It looked pretty simple, but I couldn't help thinking not everything was as simple as it looked.

Chapter 5
Present Day

The desk sergeant nodded at me as I walked into the station. I nodded back and climbed the stairs heading for the captain's office at the end of the second-floor hall. Halfway down the hall I leaned into Stosh's office and said hello to Kate. She got up and gave me a hug… or maybe I gave her one. Over her shoulder I looked at the black ribbon on the jamb of the inner-office door. Stosh's office was very empty.

Kate moved away from me and asked, "Anything I can do for you, Spencer?"

"No thanks, Kate. Just going to have a chat with the captain. Anything I can do for *you*?"

She managed a tiny smile. "Despite the obvious miracle… no."

"Well, if I figure that out I'll let you know."

She nodded.

Captain Perez came around the corner and waved at me to follow him. His secretary wasn't at her desk. He gestured to a cushioned chair, sat, and offered me some water. I declined, and he poured himself a glass.

"Anything new, Captain?"

"Nothing. But we're working on several fronts. There are two gangers we're trying to find. One is a cousin of Williams. We have reason to believe he's been a courier between Renald and Stateville."

"I'd like to do something… feel pretty helpless."

He nodded. "We all do. Find something to do to take your mind off of it. I think Rosie has some time coming. Why don't you two head up to Door County?"

"Aunt Rose suggested the same thing. Maybe I will. There's something I'd like to look into up that way."

"I have your car phone. I'll call if anything breaks loose. Until it does, just try and relax."

"Will do. Appreciate it, Captain."

He lifted his glass as I stood.

***

Rosie and another detective were standing in the hall outside Stosh's office. I walked up behind her and put a hand on her shoulder. She turned her head and smiled at me. The other detective excused himself.

"Hi, Spencer. What're you doing here?"

"Brief chat with the captain."

"Anything in particular?"

"Just wanted to see if I could help. He said he'd call if he needed me."

"I've gotta review this file. Walk with me."

As we headed to the other end of the hall I said, "He suggested I find something to take my mind off of all of this and said you might have some time coming. Can I interest you in a trip up to Door County?"

"You might. When do you want to go?"

We stopped at the detectives' room. "If you're interested, you tell me. I'm flexible. And there's something up that way I want to look into."

"Okay, I'll call you tonight. What is it?"

"I'd rather show you. How about dinner?"

"Great. Pick me up at six? McGoon's?"

"Done." We waved goodbye, and I looked at the door to Stosh's office for a few seconds before heading down the stairs.

***

We started in the bar with Guinness.

"Sorry to hear about the lieutenant, guys," said Jack as he set down the glasses.

"Thanks, Jack," said Rosie. "I still can't believe it happened."

Jack pulled a towel off his shoulder and wiped the bar top. "The papers are saying it was gang related. You agree?"

"Hard to say," Rosie said. "Sure could be. I wouldn't put it past them. But murdering a cop is even a stretch for them." She took a drink. "Every time I pass his office…"

I put my arm around her shoulder.

"My sympathies," said Jack.

"Thanks," I said.

Rosie took a long drink and said, "So what's this something?"

I took the envelopes out of my pocket and told her the story.

She took a long drink and said, "That's very odd. And your story made me hungry. Let's get a table."

Ryan seated us, and we ordered dinner and two more Guinnesses.

She shook her head. "What do you make of it, Spencer?"

I shrugged. "Not a clue. It certainly is odd. And what about Single Mother Outreach?" I told her what Carol had found out. "Make any sense to you?"

"Why would he continue paying for something he didn't get?"

"Exactly."

She gave me a coy look and asked, "Do you want to find out?"

I laughed. "Do you need to ask?"

She returned the laugh. "Nope. Just wanted to be clear."

Jane brought the food. Steak for me and shepherd's pie for Rosie. We ate for a few minutes in silence.

"So, are you up for a road trip?" I asked.

"Wouldn't miss it. Where to exactly?"

"We'll start in Green Bay with the adoption agency, but Moonlight Bay is calling." We hadn't been up to my cottage on the bay on the Lake Michigan side of Door County since Christmas.

"When do you want to leave?"

"How about Saturday? We can be up there by dinner time."

"But the agency will be closed by then."

"Exactly."

Slowly shaking her head, she smiled at me but didn't ask any questions. We finished eating, telling stories about Stosh. There were a lot of stories to tell.

Chapter 6

On the way home from McGoon's we had discussed the plan, and Rosie had talked me into meeting with someone from the agency Saturday afternoon. It didn't take much to convince me... having some knowledge of the layout of the office before wandering through it in the dark made sense. Carol called and made an appointment for Mr. and Mrs. Blaine at three on Saturday. They closed at four. That was their last appointment of the day. We would be seeing a Mrs. Peters, the same name on Stosh's letter.

We left Saturday after breakfast. The weather was perfect for a drive... sunny with fluffy white clouds. Rosie had taken the next week off, so we had plenty of time to poke around. It was about a five hour drive up Interstate 43. I usually cut over to highway 42 at Manitowoc and take that road along the lakeshore up to Door County. It's a slow, leisurely drive with beautiful views of the lake. But since we were going to Green Bay, I stayed on 43.

We stopped at a Perkins for lunch and went over our story. I had already given some basic information in a phone interview with Miss Leek. We were trying to have a child but hadn't been successful. Rosie had suggested I make a doctor appointment, but I refused. So we figured adopting would be a good alternative. We had already tried several agencies, but they had long waiting lists. A friend of Rosie knew someone who knew someone who knew of the From

Us to You Adoption Agency and had good things to say about how helpful they had been. I invested in real estate, and Rosie worked with kids who had trouble with the law. Both were true. We had decided to answer as few questions as possible and be very hesitant about making a decision. We'd have to come back.

I had been enjoying a quiet ride when about an hour out of Green Bay Rosie broke the silence.

"Spencer, have you ever thought about having kids?"

"Sure, have you?"

"Yes, I'd love to."

I nodded, knowing that wasn't the end of the conversation.

After a minute, she asked, "So, would you?"

I took a deep breath. "I would, but there's that heart thing." I sped up to seventy to pass a semi. My twin sister and I had been born with a heart problem and weren't supposed to live ten years. She hadn't. Every day I woke up I was beating the odds, but I was living on borrowed time. That didn't seem to be the type of situation to bring a child into.

She put her hand on my thigh. "You can't let that rule your life."

"I try not to, Rosie. But for long-term things like kids… and marriage, it matters."

"It's easy for me to say it shouldn't, so I won't. I do understand your point, but there's a lot you're missing. You could live forever."

I laughed.

She smiled. "Well, perhaps not forever… but just as long as the rest of us."

"Which could be tomorrow."

She punched me in the side.

We talked a bit more without reaching agreement on how to approach my life problem. The bottom line was I thought it was selfish to involve other people in my dilemma. She thought it was selfish not to.

The last hour went quickly. With a cottage less than an hour away, I had never had reason to stay in Green Bay. But, not knowing what we'd be doing, I had decided to get a hotel room. That would leave us the option of being in town if that was more convenient. At some point, we'd get to the cottage. I had made reservations for three nights at the Hampton Inn on the Fox River, only a few miles from the bay.

As 43 curved west, we had a view of the bay. Multi-colored sailboats dotted the sparkling water. I exited the highway and headed a few blocks south to Main Street. Just after crossing the East River I turned right and was at the hotel in two minutes.

It was a good choice. The hotel was a beautiful, imposing, seven-story building made of pink stone and lots of windows. Two round towers flanked the parking garage and convention center. A smiling young woman greeted us from behind the marble-topped cherry counter. We checked in, and a porter showed us to our suite with a separate bedroom and hot tub on the fifth floor. He opened the curtains, revealing a view of the river. Even with the gray sky it was a great view… a good place to sit and relax and watch the boats go by. We unpacked, washed up, and sat next to the window doing exactly that. We'd have to leave in a half hour for our appointment at three.

As a white boat with a blue stripe motored by, Rosie asked if she could ask a question. I said sure. She hesitated, so I knew it wasn't about the weather.

"Why are we doing this?"

I knew what she meant. "Sitting here? Because we have some spare time before—"

"No, not sitting here. Well, maybe yes, sitting here… instead of sitting on your deck on Moonlight Bay, having a few beers and wondering about what time to put the steaks on the grill."

"Ah… *that* sitting here."

She was quiet.

I took a deep breath and turned to face her. "I've wondered the same thing. I just need to do something, Rosie. The captain basically told me to butt out, and I do realize you all can handle the gang investigation. Until he comes up with something, there's nothing I can do… and maybe even if he does. I feel helpless. This adoption thing is just taking my mind off of it. But it is odd, and things that are odd interest me."

"I figured it was something like that." Several more boats passed us. "Not that I'm complaining," she said with a smile. "It'll be kinda fun being Mrs. Blaine."

"Be careful what you ask for."

"Oh, I always have been."

I changed the conversation to boating. I loved being on the water but had no desire to own a boat. Several friends I sailed with were proof of the saying that a boat is a hole in the water you pour money into.

At 2:20 I called the desk and asked that the rental car I had ordered and had delivered to the hotel be brought to the front. I wanted something less distinctive than a sky-blue Mustang. A black, four-door Chevy Malibu was waiting for us. On the way to the car I picked up a map of Green Bay at the front desk.

***

I drove past the agency and around the block to get a feel for the area. It was mixed commercial and residential. I went around a second time and turned into the alley to take a look at the rear of the building. I had to drive slowly to miss the bigger potholes. There were two occupied parking spaces off the alley and a single door on the rear of the building. Small single-family homes were on the other side of the alley. I made my way around to the front and parked on the street a few doors away. The agency was a single-story storefront in a brick building with a large picture window amongst other similar storefronts. Other small businesses were on the opposite side of the street. I reached into my pocket, took out my parents' wedding rings, and handed Mom's to Rosie. We had already tried them on. The fit wasn't perfect, but it was close enough. I got out and opened the door for Rosie. We had discussed the rings and decided to leave them on as long as we were up here just in case we ran into someone who might notice.

As I took her hand, I said, "Let's go have a baby, Mrs. Blaine."

She laughed. "One thing about it… from what I hear, this sure is a lot less painful."

The logo of the agency, their name in a rainbow arc with a baby in a cradle under the rainbow, was painted on the picture window.

As we neared the door a couple came out. She was sobbing. He was pushing the door with one hand and trying to comfort her with his other hand on her shoulder. I held the door. They walked away with him telling her it'd be okay. Rosie and I looked at each other with wide eyes. That certainly wasn't a good sign.

We entered and were immediately greeted enthusiastically by a smiling young woman who seemed not to have noticed the crying lady. She stood with a smile, holding out her hand to me. Everything about her was simple, from her brown hair to her clothes. She wouldn't have stood out in a crowd.

"You must be the Blaines. I'm Sarah Leek. Welcome to From Us to You."

She shook Rosie's hand and offered a seat. "Mrs. Peters will be with you in a minute. She's just attending to something."

As we sat on the green, cushioned couch, I said, "Yes, we noticed what she's attending to. That lady was pretty upset."

Sarah was flustered. "Oh, yes, she was… well her husband… it was just unfortunate. But I can't discuss our clients. Can I get you some coffee or water?"

We declined and sat. The reception area was fairly small with not much more room than for the desk and couch. It was brightly decorated in blues and pinks with pictures of cute babies on the walls. A hallway on the right side of the room led into the rear.

Mrs. Peters came out five minutes later, gave us another enthusiastic greeting, and led us down the hall to her office. It was decorated with less baby and more business. On the way to her office we passed two rooms, one with file cabinets and another a bathroom. At the end of the hall was the back door that led into the alley. We sat on a much more expensive couch.

Mrs. Peters also offered coffee, and we again declined. She opened the file in front of her and pretended to read whatever was in it. She was wearing a dark blue suit that didn't look like it was off the rack. A white blouse had a frilly collar that was pinned with a cameo brooch. She had blonde hair curling over her shoulders and wore small silver earrings.

"I see you are having trouble having a baby," she said with a pasted-on sad face that quickly changed to a broad, reassuring smile, like it was flowing out of a faucet with as much sincerity as an ice pick. "I want to assure you that we here at From Us to You can help. We have hundreds of satisfied clients." The faucet turned off as she very seriously said, "But we are very discerning about our placements. We want to make sure the babies get a good home."

I felt like I was buying a used car. *This one we just got in is perfect for you!* I was careful not to look at Rosie... I wouldn't have been able to keep a straight face.

She went over the information in the file and asked more questions, most of which we didn't answer. We made it clear that we just weren't sure about adopting, especially with someone we didn't know. She kept the attention on us.

"I see you work with kids, Mrs. Blaine. What exactly do you do?"

"I'm sort of a social worker with a private firm. We counsel kids who have had some minor trouble with the law and are going through the court system. We try and find alternatives to their lifestyles."

"Well, that's wonderful. I'm sure that's very rewarding, but if you get a child are you going to quit your job and stay home?"

We hadn't thought about that question, but Rosie handled it well.

"We've given that a lot of thought. The child would come first, but my work is flexible and so is Spencer's. We'd be able to co-parent."

"I hope that works out for you. What do you do Mr. Blaine?"

"I'm in real estate investing. That's why my time is flexible."

She nodded. "You both take all the time you need," Mrs. Peters said. She didn't seem to care what I did. "This is just a first meeting to get to know each other. I assure you you'll feel comfortable with us quickly." She did a lot of assuring. "Feel free to ask questions."

I did find the process interesting, both as to how a woman could give up her baby and how the whole process worked.

"Where do you get the babies you offer up?" I asked.

"That's an excellent question. There are a lot of mostly young women who find themselves in... shall we say trying circumstances. I'm sure I don't have to explain."

"No, but where do they come from?"

"I can't be specific, but we've built a very good reputation. We get referrals, some from clinics and hospitals and some from satis- fied clients."

"One thing we're concerned with," Rosie said, "is trouble with the woman giving up the baby. You hear stories about women changing their minds. What if someone came after us to get her baby back?"

More reassuring. "I assure you, Mrs. Blaine, that wouldn't be a problem. We—" Her intercom buzzed. "Yes, Sarah?"

"Mrs. Peters, the... um... couple is back. They'd like to see you."

"Please tell them I'm in an interview. If they'd like to wait, I'll see them when I'm done."

She turned back to us. "Where was I?"

"We were talking about someone changing their mind," I said.

"Oh yes. We screen our mothers very carefully for... well, psychological issues. That does happen, but it has never happened here. I can assure you of that!" She was very emphatic, but not very reassuring.

I'd had enough of Mrs. Peters and asked where the washroom was. I gave Mrs. Blaine a kiss on the cheek and said I'd be right back.

Rosie kept Mrs. Peters occupied so she wouldn't see me turn the wrong way down the hall. The alley door had only a lock on the knob and a pretty simple one at that. I didn't see any security alarms or any obvious cameras in the hall. I walked back up the hall, passed Mrs. Peter's office, and found the bathroom. After a few minutes thinking about babies, I flushed the toilet and ran some water. On the way back, I stopped briefly in the room with the file cabinets. There were three, four-drawer cabinets. None of them were locked, but maybe they would be at the end of the day. Even if they were, the locks were pretty standard and simple.

Rosie was talking about not being able to decide between a boy and a girl when I walked back into the office.

"How about you, Mr. Blaine? Do you have a preference?"

I shook my head. "No. Do we get a choice?"

"Well, you do, but you may have to wait longer." She laughed. "We can't guarantee the supply, you know."

I assured her I knew.

"Did you find the bathroom okay? You went the wrong way."

"I did. Just a bit confused."

"Good." She smiled, sat up in her chair, and folded her hands on her desk. "Do you have any further questions? Would you like us to start the process?"

I took Rosie's hand. "We're not sure yet, Mrs. Peters. We'll have to talk about it. I'm sure you understand."

"Oh, I do. This is a big step." She handed me her card. "Please call if you have any questions. We look forward to seeing you again."

"I do have a question," I said. "We haven't talked about money. How much is it, and if we do decide to go ahead, how is the payment handled? I assume you need a deposit."

"Yes, we do, but only two thousand dollars. The total is twelve thousand." The cost of babies had gone up. "The balance would be due when you get the baby."

"And do you handle all the paperwork with the state?"

"We do. I can assure you we make it very easy for you."

"That sounds great," I said. "We'll be in touch."

The couple was sitting on the green couch, she with red eyes and he looking concerned.

***

Rosie wanted to get in a swim before dinner, so we changed and found the pool in a large room with a wall of windows on the north side. About eighty feet of a kidney shaped pool gave Rosie a good workout. My workout was setting the back of the lounge chair at the right angle and turning pages in a book—*Crime and Punishment.*

We had dinner in the restaurant at the hotel and turned in at ten for a nap. I set the alarm for midnight.

Chapter 7

We took the rental car and parked a quarter block down from the agency. At one a.m. there was very little traffic, and the neighborhood was dark except for a few streetlights. The sky was still cloudy so there was no moonlight. I stayed in the car for ten minutes just watching the neighborhood. We saw no one, and only two cars passed us. Rosie stayed with the car. She wished me luck, and I took the long way back to the alley.

With no lights, the alley was even darker than the street. I blended in with black sneakers, jeans, and a black hooded sweatshirt. There was a faint smell of fresh blacktop in the air, but it wasn't coming from the alley... it had seen better days. I imagined the alley going on through blocks of neglected neighborhoods. Weeds were growing out of cracks, and there were potholes that were easy to walk around, but I remembered driving had been a challenge. I heard a cat somewhere in the distance, but other than that it was quiet.

I took my lock picks out of my pocket as I turned in from the alley to the back door. There was a single light above the door, but it was out. I grabbed the door knob to start working on the lock, and the knob turned. Someone had forgotten to lock the door.

I quietly let myself in and stood in the hallway listening. I heard nothing. I was looking for anything interesting, but hoped to find a folder on Stosh and his payments. I wanted to look in the file room and Mrs. Peters' office. The file room door was open. Mrs. Peters' door was closed and locked. I started with the files.

The file cabinets weren't locked. The one closest to the door was labeled "Operating Expenses." The second was labeled "Accounts," and the third had no label. Except for the cabinets and a mahogany credenza against the outside wall, the room was empty, but it wasn't a very big room. There was no window. I didn't want to chance a light so I had brought a small flashlight that I could hold in my mouth.

I thumbed through the drawers in the accounts cabinet. The first file in the top one was marked "Birth Mothers." Each folder had a name at the top and a name on the file under the stick-on label on the tab. Some had more than one name. I figured the name under the tab was the adopting family, but I had no idea why some had more than one name… perhaps references. I decided to go back and look through some of those folders once I found a file for Stosh.

The second and third drawers from the top held files starting with one labeled "Adopting Family." They were in alphabetical order. Powolski was in the third drawer. I pulled out the file and looked at the three names under the label. I was about to open the file when I felt a blow to the back of my head, and my knees buckled.

***

I woke up with a throbbing headache in a bed under a sheet and a thin gray blanket in what appeared to be a hospital room. By the bright light coming in the window I knew it was daytime, but I had no idea whether it was morning or afternoon or even what day it was. I struggled to remember why I would be in a hospital room. I heard someone clear their throat, turned my head, and saw him sitting in a chair with a smile on his face like he had thoroughly enjoyed the play. I tried to roll my eyes, but they didn't roll far.

"Chief Iverson. Fancy meeting you here."

"If I'm going to have to keep saving your butt, you'll have to put me on retainer."

"When I don't feel like a truck hit me we'll argue that point. I know what I'm doing here… but what are you doing here?"

He folded his hands over his stomach. "Got a call from Detective Lonnigan. Something about breaking and entering and a hospital, and since I hadn't seen you since that little incident in the factory, here I am."

I tried to sit up in the bed but didn't get far before my head told me to lie back down.

"I assume there's a story here," he said.

"There's always a story, Chief."

"Well, since I went out on a limb for you, I'd love to hear it. But given that there's a cop sitting in your room, perhaps you should do some editing."

I massaged the back of my head as best I could while avoiding the lump. "And what limb would that be?"

He was still smiling. "That would be the one where I vouched for you and the Green Bay police released you into my custody without filing charges for breaking and entering."

I took a deep breath and let it out slowly. "Oh, that limb."

He nodded. "And I guarantee you I'm better with that custody thing than your pretty detective. That bathroom stop at the gas station trick isn't going to work."

"Thanks for the warning. I'll think of something else." I wondered why I wasn't under arrest. "No charges?"

"Yeah. I eat breakfast once a week with Chief Snark and the county sheriff. I was able to introduce some doubt into the incident. When the police got there, you were unconscious on the floor with a lump on your head. They were able to deduce that you didn't hit *yourself*. So someone else was obviously there. The police were called by a resident across the alley from the agency. But they weren't called because of you. So someone else was in the building before you."

"Makes sense to me. But if I wasn't charged, why am I in custody?"

He smiled. "Well, it's more in theory than actual. Actually, it's all in theory. Snark needed to do something along some punitive line to appease the badge in his pocket. I have questions, but first, I'm so sorry about the lieutenant. My deepest sympathies."

"Thanks. Sometimes life isn't what you were expecting."

He nodded. "As I remember, you've had more than your share of those."

"Yeah."

We were both quiet for a minute.

"How did you get in?"

"Back door. It was unlocked. I thought I just got lucky."

"Well, maybe you did. I was able to convince Chief Snark that you had entered but you hadn't done the breaking. Perhaps you were investigating the person who *had* done the breaking."

"And he bought that?"

He shrugged. "Breakfast buddies go a long way. And what's not to buy? It's true. You didn't break in did you?"

"No."

"And you could have been investigating the person who did, right?"

"Right, if I knew who that was."

"Just so we're clear, none of us believe you were there because of the other person. But they can't prove you weren't, so you got me."

I nodded and rubbed my neck, trying to make the pain go away. I stretched my neck forward.

Iverson leaned forward. "I vouched for you. Snark asked me to keep an eye on you pending further investigation."

"Further investigation of what?"

"Perhaps whoever else was in that office." He stretched his legs out. "So, Manning. I gotta ask… why are you so far from home?"

I had been inching up slowly and had made it to sitting up in bed. "Is the cop still in the room?"

"Maybe."

"Well, when he's not, let me know."

He laughed.

"Snark?" I asked.

He laughed again. "Yup, Chief B. Snark."

"B? How bad is your first name that you have to initial it when your last name is Snark?"

"Don't know. But he won't tell."

The door opened, and Rosie came in.

"Look who's awake," said Chief Iverson.

Rosie smiled. "Well, that's a step in the right direction."

As soon as the door closed it was opened again by a nurse who came in, took my temperature and blood pressure, pronounced they were both back to normal, and said the doctor would be in shortly.

I asked if I could leave after that. She said it would be up to the doctor. I wanted to say no, it would be up to me, but my still throbbing headache reminded me that maybe it wasn't.

I closed my eyes and tried to remember what had happened. But closing my eyes made my head worse, so I put the remembering on hold. I looked around for a clock, but there was none.

"Is it morning or afternoon?" I asked.

"Three in the afternoon," said Rosie.

"Is it still Sunday, or did I miss a day?"

"Still Sunday. But you—"

She was interrupted by the doctor who smiled and put on his cheerful bedside manner. Easy for him… he didn't have a splitting headache. He took a gadget out of his pocket to look into my eyes. I knew he was looking for signs of a concussion and that was something he probably had to do, but I told him the light wasn't going to help my headache. He agreed, but said if I wanted to get out of there it had to be done. I hung on to that thought.

After torturing me, he felt the lump on my head, poked a few other places, and told me I could go but shouldn't drive for at least three days. He asked if I had someone who could stay with me.

Iverson laughed. "He won't be able to get rid of us."

"Okay," said the doc. He wrote something on the chart, rehooked it on the bottom of the bed, and wrote a prescription for pain pills. "No driving, no alcohol, and try and get some more sleep. Stop at the desk on your way out and sign out. Good luck, Mr. Manning."

I thanked him and slowly swung my legs over the edge of the bed.

"You want help getting dressed?" asked Rosie.

"If you'll just get my clothes from the closet I'll do the rest."

As she laid my clothes on the bed, she said, "The captain called your cell phone while I was driving over here. He said to tell you it will be this week, maybe Thursday… he'll let you know."

I nodded. "Did you tell him about our escapade?"

"No. I thought it best not to."

"Good."

No one was making any attempt to leave, and I didn't feel well enough to be modest, so I took off the gown and started with my pants.

Rosie stood next to the chief, and they watched me get dressed.

"I should charge admission," I said.

"If it's more than a buck, I'm leaving," said Iverson.

Rosie just watched.

Not feeling like bending over, I said, "I could use some help with my shoes."

"I'll help if you answer a question," said Rosie.

"And that would be?"

"What's Thursday?"

I took a deep breath and said, "The day after Wednesday." I got a dirty look from Rosie and looked at Iverson. "You?"

"Me too. What were you doing in the agency?"

"Nice… I'll answer that, but not here."

As Rosie was putting on my left shoe, she asked if I was hungry.

"Starved."

"Chief," said Rosie. "Will you join us for dinner?"

"He has to," I said. "I'm in his custody."

"Well, I'm not gonna be real strict on the custody thing. I figure you're not a flight risk." He turned to Rosie. "Is he buying?"

"Yup. You have a suggestion?"

"I do. Just across the river from your hotel is the Titletown Brewpub. It's in an old train depot. You'll like it."

"We need to go back to the hotel first," I said. "I think a hot shower will help my head."

Chief looked at his watch. "How about we meet there at six?"

I nodded as I rubbed my head. "Rosie, if you'll get the car, I'll meet you at the front."

Iberson started to follow her out. I stopped him. "Hang on a second, Chief." The door closed behind Rosie. "Could you get me the neighbor's description of the person they saw entering the agency? And see if the police have the file folder I was looking at."

"Sure."

I hesitated. "And there's something I need your help with."

***

Rosie had the car waiting as they wheeled me out to the carport, and an orderly helped me into the car.

"How far are we from the hotel?" I asked.

"About fifteen minutes."

"Don't hit any bumps."

In the last half hour the sunlit sky had turned dark, and it had started to rain, just a light drizzle. The dark sky helped my headache.

Rosie worked her way into traffic and asked, "Was the bump on the head worth it?"

I was silent for a few seconds, trying to remember. "I don't know." The rain came harder, and Rosie turned up the wipers. "I found a file with Powolski on it. I was looking at it when I was hit." I stared out the windshield at nothing, trying to remember the file. "I hadn't been in there very long."

"You weren't in there more than ten minutes before the police showed up. Too bad we didn't have another one of these telephones… I could have warned you."

"Sure, I'm gonna carry that damned thing around with me. Pretty useless if you asked me. Did you see anyone from the front?"

"Nope. Not until the cops showed up." Rosie turned onto Ashland and headed north. "I felt pretty helpless, knowing they'd be surprising you. But I thought it best to let happen whatever was going to happen."

"Absolutely. A Chicago cop driving the getaway car wouldn't be a good thing."

"How you feeling, Spencer?"

"The drugs are working. It's a seven instead of a nine on the pain scale."

She turned right onto Dousman and in a few blocks was crossing the Fox River. The Hampton Inn was on the east side of the river just south of the river's headwaters at Green Bay.

I was still staring at nothing out the windshield. As she turned into the hotel drive I started to remember.

"Pull over, Rosie."

"The garage is just ahead, Spencer."

"Pull over." I took a notepad and a pencil out of the glove compartment and handed them to her.

She stopped on the side of the entrance to the garage and took the pad.

I closed my eyes and saw the list on the file folder. "There was a list of names. Stosh and Francine were on the tab. There were three more on the folder under the tab." She wrote as I talked. "Harold and Carla Bell from Green Bay, Wisconsin, Benjamin and Mary Hanover from St. Charles, Illinois, and Joe and Gretchen Frey from Appleton, Wisconsin." I spent another thirty seconds trying to remember. "Then there was a space and another name… Victoria Petrace. There were dates, but I don't remember them. The last thing I remember was wanting to write them down and reaching into my pocket for my notepad and a pencil."

"That's good, Spencer. Is that all?"

I nodded. "Yes. Let's park."

I was reaching for the door handle when Rosie said, "Hang on a minute, Spencer." I turned back to her with a slight grimace. It hurt to move.

"I should know better than to ask, but…"

I took a deep breath and massaged the back of my neck. "I can't tell you."

"Can't tell me what?"

"What the captain is talking about."

"I get 'I can't tell you' when you're doing something I wouldn't... or rather shouldn't because of the police thing."

"You do, yes."

"But this is the captain."

I nodded slowly.

She looked ahead out the windshield and then back to me. "Am I going to find out at some point?"

"Yes."

"When?"

I shook my head but only for a second as each shake cued something to shoot pain through my head. "Rosie..."

She raised her hands. "Okay... okay. I hope you know what you're doing."

"That makes two of us."

"Well, three."

"Yes, three. I need a shower."

As we made our way slowly to the room, I asked Rosie to call Carol and have her get addresses and information on the three couples. I left my clothes lying on the floor of the bedroom, stepped into the shower, and let hot water pour over the back of my head.

Chapter 8

After the shower and a short nap my headache was down to three or four on the scale, so we decided to walk to the brewery. It was just across the drawbridge on Main Street from the hotel. We could see the tower from our room. As we crossed the drawbridge, the old depot came into view. The tracks were gone, but there was no doubt it had been a train depot. I could easily imagine a train waiting in front. The inside was decorated with train memorabilia and several banners, including the Milwaukee Road and Chicago and Northwestern, hung from the ceiling.

Chief Iverson waved from the bar as we walked in. We weaved through the crowd and made our way to the bar. "You guys mind sitting outside?"

We didn't.

We took one of the three open tables on the patio and looked over the beer list. A waiter arrived a couple minutes later and asked what we were drinking. They offered seasonal brews and several house beers, three of which had won medals in the Great American Beer Festival. I ordered the Boathouse Pilsner, a gold medal winner. Rosie asked questions and decided on their 400 Honey Ale. Chief already had a black German lager, a bronze medalist.

The beer arrived, and we raised our glasses.

"Easy to imagine a train depot here," I said. "Do you know anything about the history?"

Chief wiped his mouth and set down the glass. "It goes back to the late 1800s. Green Bay was the headquarters for the Lake Shore division of the Chicago Northwestern Railroad. Lake Shore track ran from here to Milwaukee. The Peninsula 400 was a regular sight. It was a daily express between Chicago and Ishpeming on the upper peninsula. Old 209 was pretty famous around here. People would come just to see it pull in."

"How long ago did the railroad close?"

"Early seventies."

The waiter was back and took our orders. Rosie ordered the wood roasted chicken salad, and Chief and I ordered cheeseburgers. Chief offered a toast to Stosh, and I took a drink of the pilsner. It offered an excellent, spicy hoppy flavor with a clean finish.

I handed Chief the documents I had found under Stosh's bed. He took in some beer while reading through them.

"Well, that raises some questions," he said as he set his glass down.

"It does."

"You guys have any answers?"

"Not yet," I said. Rosie just shook her head.

"Any guesses?"

"Nothing," I said. "I was hoping to find something at the agency, but I was interrupted."

"Yeah, you could call it that."

"Something odd going on there," Rosie said.

Bells started to clang. I looked upriver and saw a large sailboat approaching as the bridge started to rise.

"I need another look in that file drawer," I said.

Chief laughed. "If you'd like to see a jail cell from the *in*side, come on up and I'll give you a tour of mine. You get caught again, and my breakfasts aren't going to be able to help."

I watched the ship slowly approach the bridge as I weighed the consequences.

"Changing the subject before I start to think you're serious," Chief said, "the papers said Chicago cops are looking at a gang for the shooting. Anything on that?"

I was still watching the ship.

"Nothing," Rosie said. "Lots of interviews... nobody knows anything, and everybody has an alibi."

"Of course."

"We're looking for a cousin who has suddenly disappeared."

Chief just shook his head. "So senseless. I don't know how you deal with the constant shootings. I couldn't tell you the date of the last shooting we had in Door County."

"Yeah, it's tough dealing with those jaywalkers," I said.

He laughed. "Once in a while we do wander down to Chicago to lend a hand."

Rosie was looking puzzled. "What are you talking about?"

Chief Iverson had helped me catch a kidnapper in a case a few years back. It was a bit outside the rules, so he had disappeared—no one besides me and Steele ever knew he was there.

"You mind if I tell her, Chief?"

"If she's hanging around with you, she must be used to bending the rules and looking the other way, so no, don't mind at all."

I finished my beer and turned to Rosie.

"Remember when I rescued Pitcher in the basement of that factory?"

"Sure."

"Remember several people questioning my version of the story?"

"Yup. Seemed like someone else had to be in that basement."

I nodded. "Someone else was."

She slowly moved her eyes from me to Chief Iverson and back to me. "Well that explains a lot." She looked back at Iverson and said, "Thanks, Chief."

He was smiling and just nodded once, slowly and deeply. "Speaking of which, how's Steele doing? We three made a great team."

I looked at Rosie, whose face showed all the sadness of Steele's suicide.

Iverson looked at Rosie and then back at me. "What? Did I miss something?"

Rosie had tears in her eyes, so I took a deep breath and told him. "Steele comitted suicide a couple years ago."

Iverson's mouth opened, but there were no words.

"We were working a case involving missing kids and cornered one of the kidnappers at Riverview as he was in the process of taking another kid. He was one nasty bastard. The guy ended up on the floor with Steele standing over him. I can still see the arrogant smirk on the guy's face. Steele leaned down and put the gun to the guy's forehead and told him how worthless he was. The smirk didn't disappear... he knew a cop wouldn't pull the trigger. He was laughing at Steele."

Iverson shook his head. "I can't imagine the tension in that room. Was the guy found guilty?"

I thought about that. "Yeah, by a jury of one. Steele pulled the trigger."

Iverson's mouth was open again for several seconds before he said, "Jesus... then what?"

"While I was dealing with the guy on the floor and the kid, Steele went into a back room and killed himself."

"I can't imagine. Did you ever find out why?"

I nodded. "I knew why. When his son was little he was kidnapped. Steele said he was over it and had moved on, but I guess not."

"I guess *not*," Iverson said. "Maybe you never get over something like that. What a shame."

Rosie had dried her eyes with her napkin and finished her water.

The waiter dropped off the bill, and we all left money on the table.

As we stood up, Chief told me not to do anything stupid. I said I'd try. He offered a ride back to the hotel, but it was a nice night for a walk. We parted on the sidewalk but hadn't gone far when Chief called my name.

"Spencer, I almost forgot. The description of the person who hit you… not going to help much. Average build and short, not much more than five feet. Dark pants and a dark hooded sweatshirt."

I nodded. "How about the file folder?"

"The police don't have it."

I thought about that. "I don't know about Green Bay Police, but if I find a guy passed out on the floor with a file folder next to him, I'm taking the file as evidence."

He agreed.

"So where's the evidence?"

Rosie spoke up. "Are you sure you didn't put it back in the drawer before you were hit?"

"Positive. I didn't even get a chance to open it."

"Then either the person who hit you put it back in the drawer, or took it, or there's something your breakfast buddy isn't sharing with you, Chief."

He shook his head. "It's not the third."

"Okay," I said, "but why would it be the first or second?"

Iverson slapped me on the shoulder. "That's why you get the big bucks, kid. Good luck finding out."

"Thanks, I'll do that."

He waved goodbye over his shoulder as he walked away.

***

As we neared the bridge we passed the edge of the last building and saw our hotel lit up with multi-colored floodlights. I stopped halfway across the bridge and leaned on the railing. Rosie put her arm around my waist, and I pulled her closer. We watched the boat lights on the river for a few minutes before she spoke up.

"You're going back to the agency, aren't you."

It wasn't a question.

"I'd sure like to have a look in that folder."

"Yeah, I was afraid of that. I also know when the best time to do that is."

"By tomorrow they'll have someone changing the locks and putting on deadbolts and installing an alarm system. Who'd expect another break-in the next night?"

"Me."

"Well, luckily you're not running the agency."

A large boat with a fly bridge barely cleared the bridge. I thought it was going to hit.

"Spencer, how do you think the first person got in?"

I shrugged. "Either picked the lock or the door was open."

"The second isn't very likely."

"No, probably not. But it's a simple lock. Would only take a little skill to pick it."

"For you, but that's not a skill most people have. So what's our plan?"

"My plan is I'm heading back after midnight. You're staying at the hotel and getting some sleep. You have a career at stake."

She was quiet for a minute. "As much as I hate to agree with you, I agree with you. But I'm not going to get any sleep. What's the rest of your plan?"

I laughed. "I'll let you know after I come up with one."

She didn't laugh. "I'm a little chilly. Let's head back."

***

I waited until two, took the rental car, and parked a block away in a lot next to a hardware store that had three other cars in it. Since there was obviously someone up late in a house on the alley, I had decided to chance the front door. It had a more sophisticated lock than the alley door, but it only took me thirty seconds to get in.

I went right to the file drawer with Stosh's file. It was gone. Not long after I started in this business, I found out that the reason something didn't make sense was that I didn't have the facts. Once I found them, every case had made perfect sense. I just had to put together the pieces of the puzzle. But first I had to find the pieces. Why would someone take it? I had pieces to find.

As I was about to close the drawer, I thought they may have misfiled it in their hurry to leave, so I thumbed through the whole drawer. It wasn't there. The single name under the three names on Stosh's folder was Victoria Petrace. I had given some thought to the filing system and thought Petrace might be the birth mother. So I pulled open the "Birth Mother" drawer and looked for a Petrace file. I didn't find one. Maybe the names meant something else.

I felt like I was pushing my luck but wanted to take a look at Mrs. Peters' file and opened the employee drawer. The file was there. And right behind it was a file for Victoria Petrace. I jotted down some information from Peters' file. She'd been with the company since 1979, first name Cynthia. I got her address and home phone.

Victoria's file was more interesting. She had been hired in 1982 and let go in February of this year. It didn't say why. Specifically, it said "separated." I got her address too. It was in Green Bay.

As I was closing the drawer I had another thought. Stosh's file had the names of three couples under the tab. Beneath that was Victoria Petrace. I thought for a few seconds and remembered the first names, Harold and Carla Bell. Given enough time, I probably could have remembered the others, but I didn't have to.

I pulled open the "Adopting Family" drawer and didn't have to look hard for Bell… it was the first one. "Bell, Harold and Carla" was on the tab. On the folder, under the tab, were three names. One of them was Stanley and Francine Powolski. Petrace's name was under the list. I didn't want to take time to think about it… I needed to leave. I had passed my comfort level for being somewhere I didn't belong about when I had found Victoria's file.

I made sure everything was the way I had found it and walked into the hall and listened. Quiet. I looked both ways out the picture window and saw no cars. I stepped outside, made sure the door closed behind me, and listened again. Nothing but the quiet of three in the morning. I liked that peaceful window, the time between the humans going to sleep and the birds waking up.

***

I parked and entered the hotel through the convention center to avoid the lobby and took the stairs up to the fifth floor. Rosie had said she'd be up waiting, but I quietly opened the door. She was sitting in the chair in front of the windows… sound asleep. No boats on the river. I touched her shoulder, and she slowly opened her eyes. She smiled, stood up, and put her arms around me. I returned the favor.

"Glad to see you. No trouble?"

"No trouble."

"Find anything?"

"Yup."

"Tell me about it in the morning. Let's go to bed."

"Right behind you."

Chapter 9

The phone woke me up at a little before ten. I heard Rosie answer it in the main room. I washed up and got dressed. Rosie was looking out the windows in a room full of sunshine.

"Good morning, Mr. Blaine."

I smiled. "Good morning, Mrs. Blaine."

"Hungry?"

"Starved."

"There are rolls and coffee in the kitchenette, or we can go down to the restaurant."

I joined her in front of the window and wrapped my arms around her from behind.

"Let's stay here. Hard to beat this view, and there are liable to be other people in the restaurant." I smiled. "Did you eat?"

"I did, but I'll have some coffee."

"Who was on the phone?"

"Carol with information on the names. And more about the agency. And a bit more."

We sat at the table, and she handed me a slip of paper. It had addresses for the three couples and another name and address—Justine Trainer.

"Trainer is the owner. She was a nurse at a local hospital for twenty years up until 1970 when she opened this adoption agency.

Obviously still in business after fifteen years, so the baby business must be doing okay."

I dunked a roll in the coffee and took a bite. "Good. What's the more?"

She took a sip of coffee and pointed at the list. "Mary Hanover."

"What about her?"

"She's dead. Murdered about four months ago. Shot as she was walking from her garage to the house."

I was about to take a drink but put down my cup. "Well, I wasn't expecting that."

"No. I would think not."

"Any more about it?"

"Nope. Just what you see on the list. She and Harold live, or lived, in St. Charles."

I thought for a few seconds and said with a smile, "Nice day for a drive."

"I figured. But I was hoping for some time in the whirlpool tub."

"I think I can arrange that," I said with a bigger smile.

"Do you know someone in St. Charles?"

"No, but I know a certain detective who would probably be willing to make a call."

"She may be more willing after some time in the tub."

"Exactly! See if we can see someone in the morning. If we leave after lunch we'll have plenty of time to get home and spend a quiet evening. I'm going to call the agency and make another appointment for us on Wednesday."

"After breaking in?"

"If they got a record of the incident, it had my name, not Blaine. And I wasn't arrested, so would my name even be on it?"

"Probably not. What's the purpose for going back there?"

"I have two days to think of something."

She laughed. "Do you want me to cancel the room for tonight?"

"No. I think I'd like to extend it till the end of the week. I'll call and do that. You start the water."

"I was hoping to spend some time at the cottage," she said.

"We will. But we might get spoiled by this tub."

She laughed. "Nice to have choices."

"Indeed."

I took care of the room, and it was only a second after I hung up that the phone rang.

"Hello, Spencer, it's Kate."

"Good morning, Kate. How are you holding up?"

"As best as can be expected. The place just isn't the same. They have me working with the captain since Lieutenant…" Her voice broke.

"I'm sorry, Kate."

After a pause, she said, "I'll be all right. How are you?"

"The same. Trying to stay busy. What can I do for you?"

"They found the cousin this morning. He was hiding in a cellar. We got a tip."

"Well, that's something. But I'm not real hopeful."

"No? I'm trying to be."

"Hang onto that, Kate. You never know."

"I'll try."

Rosie came out of the bathroom and waved.

"Rosie says hi."

"Hi to Rosie. You two have fun."

"We're about to do that. Bye, Kate."

"Bye, Spencer."

The water was too hot, and it took me several minutes to get all the way in.

While we were soaking, I told her what I had found at the agency.

"That answers a few questions," Rosie said.

"Yes, Petrace was an employee and handled the adoption. But why are there extra names on the folder?"

"Still pieces that don't fit." She added water to the tub and sunk up to her chin. "And Petrace didn't start there until eighty-two, long after Stosh's adoption date."

"Probably just took it over from whoever was there before."

"Probably."

I moved so that a water jet was in the middle of my back. "Now, if you don't mind, I'm going to close my eyes and not think about anything but you and the water."

She smiled. "I don't mind at all."

***

We were on the road by one, after a brief discussion about doctor's orders and who shouldn't be driving. The discussion ended with Rosie rolling her eyes and getting in the passenger seat. We were back home in Chicago by seven. I ordered a pizza from the car, and it arrived five minutes after we did. We spent the evening watching television and chatting about memories. We turned in at ten and got a good night's sleep.

Chapter 10

The birds woke me up at a little after five. The sky was lightening, and it promised to be a nice spring day. The weatherman predicted a high in the mid-seventies. Rosie had made an appointment with a Detective Springer for eleven a.m. We got there fifteen minutes early. St. Charles was a quaint town, on a different Fox River, full of stately old homes, shops, and restaurants. The station fit right in with its fancy old brickwork.

We were shown to Springer's office. He was on the phone and waved us in. Numerous pictures on the wall showed Springer's history through the years. They started with him and a partner in patrol uniform next to a squad car. Above the police photos was Springer in a marine uniform. The version behind the desk was dressed in brown dress slacks and a long-sleeve shirt and sported a crew cut that was a bit grown out but still neat. I wondered whether his tan was from tennis or golf. I decided on golf. A sport coat hung on a hook next to the pictures.

After introductions, he offered us seats and apologized for the décor.

"Yes," Rosie said, "it's sure a step down from my palace in Chicago."

Everyone laughed. It was a good ice breaker.

"My sympathies about Lieutenant Powolski," he said.

"Thanks," we both said.

"Did you work with him?"

"I did," said Rosie. "He was my boss. With Spencer he was more like a favorite uncle. Spencer's father was chief of police, and the lieutenant was like a part of the family."

He looked at me with a different look. "Oh, that Manning. My sympathies about your folks, Spencer. This job is pretty damned sad sometimes."

I just nodded and changed the subject.

Telling him how Mary Hanover fit in, I explained some of the case to Springer and asked what they had.

He shrugged. "Not much. She was shot twice at close range in the chest with a .22 as she walked with groceries from her garage to the house."

"What time?"

"Doc puts it somewhere around ten p.m."

"No one saw anything?"

He shook his head. "They live out in unincorporated horse country. Five-acres-plus lots."

"No one heard the shots?" Rosie asked.

Springer sighed. "Yeah, two people said they heard something but said they'd been having trouble with coyotes and figured that's what the shots were. A real shame. Doc said she would have survived if someone got to her soon enough. Neither wound would have killed her, but she bled out. She crawled about twenty feet from where she fell."

"Her husband wasn't home?" I asked.

"Nope. At a meeting of chicken farmers. They raise them."

A female cop came in and dropped a file on Springer's desk.

"Thanks, Betsy."

She nodded in our direction and left.

"Any attempts on the husband's life?"

"Nope." He leaned back in his chair. "So you think this is tied in with the adoption thing?"

"Do you like coincidences?"

He smiled. "Not much. Have you checked the other two names?"

"That's on our list."

"Where do they live?"

"Both in Wisconsin. The Bells are in Green Bay and the Freys are in Appleton. We're heading back up to Green Bay from here. Did your investigation come up with anything?"

"Only a couple of longshots. There are two people who were not happy with the Hanovers. One was part of this chicken group. Some sort of feud about selling eggs. The other was a neighbor. Seems one of their chickens turned out to be a rooster that could crow with the best of them. Threats had been made, but mostly to the rooster."

"Hardly seems worth killing over," I said.

"You never know what pushes someone's buttons."

We agreed.

Springer handed Rosie a card, and I gave him one of mine.

"If there's anything I can do to help, you've got my number," he said as he stood.

"And vice versa," said Rosie.

He stopped us as we were walking out. "What was the bullet with the lieutenant?"

"A .22," Rosie said.

"Another coincidence."

"Add it to the list," I said.

He nodded.

Chapter 11

We stopped for lunch and by one were heading north toward the tollway. Stopped at a light in Elgin, I asked Rosie what she thought about a detour to Appleton.

"It's your gas."

As I pulled away I said, "It's not too far out of the way... just south of Green Bay and a bit west. We've gotta head north anyway."

She agreed.

I turned on the radio. The Cubs were playing the Giants. They were in the bottom of the first.

"Speaking of gas, it's a good thing that leaded gas ban didn't go through," Rosie said.

"Well, a good thing for the Mustang. But not so good for the environment."

She laughed. "Money doesn't care about the environment, Spencer."

"Nope. Lead has been a known poison for fifty years. But it makes a lot of money for the gas companies. One of these days we'll succeed in making this planet an unfit place to live."

"Well, aren't you a ball of sunshine."

"Just a realist."

"And a hypocrite, if you don't mind my saying."

"I do mind, but only because you're right."

I turned onto the westbound entrance ramp to I90 and headed toward Rockford.

When we reached Rockford and turned north, Rosie asked, "So, when we get to Appleton what do you have in mind?"

"If they have a Dairy Queen I'll buy you a cone."

"That would be wonderful. But I was more asking about the Freys."

"Not sure. For the moment, I'd just like to make sure they're alive."

That led to a philosophical discussion that lasted all the way to the Janesville exit as to whether we should even tell the Freys about the situation. The simplest plan would be to knock on their door and see if they were both alive. But if someone knocked on my door with that purpose I'd want to know why, which would certainly lead to some concern. Did we want to cause them concern… perhaps unduly? But if we didn't let them know and one or both of them ended up dead that certainly would be worse than causing concern. That led to Rosie's next line of thought.

"We're assuming there's a connection because two of the people on the file folder are dead."

"Well, a bit more than that," I said. "Both murdered… same caliber bullet."

"Yes, but why?"

"Of course. If we knew why, this wouldn't be an issue." I thought about it as I drove. "Another question is why are there so many names on the folders. One birth mother should be tied to one adopting client. Victoria's name was written under the other names on both folders, but the names on the tabs and the list under the tabs were different."

"But different only in that they were switched around," I said. "The same names were on all the folders."

"Correct."

"The only name in the same spot on both folders was Victoria's."

"Correct again," Rosie said. "And we know she was an employee. Maybe she was the one who handled both cases."

"When did she work there?"

I tried to remember. "From 1982 until early this year, I think. Three years."

"And when did Stosh and Francine start the adoption?"

"I think it was 1975."

"So," Rosie said, "Victoria didn't work there until much later. So she couldn't have handled the cases."

"Then she took it over," I said. "Someone had to handle Stosh's checks. It's unlikely that the same employees would be there that long."

"Maybe, but why are there so many other names on the folder?"

"Good question."

"And what do we do about the Freys?" she asked.

"How about we stop at the police station and let them decide?"

"That's a pretty lame solution," Rosie said.

"You have a better idea?"

She just stared out the window.

"And we have to find out where the Freys live," I said.

"Okay, we'll have a chat with the police. But this is going to sound pretty lame. In St. Charles we had a murder to be wondering about. Here we just have a pretty far-fetched story."

I turned up the radio. Scoreless in the third. WGN was starting to be covered by static, and we'd lose the signal before long.

I agreed with her. "But I'm thinking we need to let somebody know. The more networking the better. And I'm thinking the best option is the police. Let them decide."

"Okay by me."

The farm fields gave way to the suburbs of Madison. I turned east on 151 and headed toward Lake Winnebago and Appleton. I drove down country backroads that wound around lakes and hills through the glacial terrain of Wisconsin. Planted around the lakes were farmers' fields, green crops barely showing above the soil.

***

We passed a large dairy farm with the late afternoon sun sparkling off of silver roofs and followed the curving road into Appleton. It wasn't as big as Green Bay, but it was a fair-sized city, much larger than the small towns that dotted the farm fields along the highway, many of which didn't even have stop signs. I stopped for gas at the edge of town and got directions to the police department.

We turned onto Main Street, and I got the feel of small-town America as we passed shops that had probably been there for a hundred years. What caught my attention the most was Matt's Hardware. The painted sign above the door and the window displays jammed with merchandise brought back fond memories of the neighborhood hardware store Dad let me wander around in, with the wooden bins full of treasures and sawdust on the wooden floors. And then there was the one fellow who had been there since it opened, it seemed, who knew where everything was. When I was a kid, that guy was one of my heroes. Whatever they sold, he knew which bin it was in. Two blocks up we found the police department, and I pulled the Mustang into an angled parking spot in front. It was a brick structure with a parking lot on one side and a coffee shop on the other. "Appleton Police" was stenciled on the window. Next to that was a red apple.

The inside was a bit dim as the front faced north and didn't get any direct sun. There was a large man in jeans and a flannel shirt standing at the counter talking to a woman in a dark-blue uniform at one of three desks. His belt was holding up his stomach. I stood next to him and waited for him to stop talking.

"Can I help you?" the woman asked with raised eyebrows.

"Yes. We'd like to talk with the chief, if he's available," I said.

She smiled at the man at the counter. "I'll see if he's available." I expected her to get up, but instead, still looking at the man at the counter, she asked, "Chief, are you available?"

He smiled back at her. "I'll have to check with my secretary. Officer Mills, am I available?"

They both laughed. This evidently wasn't the first time they had pulled this routine.

"Sorry," he said with a smile, holding his hand out. "I'm Chief Werth, Yancy."

I introduced myself and Rosie as Detective Lonnigan from Chicago.

"Detective, eh? Well, follow me. Would you like some coffee?"

He led us around the counter to an office at the rear of the room.

"Officer Mills, would you like some coffee?"

"No thanks, Chief."

There was a pot percolating on a shelf to the right of his desk. Rosie took a cup… I declined.

"What can I do for you?" he asked as we all sat.

I held my hand out to Rosie, and she took five minutes to explain the situation. She covered everything except the Freys and my nighttime visits to the agency. She told him about the folders but not how we knew. He didn't ask.

Chief Werth folded his hands over his stomach, let out a few um hmms, nodded some, and for the most part looked like he was giving it some thought.

When Rosie was done, he took a deep breath and let it out slowly. "First, I'm sorry about Lieutenant Powolski. I often wonder why we do this. Second, that's all very interesting, but why are you sitting in my office?"

I responded. "One of the names on the folder was Frey, Joe and Gretchen."

His eyebrows went up. "Well, that does make it a bit different."

"Do you know them?" Rosie asked.

He nodded. "Very well. Joe Frey is on the city council. We have coffee every so often."

"Can we assume they're both alive?"

He laughed. "Last I checked. Though there are some on the council who may at times wish otherwise."

We both laughed.

Officer Mills leaned in the doorway. "Tracy is taking a half hour for dinner, Chief."

"Okay. Thanks Ellen."

"We were wondering whether or not we should tell the Freys about this… situation," I said.

He sat up straight and said, "I think so. As a matter of fact, I already know a little about this agency. Joe talked to me about adopting a child. They were having trouble and getting older every day, as he put it. Someone recommended that agency in Green Bay. Everything was going okay... they got a letter and a call saying they had found a baby for them. But then it fell apart for some reason, and Joe came to me."

"What fell apart?"

He finished his coffee and said, "I think I'd better let *them* tell you that. Do you have time for a drive?"

"How long a drive?" I asked.

"They're about fifteen minutes out on the edge of town."

"Sure. Let's go."

He stood. "We'll take the squad car."

We went out the side door and got in a silver car with a whip antenna and "Appleton Police" on the side with an emblem that included the red apple.

***

We chatted as we drove and learned that Joe had grown up in Appleton and Gretchen had come here ten years ago looking for a job. Both were schoolteachers.

The Freys' place really wasn't even on the edge of town. It was around a bend in the road from the last house. From their drive I couldn't see any other houses. It was an old Victorian farmhouse that looked like it had been given lots of loving care. It was the last structure except for the arched, black iron entryway to the cemetery on the north side of the house. Beyond that were green fields and forest as far as I could see.

The chief pulled into the gravel drive and said, "They're home. That's their car in front of the garage."

Gretchen answered the door with a smile for Chief and asked us all to come in. Joe walked into the front room while Chief was introducing us to Gretchen. She asked if we'd join them for an early dinner. We all thanked her but declined and asked if we could have a few minutes. She offered seats. Rosie and I took the couch. Chief sat in the rocker. The Freys sat on the love seat.

I looked around the room. Stairs were off to the left of the front door. Two exterior walls were covered with floral paper, and the inside walls were done in dark paneling with gas wall sconces hung on the wall that made up the side of the enclosed stairs. The ceiling was plaster with carved molding. Several pieces of period furniture were placed around the room.

"What's this all about?" asked Joe with a worried look.

Rocking slowly, Chief said, "These two came in with a story that involves you two." He looked toward Rosie. "Detective?"

Rosie once again told the story she had told to Chief Werth, starting with Stosh and my finding the envelopes. When she told about Mrs. Hanover, Gretchen took her husband's hand. Rosie finished with our chat with Chief Werth.

"That's pretty disturbing," said Mrs. Frey.

Joe let go of her hand and put his arm around her shoulder. "Do you have any evidence tying the agency to the murders, or is this just a theory?"

I had sunk into the couch cushion and moved forward on the edge so I could sit up straight. "We have no evidence, but I'm not a believer in coincidence. I'm going to pay attention to the fact that two people involved with that agency are dead."

Gretchen sighed and shook her head. "I'd rather we weren't the next customers next door." She pointed toward the cemetery.

Joe pulled her closer. "What do you think we should do about this, Chief?"

He stopped rocking. "I'd say just go on with life but be careful. Try not to go anywhere alone or be out late at night."

"That's an awful way to live," Gretchen said.

"Yes," I agreed. "But it's a good way to stay alive."

Chief started rocking again. "Joe, I told them you had some concerns about the agency. Tell them about that."

Before he could start, Gretchen asked if anyone wanted coffee or something else to drink. We all declined.

Joe took his arm from around his wife and crossed his legs. "Everything was going fine. The process had taken almost a year, but we were happy with them and got a letter saying they had found a baby. We were thrilled. We got a phone call from Mrs. Peters telling us we should send a check for the balance."

"Did you?" I asked.

"Yes, the next day."

"How much was it?"

"Six thousand dollars."

I nodded. That and the down payment was the same amount as Stosh's payment. "Then what?"

"Well, about a month later we got a letter stating that there had been a problem. The birth mother had changed her mind and wanted to keep her baby."

Gretchen was wringing her hands in her lap. "That was hard to take… we were so disappointed. But we were happy for the mother. We decided it was always best for a baby to be with its mother."

I didn't agree but said nothing. "So what was your concern?"

Gretchen explained. "The letter said that they would keep looking and would put us at the top of the list. It said they would refund our check if we wished, and we could write a new check when they found another baby. We decided to not get the refund, hoping it would be soon. Then a few weeks later we got another letter from the agency." She took a deep breath and turned to Joe with a concerned look.

He looked at her with a frown and then turned to us. "That letter said that the birth mother was having trouble making ends meet and was struggling to keep her baby. It said they were associated with an organization called Single Mother Outreach and also had a house they used for single mothers having trouble. It asked us for a donation to go to the mother to help her get on her feet. The letter said the agency was helping and suggested, if we were interested in helping, that we set up a monthly payment plan for whatever amount we were comfortable with."

Rosie and I looked at each other with raised eyebrows.

"What?" asked Chief, looking at me.

Rosie hadn't mentioned Stosh's checks. She nodded to me.

"There were nineteen canceled checks in Stosh's envelope written every six months or so for ten years," I said, "...made out to Single Mother Outreach."

Joe and Gretchen looked puzzled. "So what the hell does that mean?" Joe asked. "What are the chances that would happen with two mothers?"

I shrugged. "I guess it's possible, but, again, I'm not fond of coincidences."

"So if it's not a coincidence what the hell's going on?" Joe asked.

Chief Werth replied. "There are all kinds of confidence scams out there. This may be one of them."

"With babies?" Gretchen asked, incredulous. "With people's hearts?"

"That's the best kind for the scammer," Chief said. "People part with money when their heart strings are tugged."

"So what did you do?" Rosie asked.

Joe turned to us. "We talked with Yancy and decided to do nothing."

"You didn't ask for your down payment back?" Rosie asked.

Joe shook his head. "Not right away. We thought they were sincere. They *had* offered to return the down payment, so we didn't suspect anything funny."

"You said not right away," Rosie said.

"Yes. After a month of not hearing anything from them, I called and asked Mrs. Peters if there were any possibilities. She said no, but they were trying. We talked it over and decided to stop for a while. It was too emotionally draining. They refunded our money."

I agreed. "Did you hear any more from them?"

Joe shook his head. "Nothing. And we've given up on adopting."

Gretchen moved forward on the love seat and held out her hand. "So, we have here two police people and a private detective. Do you all think we're in danger?"

"As I said," responded Chief, "I'd just be careful for a while."

"That doesn't answer my question. Detective?"

I was glad she asked Rosie first. There wasn't an easy answer. We didn't want to scare them unduly, but we wanted to get their attention.

Rosie spread her hands out. "I wouldn't go that far, but I agree with Chief Werth… be careful."

Chief placed his hands on the arms of the rocker and pushed himself up. "Tell you what. I'll have the patrol cars make a few extra trips out here each night. And, Joe, you have my home phone. Call me anytime, especially if you see someone you don't know hanging around."

An angry look had replaced Gretchen's concern. "We live next to a cemetery. We see many people we don't know." She clenched her jaw. "All we wanted to do was give a baby a home, and this is what we get?"

There was no good answer to that, and no one responded.

"How long do we have to be *careful*?" she asked.

There wasn't a good answer to that either, but I tried.

"We're going to keep working on this, Mrs. Frey. Hopefully we'll catch the person and this will be over."

She still looked angry. "Do you have any idea why these people were killed?"

I would have liked to have had an answer to that question but just shook my head. "No."

"I'm just a schoolteacher, but I would think it's hard to catch someone if you don't have a motive."

I couldn't disagree. My only answer was, again, "We'll keep looking." I had a thought that might help, but I didn't want to share it with them. We needed to get ahold of Detective Springer and find out if the Hanovers had the same experience with the agency.

Mrs. Frey was angry and afraid. I knew it was at the situation and not us, but we were the ones there. She had to take it out on someone.

"You're going to keep looking," she said. "That's great. Who's going to protect us... the dog?"

I was sure the rest had the same reaction as I did, wondering what she was talking about.

Her husband, Joe, looked as confused as we did and gently asked, "What dog are you talking about, honey?"

She looked disgusted. "You know, the black dog that sits at the cemetery gate."

It was obvious he still didn't know what she was talking about and tried to comfort her.

"It'll be all right, dear. Don't worry about the dog."

"Don't patronize me! You can't tell me you haven't seen the dog. He's there almost every day when we go to work."

He was still confused. "I do remember you mentioning a dog a while back, but—"

She was getting more and more disturbed.

"Don't tell me you've never seen the dog. I'm not making this up! I'm not crazy!"

He took her hand. "No, honey, you're not crazy. It's the stress of this. We're all worried."

She just glared at him.

We were all uncomfortable. Chief Werth suggested we go, and we all stood. He again told them it would be okay and to call if anything suspicious happened, no matter how trivial. Joe thanked us all for coming and wished us luck.

On the ride back I shared my thought about checking with the Hanovers.

"The answer to that question will be helpful... but not conclusive," Chief Werth said.

"Nope. But helpful is all we have at the moment."

Werth pulled back into his spot. Before we got out I asked if there was a Dairy Queen in town.

He smiled. "What's a town without a DQ? Up two blocks, turn right on Baker, and down three blocks."

"Do they have food?"

"Nope, just ice cream. But there's a diner right next door I can recommend."

"Thanks, you wanna join us?"

He laughed. "Thanks for the offer." He patted his stomach. "I'm trying to stay away from ice cream."

"Good luck with that," I said. "How long a drive to Green Bay?"

"Less than an hour. Go south a block from DQ and you'll hit College Avenue. You'll pass Lawrence University and cross the Fox River. A couple miles after that, turn north on 441 and that'll take you to 41 and up to Green Bay."

"Great. Thanks, Chief. Nice meeting you," I said. We all shook hands.

"Keep me informed, and let me know if there's anything I can do."

"Will do."

We had a burger at the diner.

"Well, one mystery solved," Rosie said. "Now we know about the payments."

"Yup," I said.

"But poor Mrs. Frey. She's pretty scared."

"She has reason to be. It's a helpless feeling."

"And what's with the dog?" Rosie asked and then picked up her root beer.

"You're not going to like my answer."

She smiled. "Nothing new about that. Try me."

"Well, first of all, a dog with a lot of bark would be a big help."

"Maybe the black dog would be a watchdog."

"It might if it was."

She was about to take a bite of her burger and stopped. "What the hell does that mean?"

"This is the answer you're not going to like."

She just looked at me with squinted eyes.

"I think Mrs. Frey is the only one who can see the dog."

She looked at me some more. "Are you saying the dog is a ghost?"

I nodded and took a bite. "Greek mythology holds that a three-headed dog named Cerebrus, also called the hound of Hades, guarded the gates of hell to keep the dead from leaving. There have been many reports of dogs, usually black, seen around cemeteries and places where executions have occurred. They're known as hell-hounds, and they're a bad omen."

"So it's not going to protect Mrs. Frey."

"Probably not." Rosie was taking it better than I thought she would. "It could also be the pet dog of someone buried in the cemetery."

"I'd like to look into that some more," Rosie said.

"So would I." I finished my burger. "I've done some reading, and these old towns usually have pretty good records. It would be interesting to come back and spend some time in the archives."

"That would be fun. Let's do it."

We stopped at DQ and had cones for dessert and then headed back to Green Bay.

We crossed the river twice, and when we got to 41 Rosie asked, "You want me to call Springer in the morning?"

"Sure."

We were quiet for a minute before I asked, "Do you remember Joe's question about the chances of the payments happening with two mothers?"

She nodded.

"Maybe it's the same mother. We need to find out about the Hanovers."

A half hour later I was pulling into a space at the hotel and looking forward to the whirlpool tub and a relaxing evening watching the river boats.

Rosie noticed the flashing message light on the phone. "I'll check messages, Spencer."

"Okay. I'll start the tub."

The whirlpool was in a large room outside the bathroom. It was about half full when Rosie came in.

"A message from the captain. He says Friday. And also they got nothing from the cousin. The gang interviews got them nowhere. They're still looking, of course."

"Okay. Thanks." I wondered if she was going to ask, and she did.

"So, when Friday comes do I get to find out what the hell is going on?"

I laughed. "I promise to clear up the mystery at some point, but I don't know when."

"Will it be before I shoot you?"

"Hopefully."

"Remember we have an appointment at eleven at the agency."

"Yup. Thanks."

We got into the tub slowly, adapting to the hot water, and I turned on the jets. A couple of beers and an hour watching the lights on the river were a perfect way to wind down as we held hands and talked about our strategy for the meeting.

We were both nodding off around eleven and decided we had reached the end of a long day.

As we were turning down the bedcovers, Rosie said, "I have a request."

"Which is?"

"This is a nice room, but I miss Moonlight Bay. Can we stay at the cottage tomorrow night?"

"I've been thinking the same thing myself," I said. "Absolutely." Nothing is ever for sure, but I was hopeful.

She came around the bed and put her arms around me. We had to cut the hug short before we fell asleep standing up.

Chapter 12

Rosie got ahold of Detective Springer a little after nine. He said he'd check with Mr. Hanover and get back to us. Indirect sunlight filled the room as we watched the sun sparkling on the water. We took the rental car and arrived at the agency right on time.

"Good morning, Mr. and Mrs. Blaine," Miss Leek said with a smile. "It's nice to see you again."

We both returned her good morning.

"Have a seat. Mrs. Peters is running a little late. She just called and said to tell you she'd be here in a few minutes."

"No problem, Sarah."

"Can I get you something to drink?"

We both declined.

"While we're waiting," I said, "I'm wondering about something that happened the last time we were here."

"What's that?" She looked concerned.

"When we came in there was a couple leaving, and the woman was crying. Mrs. Peters' explanation wasn't too convincing. Do you get many upset clients?"

She looked at everything in the room except me and was obviously flustered. "No, we really don't... not... well..."

I let her pause.

"I've only been here a year so I haven't seen a lot of clients, but that was the only one I've seen upset. I…" She looked unsure of herself.

I leaned forward on the couch. "What were you going to say, Sarah?"

"Well, we did have trouble with a mother, but I—"

Sarah stopped as we all heard the back door open and close. Mrs. Peters had arrived.

***

Mrs. Peters had her smile turned on by the time we walked into her office. She offered us a seat and told us how nice it was to see us again. I was trying hard not to walk out. If I was there to actually adopt a baby, I would have.

"So how are you coming along in your decision?" she asked.

Rosie answered, "We're still weighing all the factors and trying to make a good decision."

Peters nodded in agreement. "It is an important decision, and I'm glad you're taking time to think about it. This isn't something that should be rushed into. How can I help?"

Rosie looked at me lovingly and then back at Peters. "Well, the decision about whether or not we want to add a child to our family is a personal one, but the decision of what agency to use certainly involves you."

Peters nodded with her cutting smile. "Didn't you say last time that you were having trouble and came here because someone recommended us because we produce results?"

"Yes, that's true. But we're still upset about what happened the last time with that other couple."

The smile disappeared and Peters looked confused. "What couple was that?"

"As we came in a couple was leaving, and the woman was crying."

"Oh yes, I remember. It was a personal disagreement between the two of them. I can see how that would upset you, but as I said, I can't discuss our clients. I will show you the same courtesy."

Rosie raised her hand. "I totally understand. I'm just letting you know that was a bit disturbing. Adopting should be a happy occasion."

The smile was back. "Well, I'm sure it will be for you. You seem to have a supportive husband."

"Oh, I do. But we're looking at another agency. This is such a big decision."

She was still smiling, but it wasn't all that friendly. "I understand completely, but we're known for solving problems, not creating them. After all, someone did recommend you. By the way, who was that?"

"Oh, no one you'd know," Rosie said. "A friend of a friend of a friend type of thing."

"I see. But still, a recommendation is valuable."

We sat in an uncomfortable silence for half a minute.

"So if you aren't yet ready to decide, what was your purpose for coming here today?"

"Just for some reassurance."

"I hope I've been able to do that. Do you have any questions?"

Rosie shook her head. "No, I don't think so."

Peters turned to me. "And you, Mr. Blaine? You've been awfully quiet today."

I gave her my best fake smile. I was sure it was better than hers. "No, we just need some more time."

"Well that's no problem. But we do have a few possibilities we're working on. I should know more within the week. Do you think you'll be able to decide by then?"

"I believe we should be able to," I said.

"Wonderful. We'll be in touch. Thanks for coming in again." She stood, walked out from behind the desk, and offered her hand.

Miss Leek gave us a smile and wished us well as we passed her desk. She hadn't been taught well by Peters... hers was genuine.

***

A s we pulled away, I asked Rosie what she thought of Peters.

"She's about as fake as you can be. But I guess she's a good salesman. Tells you what you want to hear and solves all your problems. What do you think?"

I laughed. "That pretty well sums it up. I wouldn't buy Girl Scout cookies from her. Why would anyone trust her with adopting a child?"

"You have to remember, Spencer... there's one big difference here." She paused as I turned a corner. "We're not actually looking for a baby. We have no emotions in the game. Someone who has hopes and dreams is going to be much more susceptible to Peters' sales pitch. They *want* to hear that someone is going to solve their problems. And they'll overlook the fake smile and the sleezy pitch."

I took a deep breath and let it out slowly. "I guess. That's kinda sad."

"It is. It's sad that Peters takes advantage of that."

We drove for another block before I asked, "And what do you think of Sarah Leek?"

"I like her. She doesn't fit in that office, but a job's a job, and she probably does her job well and doesn't have to spend much time with Peters. You?"

"I agree. But she's got something stuck in her throat."

"It does appear that way. How do you want to go about unsticking it?"

"Let's think about it over lunch. You good with Titletown?"

"Sure. The walk will be nice too."

Twenty minutes later we were trying a couple of different beers and waiting for ribs. They were well worth the wait. I was ahead of Rosie six to three.

"If you don't eat faster you're not going to get your share," I said.

She put down her stein and said, "I'm not worried about it. Some of us have figures to watch. And I have this quirk about eating... I like to actually taste my food, especially when it's this good."

That wasn't going to slow me down. "Okay, I warned you."

When we finished, we ordered two more beers and took them out to the patio. It was a good day to be outside… temperature in the seventies and fluffy, white cumulus clouds drifting slowly southeast.

"So what do we do about Sarah?"

"I think one of us needs to run into her outside of work."

She let me think as she lifted her beer. "Which one?"

"I'm open for suggestions. The which may depend on how we're going to run into her."

The bridge bells started to ring. I looked downriver and saw a large sailboat heading toward the bay. Gates went down, lights flashed, and ten seconds later the bridge leafs started to rise.

Rosie drummed her fingers on the table. "How about one of us picks her up after work and follows her home, or wherever she happens to go."

I nodded. "Our only chance is if she goes somewhere besides home. A shopping center would work, or a restaurant. We can hardly claim coincidence by ringing her doorbell."

"Right." She finished the beer. I had beat her by ten minutes. "So who goes?"

"It seems to be more up my alley, but I'm okay with you going. She might relate better to you as the poor woman who can't have a baby. She seems the sympathetic type."

"Okay, I'm game."

We watched the boat motor through the bridge opening.

"How about this, Spencer. We both go. You drive, and I follow her on foot if she stops somewhere."

"Sounds good to me. They close at five. So the next question is today or tomorrow?"

"Hmm. I'm torn. No time like the present, but I'd really like to spend some time at the cottage. And we have no idea how long this might take."

I had been drawing patterns in the moisture on the outside of my stein. "Right. You talked me into tomorrow. There's no hurry."

"That we know of."

"Yeah, well, at the moment I'm voting for the cottage. If something happens between now and tomorrow night, we'll figure it out tomorrow. You ready?"

She nodded. We stood, and I left money on the table. By the time we got to the street the bridge had lowered.

Chapter 13

We packed a day's worth of clothes and headed east out of town to 57. We hit Sturgeon Bay at ten after three, crossed the canal between Green Bay and Lake Michigan, and continued north on 42 into the upper part of the Door County peninsula, which technically was an island as it was separated from the mainland by the canal.

I asked Rosie if she wanted to make a slight detour to the eastern end of the canal and see the Coast Guard station. She said she'd like to at some point, but right now she wanted to be in a lounge chair on my deck.

I turned right onto 57 and headed north. We stopped at the market in Baileys Harbor and stocked up on some food. I got steaks for dinner. Rosie picked out the trimmings.

As we turned out of the parking lot my phone rang, and Rosie answered.

"Hi, Captain."

I tried to figure out the conversation from Rosie's side and thought I had a pretty good idea. After a few minutes, she told him she'd tell me and hung up.

"They have another lead on Stosh. They found someone who hinted that there may have been an initiation that involved shooting a cop."

"Any names?"

"No, but there are a lot of people looking."

"That would solve the gang's problem. Shoot a cop and here's the one we want you to shoot."

Rosie shook her head. "That that's okay to someone is still amazing to me… even after all these years."

"Well—"

She cut me off. "I know the reasons. No mother or father, or useless mother or father, a system that has let them down, and someone finds a way to be important with the Prophets. We run after-school programs and clubs and sports events and still some choose the gangs."

"Not an easy problem, Rosie. He's still okay with you being up here?"

"Seems to be. Says they have it covered."

Just north of Baileys Harbor, I turned onto county Q and immediately felt at home in the forest. Five minutes later, we looked out over Moonlight Bay onto Lake Michigan, and five minutes after that turned onto Moonlight Bay Drive where the homes were partially hidden in the dense pine trees. I turned into the gravel drive I shared with the cottage next door and felt like I always did when I pulled into that drive—the rest of the world didn't exist.

"Spencer, your neighbor's cottage is sold!"

It had been vacant and for sale for most of the last year.

"I wonder who bought it," she said. "Hope it's not someone who likes loud parties."

I pulled up to the side of the cottage and turned off the Mustang. "Shouldn't be a problem, Rosie. That kind of person doesn't like this kind of living."

"I hope you're right."

"I'm pretty confident."

"You can be confident all you want. This you have no control over. I hope it's someone you can get along with."

I told her I wasn't worried. I picked up two bags of groceries and led the way to the front door. After stowing the food and our bags, I said, "Let's open the windows and air this place out. Then I think there are a couple of chairs on the deck with our names on them."

When the temperature started to drop as the sun dipped behind the trees, I suggested we start dinner. Rosie was as hungry as I was.

While we were eating, we talked about Sarah. Rosie added a twist to the plan. If she got the chance to talk to Sarah, depending on how that went, she'd tell Sarah I was waiting out in the car, and I'd like to talk to her too. I agreed.

As I took my last bite of steak, I said, "At some point we need to switch from concerned adoptees to detectives."

While she was cutting her meat, Rosie said, "We'll have to play that by ear."

"Yup. I wonder if she knows two of their clients have been murdered." I watched Rosie finish eating. "But for starters I want to know about the trouble with a mother. That'd be a good ice breaker for you."

"It would," she said. "Let's clean up and take a walk."

"How long a walk do you want to take?"

"I need to work off this steak. What do you have in mind?"

"It's about a forty-minute walk to the lighthouse out on Cana Island."

She agreed. "It's a nice night for a walk."

***

We grabbed flashlights and jackets and headed out a little after eight. The little bit of yellow and light-blue twilight turned to dark blue and then to black. Night came quickly up here. As there were no lights on the road to interfere with the dark, the only light came from far-spread homes tucked back in the forest.

"Do we need to worry about animals?" asked Rosie.

"If we stay on the road and keep our flashlights on they'll stay away from us."

"It's so quiet," she said.

"Yeah, the rest of the world doesn't exist here."

After a half hour we came out of the woods into an opening with the island in front of us. To our right was Moonlight Bay, and Lake Michigan was to our left. And a sky full of stars was above.

"I've never seen so many stars," said Rosie.

"Yes, it's beautiful. Civilization tends to cover up things like that."

We started across the gravel and stone causeway between the mainland and the island. The only sounds were the crunch of our footsteps on the gravel and the gentle wash of waves on the shore. Halfway across we heard the plaintive cry of a loon.

"The lake is low this year," I said. "There were times when I was a kid we waded through water almost to our knees to get across here."

"Is this the only way?"

"It is."

"Where's the lighthouse?"

"You'll see… and you're in for a surprise."

I took Rosie's hand as the narrow path wound into dense trees. And then after a short walk the Cana Island lighthouse came into view as we walked into a clearing. As the light swept over the tops of the trees, I told her the white, steel-clad tower was eighty-nine feet tall, and the light had been in operation since 1869.

"It's beautiful. This is a wonderful surprise, Spencer."

I laughed. "It is, but it's not the surprise I had in mind."

"And what would that be?"

"You'll see."

We walked around the grounds, and she read the informational plaques. Looking up, she said, "I bet the view is spectacular from that walkway." There was a watch deck around the tower just below the lantern.

I took her hand and led her out to the beach where four multi-colored, wooden chairs rested on a little rise above the sand. We sat on the two in the middle.

"This is so peaceful," she said as she looked out over the lake. "I can hardly tell where the water ends and the sky starts."

"Yup, pretty dark. But you'll be able to tell soon enough."

"What do you mean by that? Sounds pretty mysterious."

I just smiled and told her to keep watching. I was dozing a bit when, ten minutes later, Rosie shouted, "Spencer! The water's on fire!"

I laughed. "That's a bit of an oxymoron. But you might think so." Almost directly ahead of us, a red line had appeared at the water's edge. As we watched, the line quickly turned into an enormous red ball rising out of the lake. The full moon was one night away, but this one was still sensational.

Rosie couldn't take her eyes off the water. "That was spectacular, Spencer. Did you know that was going to happen?"

"Yes. I looked at moonrise in the paper. But we got lucky with Ma Nature. A clear night and no wind set the scene."

"Why does the wind matter?"

"Waves would have ruined the effect on the horizon."

We watched for a few more minutes before I reminded her we had to walk back. She reluctantly got up and took a last look up at the rotating light. As we reached the causeway we again heard the loon.

"That's such a sad sound," Rosie said. "But it's mesmerizing."

"That it is. There are Indian legends about the loon that are just as sad as the cry." I told her about the boy whose sight was taken away by his selfish, evil mother and then restored by a loon. "The cry is partly a warning during mating season of a pair protecting their territory."

Halfway across, Rosie stopped and turned to me with tears in her eyes.

I held her shoulders and asked what was wrong.

"They may be protecting their territory, but I think the cry is for Stosh."

I pulled her close to me, and we stood listening for a few minutes before heading home.

The walk back was uneventful. As we were getting ready for bed, Rosie put her arms around me and said, "I'm glad we decided to come here tonight, Spencer. That was a wonderful evening."

"Me too. Tomorrow back to work."

Chapter 14

Thursday started with the sound of rain on the roof at four a.m. I had planned on getting up early to watch the sunrise. Now I was just getting up early. I picked up the book I had brought with me, stretched out on the couch, and listened to the music of the rain. I was on the third chapter of *The Stories Insects Tell,* by Garf. A friend in Hawaii had sent it to me. It was a book about the new field of forensic entomology, the importance of insects as evidence at a crime scene. I found it fascinating.

The rhythm of the rain put me back to sleep around five, and Rosie woke me up at ten after seven by sitting crosswise on the couch and draping her legs on my lap.

"Good morning, Mr. Blaine. Was Mrs. Blaine snoring?"

"No," I said with a smile. "The rain woke me up."

"And then put you back to sleep, it looked like."

"Evidently."

"Watcha reading?"

I handed her the book.

"I've read a couple articles about this," she said. "Sounds interesting."

"It is."

"But the official take is even if it makes sense, it would be impossible to use as evidence in court."

I stretched. "I imagine. But fingerprints were a novelty, too, a while back."

She shrugged. "Breakfast?"

We made scrambled eggs with cheddar cheese and crumbled bacon and ate on the deck under the overhang. It was still drizzling. As we were cleaning up, I said, "I have some phone calls to make, then we have the morning to relax."

"What time do you want to leave?"

"Well, let's make it one thirty. That'll give us enough time to get settled back at the hotel and get to the agency by five."

"Okay. I'll finish up here. Make your calls."

***

The first was to Carol. There was nothing important on her end.

"I have a chore for you," I said.

"Good. I need a distraction from the stress of trying to find something to do."

I ignored her. "Get ahold of Paul. I need him up here by Sunday afternoon. I have a day job that may last a week. Get him our usual rental car and a camera and one of the cell phones. Let me know what the number is. Give him the address of the hotel… tell him I'll reserve a room."

"Will do. Watson misses you."

"Sure he does. Does Billy play with him every day?"

"Of course."

"Does he get fed twice a day?"

"Sure."

"Then he doesn't miss me."

"You just wait and see the greeting you get when you get back."

"Okay. Good luck with that. Oh, one more thing." I explained that I wanted her to be the clearing house for information and to keep her usual notes. She would receive information and get it out to the rest of those involved.

The second call was to Captain Perez to give him an update. He was interested and told me not to get Rosie into any trouble. The third was to Chief Iverson. I let both know about Carol's clearing house assignment.

"Nice of you to check in, Manning," he said, sounding a bit edgy.

"Pardon?"

"I left a message yesterday afternoon."

"Where?"

"At the hotel. Snark is looking for you. He left a message, too, and called me when you didn't return the call."

"Ah, well, we're not at the hotel."

"Avoiding the law?"

"More like if you have a place on Moonlight Bay you might like to spend a day or two there once in a while."

He laughed. "Can't argue with that."

"What's Snark want?"

"He didn't share. But my guess would be he's not quite satisfied about the little incident at the agency and wants to chat."

"Don't see why he wouldn't be satisfied. His breakfast buddy vouched for me."

"No, nothing about that was at all questionable."

"Have you told him more about the agency?"

"Nope. Why would I?"

"Figured it would make good breakfast talk."

"Nah, not my county... not my problem."

"Chicago wasn't your county either."

"No, it wasn't. But that wasn't work. It was something that sounded like too much fun to pass up."

I laughed. "We've been busy. I have more on the agency files."

"Like to hear it, but call Snark first before he issues an arrest warrant."

"You trust him?"

"No reason not to."

"Give me his number." He did.

"I'm guessing he'll want to see you today. Are you planning on going back to Green Bay?"

"Actually, we're going back this afternoon and will be staying at the hotel tonight."

"Well, see if you can work him in. I'm kind of out on a limb here."

"Sure. Is it raining on your side of the county?"

"Yup. Supposed to last all day."

"Well, stay dry. Take the day off."

"Right. Everything good for tomorrow?" Chief asked.

"It is. Thanks for your help."

"My pleasure. Try to behave with Snark."

"I'll do my best."

Rosie had finished up in the kitchen and was sitting on the couch with my book. I told her about the call from Snark.

"Not surprised," she said. "I'd have called you before this."

"That's just because you have a thing for me."

"Snark may have a thing for you too. But probably not the same kind of thing."

I laughed and sat at the kitchen counter with the phone.

As I was dialing, she pointed at the book and said, "Some of this is disgusting. Don't think I'd be fond of maggots crawling in my nose and feasting on my brains."

"If it came to that, I'm thinking you wouldn't be in a position to care."

I had one more call to make before Snark. Maxine answered.

"Hi, Max… how's things in paradise?"

"Hi, Spencer. Just as you'd expect paradise to be. Are you doing okay? I can't imagine. I'm so sorry."

"Doing as good as can be expected. Is Aunt Rose there?"

"She's shopping. You need anything in particular?"

"Nope. Rosie and I are over at the cottage, but we're also spending time in Green Bay looking into something. How's business?"

"It's too good. We're actually looking to hire another person."

"Not a bad problem to have. Tell Rose we'll be by sometime over the weekend. Our love to you both."

"And to you, my knight in shining armor."

I hung up with a smile on my face and passed on the news to Rosie.

***

I dialed Snark's number. As it was ringing, I thought about bugs feasting on my brain. A woman answered, and I got Snark after waiting a few minutes.

"Nice of you to check in, Manning. I left a message yesterday."

"Haven't been at the hotel since yesterday morning. What can I do for you?"

"Need to have a chat. All I got is what Iverson fed me, and that didn't exactly take care of my appetite. I need you here in an hour."

"I'm up in Door. I can be there at three. But I've got a five o'clock appointment."

"Only if I'm done talking. Don't be late." He hung up.

I sat down next to Rosie and told her about the calls.

"Want to leave earlier?"

"No, we'll have enough time."

"Do you know where the police department is?"

"Nope. We'll get it from the front desk."

"What if he keeps you too long to make our appointment?"

"Not going to happen."

"It will if he says it will."

"He'd have to arrest me, and I don't see that happening after all this time and with Iverson going to bat for me."

"He can hold you as a witness."

"Not without me raising the kind of hell he probably doesn't want."

"This isn't Chicago, Spencer. The only friend you have isn't even in the same county."

"I know. But justice is on my side."

"Don't know if you've seen Miss Justice lately... she's got that blindfold over her eyes."

"I do recall that. I'll be nice, and we can always postpone Sarah if we have to."

***

S nark kept me waiting. A uniformed officer gestured at me at twenty after three, and I followed him into Snark's office. He didn't bother to stand.

"You look different standing upright without a sheet on you."

"Yeah, I prefer this look."

He was short and pudgy, and his lower jaw stuck out just enough to be noticeable. A receding hairline was making good progress toward the back of his head. There was no color in his eyes... unless gray was a color. I sat without being offered a seat, and we stared at each other for a good minute. Finally, I broke the stalemate.

"Like I said, I have an appointment. If you have something to talk about..."

"And like I said, you might make it and you might not."

"If you have questions, ask. Otherwise I'm leaving. I've had more than my share of staring contests."

"Think you're pretty smart, huh?"

"I've found that preferable to being dumb."

"Yet you come up with a story like what Iverson fed me?"

Technically, I didn't come up with the story, Iverson did, but I didn't see any future in pointing that out. I knew it was a story Iverson had come up with on the fly, but I knew as well as Snark that the story had as many holes as Swiss cheese.

"Let me see if I've got this straight," said Snark. "You saw someone breaking into the back door of the From Us To You Adoption Agency, and you followed because you're a responsible citizen wanting to stop a crime."

Sounded good to me. I nodded.

"And you, who lives in Chicago, just happened to be in an alley in Green Bay at two in the morning."

I was hoping he wouldn't bring up the Swiss cheese part of the story. "You find that odd?"

He just stared at me. "Perhaps just as odd as someone who has a cottage on Moonlight Bay staying at the Hampton Inn in Green Bay."

I was trying, but it was hard not to see his point. I had always tried to check with my brain first before I opened my mouth, but this time my brain had nothing to add, so I kept my mouth closed.

"Cat got your tongue, Manning?"

I just repositioned myself in the chair and crossed my legs.

"What were you doing there?"

The story was dumb as hell. He knew it, and he knew I knew it, but I needed to know more, both about Snark and the agency, before I shared my opinions. So far all I had was coincidences, and Snark wasn't giving me any reason to be friendly.

I tried to look like I was thinking and slowly shook my head. "You know, I've been trying to remember what happened. That blow on the head seems to have affected my memory. I'm very concerned."

"I bet you are. What do you know about the adoption agency?"

"Beyond they probably arrange adoptions... nothing. Why? Do you suspect them of something?"

"I suspect *you* of something, but I don't know what it is." He leaned forward and folded his hands together on top of his desk. "I'll level with you, Manning. Something was going on. I think you were planning on breaking in, but somebody beat you to it. I'd like to know why."

I spread my hands apart. "I'd like to help, but I just don't remember. I was in the hospital, you know."

"That's the hand you're playing with?"

At the moment, it was the only hand I had, and I wasn't too happy about it. I shrugged.

"What do you know that I don't?"

"Probably lots of things, but since I don't know what you know, that's a pretty hard question to answer."

"Okay, be a smart-ass. The only reason you're not under arrest is Iverson stuck up for you."

"What would you arrest me for?"

"I'd find something." He stared at me some more. "I did some checking up on you, Manning. You've made quite a name for yourself up here." He continued when I didn't respond. "A little matter a few years back with the mayor of Chicago's wife shot by you up here at his summer place."

My brain was still recommending my mouth stay shut.

"Seems like a lot got swept under the rug… left a lot unexplained."

It was a very strange and sad case, and when I'm shot at I shoot back. Everyone who mattered had been satisfied, including the mayor. And the sweeping under the rug had been done for his benefit, not mine. But that was something very few people knew about and certainly not something I was going to share with Snark. I had told Iverson the story, but Iverson evidently hadn't felt the need to tell Snark either.

"No answer, Manning?"

"First, I shot in self-defense, and second, you didn't ask a question."

He scrunched up his lips and tapped his fingers on his desk.

We danced around and around for another hour before he told me to get the hell out of his office and warned me that he was looking into this. And if he found one hair out of place I'd be back in his office, perhaps in cuffs.

I stood. Not wanting to appear uncooperative, I said, "If I remember anything I'll let you know."

"I'm sure you will."

As I got to the door, he added, "I'm going to find out what's going on." I stopped walking and turned back.

"Do I get a question?"

He just stared at me.

"Were there any forced entry marks on the door?"

"The door?"

"The door. The person I was following got in first. How did they get in? Were there any marks of forced entry?"

He still stared.

"I could go back and look."

He thought about that for a few seconds and said, "No, there weren't."

I smiled and walked away.

***

Rosie saw me coming and started the Mustang as I hurried down the walk.

"Are we going to make it?" she asked.

"It'll be close, but we should."

She ran a couple of yellow lights, and we got there just in time. Traffic was light. We had just pulled into a parking spot on the street a few doors down from the agency when Sarah walked out the door and locked it behind her. She was wearing a raincoat and carrying an umbrella, but the rain had stopped. We watched as she walked up the street away from us and stopped at the corner at a bus shelter.

"That'll make it easier to follow her," I said.

"Wonder which way she's going."

"It shouldn't matter. Even if we have to turn around, we shouldn't lose a bus."

The bus came at eight after and headed away from us. Rosie pulled out and followed.

Chapter 15

Rosie had to be careful at stops to make sure Sarah didn't get off the bus. About ten minutes later, she did and transferred to another bus that headed west. The bus made for another addition to the plan that Rosie and I had discussed. If she went somewhere besides home first, Sarah would need a ride home. We could offer her dinner and a ride and have time to chat.

Five minutes later, the bus stopped in front of Target, and Sarah got off. Rosie pulled into the parking lot and found a spot close to the doors. As Sarah went in, Rosie followed her. As I watched the customers I thought about Snark and wondered how I could find out what his first name was. I tried to come up with something worse than Snark, but I came up empty.

Twenty minutes later, Rosie opened the passenger door.

"You talk to her?" I asked.

She nodded emphatically. "Yes. We're all set. She smiled when she saw me and seems anxious to talk. She's finishing shopping and will meet us out here."

"Did you ask about dinner?"

"She liked that idea. I think she's lonely."

"Good, we'll unlonely her for the evening."

"Unlonely?"

"Did you know what I meant?"

She shook her head and rolled her eyes.

The rain started again, this time a bit harder than the steady drizzle that had been falling most of the day. I pulled in the loading area under an overhang close to the doors so Sarah wouldn't have to use her umbrella. She came out a few minutes later.

"Thanks for moving the car," she said. "What a dreary day."

"You remember Spencer?" asked Rosie.

"Yes, of course. Hello, Mr. Blaine."

"Hello, Sarah. Please call me Spencer."

She smiled. "Okay. This is a very cool car!"

"Thanks. I'm pretty fond of it… almost a member of my family." Actually, since Dad had given it to me, it *was* a member of my family. "Rosie says you'll join us for dinner."

"Yes, that would be very nice."

"What would you suggest?"

Someone behind me honked. I looked in the mirror and saw a man gesturing for me to move. I pulled up so he could get under the overhang.

"Well, I like Perkins. They're pretty popular up here."

"We've been to Perkins," said Rosie. "That would be fine."

It was fine for Rosie… she didn't mind dinner without beer.

Sarah gave me directions, and we chatted about the weather and made small talk during the fifteen-minute drive.

The restaurant wasn't very crowded, and we were seated in a booth by a hostess who seemed glad to see us. The waiter took our drink order and left us to the menus. As I looked at the dinners, I watched Sarah looking nervously around the room. I had the feeling she was concerned about being seen with us.

Rosie asked what we were going to have, and I made a comment about bangers and mash. Sarah gave me a puzzled look, and I told her about McGoon's. I extended an invitation if she was ever in Chicago and asked if she had ever been there.

She shook her head and looked down. "I'm afraid I'm a small-town girl. I don't think I'd like Chicago… the things I hear… the murders…"

"Green Bay is hardly a small town, Sarah."

"But it's not *that* big, and even *it's* too big for me."

"Where did you grow up?"

"My family has a farm in Readfield, west of Appleton. About three hundred people. I love it there."

"Then why are you in Green Bay?" I asked.

"The farm isn't doing so well. I needed to get a job. There aren't any in Readfield."

"I'm sorry to hear that, Sarah." I started on my coffee. Sarah had tea. "Do you like working at the agency?"

She hesitated and reached for her tea. "It's a job, and it helps out at home. They wouldn't be able to make it without the money I send. But I really don't like the city."

"No brothers?" I asked.

"Yes, but he's only fourteen. He does his chores, but that doesn't pay the bills."

We both wished her family luck as the waiter passed out the food. We all got in a few bites before Sarah said she wanted to tell us something. It was obvious she was having trouble with it.

"I'm not sure how to say this, so I'll just say it and hope I'm not being... well..."

Rosie touched Sarah's arm. "Just go ahead, Sarah. We're all friends here."

"Well, I see a lot of couples at the agency. We always require both people come in. A lot of them are... well, what I want to say is, you two are the nicest couple I've met. It's obvious how much you care about each other. Mrs. Blaine... Rosie, I saw the way he looks at you. I hope I find someone who looks at me that way."

Rosie laughed, and I think Sarah blushed.

"I'm sorry, Sarah. That was lovely... thanks. My laugh was because you don't know Spencer. Two things. One, he looks at his Mustang the same way, so I don't get too excited. And two, I'm sure you'll find someone. You're a lovely person. Some guy will be lucky to have you."

She blushed again.

As we got back to the food, I turned the conversation back to the agency.

"When we were at the agency you were saying you had trouble with a mother."

She wiped her mouth. "You have a good memory."

"When he wants to," said Rosie with a smile. "We *have* been wondering what you were going to say."

She looked around the room again. "Well, we had a mother who gave up her baby but changed her mind."

"We asked Mrs. Peters about that. Does that happen much?"

She shook her head. "Not much. That was the only time since I'd been there, but then I haven't been there long, so I don't know about before."

"What happened?"

"I really don't know much about it. Mrs. Peters doesn't tell me about the clients. I just take care of the front desk. But Victoria has been…" She stopped and put her hand over her mouth.

"What's the matter, Sarah?" I asked. I made sure not to look at Rosie.

"I shouldn't have said her name. Please don't tell Mrs. Peters I told you. Mothers' and clients' names are confidential. She'd fire me." She looked scared.

Rosie patted her arm again. "Don't worry, Sarah. We'd never say anything. To tell you the truth, we're not very fond of Mrs. Peters."

She let out a long breath and looked relieved. A little smile replaced the fear. "To tell *you* the truth, I'm not either."

We all laughed.

"Do you know any more about it?" Rosie asked.

"I just overheard yelling. Normally I can't hear what goes on in Mrs. Peters' office… she usually keeps the door closed. But Vic…" she looked at both of us.

"It's okay, Sarah," said Rosie.

Sarah nodded. "I could hear because Victoria was yelling. She wanted to know who had her baby. They're not supposed to know that."

"Of course not," Rosie said. "Did you hear anything else?"

"No. A few minutes later Victoria left. She didn't look at me. Mrs. Peters came out and told me there had been a misunderstanding, and Victoria should not be allowed in if she came back and not to make any appointments with her. She told me we were going to keep the doors locked for a few days."

"She didn't call the police and report it?"

She shook her head. "No. I suggested that, but she didn't want to. She said she just needed to blow off some steam and that was probably the end of it."

"And did she ever come back?"

"No, but I was pretty scared. But I felt better with the doors locked."

I was beginning to think she *had* come back, and was hoping I'd get to thank her some day for the bump on my head.

"There's something else about Victoria," Sarah said. "The agency owns a house that we let mothers live in if they need help while going through the process. Victoria lives there."

"Okay, Sarah, thanks. One more question. We heard there was a break-in a few days ago. Were there any others?"

She looked puzzled. "Not that were reported."

"What does that mean?" Rosie asked.

"About six months ago Mrs. Peters asked me if I had been in the office after hours. I told her I hadn't and asked why. She said a file drawer was slightly open. Why do you ask?"

"No special reason," I said. "It just seems that odd things are happening there."

When Sarah didn't continue, I said, "We're very concerned about using your agency. We're leaning toward looking somewhere else."

She looked worried. "I hope I didn't—"

Rosie reassured her. "No, we had concerns after the first time we talked with Mrs. Peters. You've just confirmed what we already thought."

It was time to change the subject. "Do you go back home, Sarah?"

She immediately brightened up. "I go back on the weekends. I don't think I'd be able to stand it if I didn't."

"What do you miss about it the most?" Rosie asked. "I mean besides your family."

Sarah looked wistful and smiled slightly. "Hootie," she said softly.

"Hootie?" I asked.

She nodded. "When I go to bed, I listen to the crickets. It's so peaceful… no traffic noise or radios. And we have a barn owl. He says goodnight to me every night." She frowned a bit. "I know that sounds silly, but I miss that."

"Not silly at all," said Rosie. "You're lucky."

She looked uncomfortable.

"Is there something else, Sarah?" Rosie asked.

She folded her hands on the table top and looked down at them. "I've never told anyone this."

We waited.

"I think the owl is…"

After some silence, Rosie said, "It's okay, Sarah. You don't have to tell us if it's hard for you."

I had no idea what she was trying to say, but it seemed like Rosie did.

Sarah looked up at Rosie. "No, I'd like to. I've never told anyone." After some more silence and a glance at me she continued. "I think the owl is me. I seem to know what he's thinking. Sometimes I think he's me in a past life." She let out a long sigh, like she had just gotten something off her chest. She glanced briefly at me and then looked back at Rosie. "You probably think I'm crazy, but no matter what happened during the day I went to sleep happy."

Rosie shook her head. "No, not at all. I've read some about that. I think there are things that we just don't know about… that there are no good explanations for. I think it's very special that you have that relationship with your owl… no matter what the explanation is."

Sarah looked relieved.

The waiter started clearing the table and asked if we wanted dessert. We all ordered pie. Sarah was hesitant about spending our money, but Rosie reassured her dinner included dessert. I wanted to tell her it also included beer, but…

Sarah thanked us profusely for dinner as she guided us to her apartment building. It was four units on a block of buildings that were all alike. They were nicely kept up, but I could imagine she missed the farm every time she came home. She waved after she unlocked the door.

As soon as we were back in the car I said, "An owl in a previous life?"

"Come on, Spencer. There are lots of stories about things that there are no explanations for."

"Like ghosts?"

"Sure, like ghosts… and near-death experiences where people see their loved ones in a bright light, smiling and beckoning to them. There are things beyond simple explanations."

"Well, none of that has ever happened to me."

"No? Maybe not those specifically, but what about all your feelings about cases based on just gut feelings and no evidence?"

"That's different. That's real life."

She shook her head. "The situations are real, but your assumptions are based on something other than reality most of the time. And you're always right."

I smiled. "That's because I'm good at what I do."

"Not saying you're not. But something is guiding you, and you can't give me a good explanation for it."

I thought about that and pulled away from the curb. I had read a book about ghosts and spirits, but I didn't know what to believe. We had driven about a block when Rosie said, "So Victoria wasn't only an employee."

"Right. Interesting. She was also a birth mother, and I'm betting we've found the mystery person who clobbered me."

"And we know why she was there. She was trying to find out who had adopted her baby."

"Maybe."

I turned and headed north.

"Maybe?"

"Still trying to fit the pieces together, Rosie. If that was her, who was there two months ago? And we know something Sarah doesn't."

"Right. Victoria wasn't only a mother, she was an employee."

"And a mother who wants her baby back."

"And isn't getting it."

I stopped a bit suddenly as a light turned yellow. "Mrs. Peters told Sarah Victoria was just blowing off steam. I wonder if the pot is still boiling."

"And how much steam is still blowing?" Rosie said.

"Enough to kill someone?"

"We've both seen enough to know it doesn't take much steam to kill someone, Spencer. All it takes is one heated conversation, and this is a lot more than that."

"Snark said there weren't any signs of forced entry on the door. Employees have keys. Maybe both times were Victoria."

"And you think they didn't change the locks after the first incident?"

"It's possible," I said. "Sarah would know."

"I bet they're changed now."

"I bet they are."

"Sarah would know that too," Rosie said.

"She'd also know why there were multiple names on the folders."

"Yes, but you'd have to explain how *you* know that. Unless you can come up with something, you'll have to tell her you were the one who broke in."

"Well, technically—"

She waved her hand. "Yeah, yeah. I know, you didn't break in."

I drove another block. "I'd really like to know." I pulled into an alley and turned around.

"You've got fifteen minutes to think of something," said Rosie.

"I'll try and do that while you enjoy the scenery."

She laughed.

Chapter 16

I hadn't thought of anything. I rang the doorbell, and a minute later Sarah moved a curtain and looked out the window. She let us in with a puzzled look.

"We're sorry to bother you, Sarah, but we have a couple more questions."

"Okay, please sit down." She pointed to the couch. There wasn't a lot of furniture. My guess was the place came furnished. There were a few homey touches, like a picture of her family on the table, but there weren't many decorations. Sarah wasn't making this home.

"Can I get you anything to drink?" Sarah asked.

We declined.

"Sarah, there are a few more things we'd like to ask you about." I took a deep breath and looked at Rosie. She just raised her eyebrows and shrugged just enough for me to notice. She hadn't thought of anything either.

I decided I had to level with her. "We haven't been quite truthful with you, Sarah."

Her look turned from puzzled to a bit wary and maybe afraid. I quickly explained.

"We *are* from Chicago, but we're not looking for a baby. Rosie is a police detective, and I'm a private detective. We're looking into something that may involve your adoption agency." I showed her my license and Rosie showed her badge. I wouldn't have blamed Sarah if she asked us to leave, but she seemed to calm down and the puzzled look was back.

She asked what we were looking into, and we told her we weren't totally sure yet so couldn't say any more. She asked what else we wanted to know.

Rosie told her we were wondering if the locks had been changed after the suspected break-in.

"No. Mrs. Peters said they were going to, but they didn't. But they did on Monday after the break-in over the weekend. I have new keys."

"Okay, that's good." I didn't mention that the new locks would stop Victoria but not me. "The other thing we'd like to know is why there are several names on the file folders."

She started to answer and then, suddenly, the puzzled look was back. "How do you know about the file folders?"

Of course. I decided the truth was sometimes the best answer.

"Because I was the one who was in the office Saturday night."

"You were? You broke in?"

I nodded. "I was, but I didn't break in."

"Then how did you get in?"

"The door was already unlocked, and somebody was already inside. And that somebody hit me on the head and knocked me out."

"Who do you think that was?"

The truth wasn't always the best answer. "I don't know." I may have had the truth, and I may not have. "Someone obviously looking for something. I saw two folders with multiple names on them. There was one name on the tab and then three other names. Under that was the name Victoria Petrace. Do you know anything about that?"

It took a minute for her to process all the information, and I still wasn't sure she wouldn't ask us to leave. She finally answered.

"Yes, when I was learning the job, Mrs. Peters told me the names were the possible adopting families. I was responsible for the filing. Not all the files had multiple names. Some only had one."

"And how would you know who the adopting family was?"

"That would be the name on the top tab. If for some reason that didn't work out, we'd call the next person."

I looked at Rosie. She was watching Sarah.

"Sarah, were there adoptions that didn't work out?" asked Rosie.

She sat up in her chair. "Sure. Once in a while."

"And do you know anything about the adopting families being asked to pay to help support the mother?"

By the look on her face, she didn't. "Pardon? I'm not sure what you're talking about."

"Well, we've met a couple families who didn't get the baby who were told the mother wanted the baby back, but she had no money. The families were asked if they would be willing to donate money to the mother."

Sarah vehemently shook her head. "I don't know anything about that. I can't imagine... is that what you're looking into?"

I said it was, and she seemed satisfied. At the moment, I decided telling her about the murders would only needlessly scare her and asked if she had ever heard of Single Mother Outreach. She hadn't.

She grasped her hands in her lap. "With all these break-ins, do you think I'm in any danger?"

I didn't think so, even with the part we hadn't told her. Victoria wouldn't show up during business hours.

"No, I don't think so. I think whatever was going on is over, but if you ever feel uncomfortable, call the police... and us." I wrote down our numbers and explained about my car phone. "And we're looking for Victoria, so call if you see her."

She seemed satisfied.

"Sarah, would you give us a description of Victoria?"

She did... short, short brown hair, and a round face.

I asked if she had any questions. She didn't. But she did say she missed life on the farm. I would have too.

***

When we got in the car I asked Rosie to get my notebook and the map out of the glove compartment.

"Victoria?"

"Yes. Her address is in the notebook. There's a list of the streets on the back of the map."

Rosie found it, and we headed west.

"So Victoria isn't getting in anymore," she said. "Either she has the information she needs or she's still looking and won't get it from the agency."

"I'm wondering why she broke in twice."

"Maybe she was interrupted the first time before she found what she wanted. Maybe she just found a couple of names."

"Yeah, Powolski and Hanover. And she hasn't found her baby yet."

"And if she hasn't found her baby, maybe the steam still has a bullet in it."

Rosie hesitated before saying "maybe."

"And if she found the other names this time…"

"We need to make some phone calls."

***

We found Victoria's address and parked on the street across from it, in front of a house that had a for rent sign in the window. The whole neighborhood was depressed, but her house was the worst. It was a small, wood frame house that needed a lot of work. The agency wasn't putting a lot of effort into being a landlord. A shutter was hanging at an angle, it badly needed a paint job, trees and bushes were overgrown, the yard was full of weeds, and there were three newspapers on the walk leading up to the house. The house was dark.

Rosie used my car phone to call Detective Springer and Chief Werth at their home numbers to tell them about Victoria. They said they'd talk to Mr. Hanover and the Freys and get them some protection.

When Rosie disconnected from Chief Werth, she asked me about the other couple. The Bells lived in Green Bay.

"I guess we need to call Snark," I said.

"And tell him how we know all this?"

"I'd rather he not have anything that's going to end up with me in jail."

"If it was me," Rosie said, "I'd be willing to overlook that for what we're giving him."

"But it's not you. He's not a member of my fan club."

A car pulled into a spot on the other side of the street, and two people entered the house next to Victoria's.

"So maybe I contact him and tell him I uncovered this information along with a case I've been working on in Chicago," she said.

"Maybe. We need to do something about the Bells. Call him."

She called the Green Bay police and was told they would try and get ahold of the chief, but he was at a banquet so it might be a while. More than likely he would call in the morning. Rosie tried to convince the person on the other end of the line that this was a matter of some urgency. When I heard Rosie say "No, it's not an emergency" I knew we weren't going to get through to Snark. But I knew they could get ahold of the chief if they wanted to.

"Sounded like that didn't go too well," I said.

"I tried."

We sat for another ten minutes and decided, especially given the papers, that Victoria wasn't coming home tonight. But I suggested I check with the neighbor. Rosie agreed. I rang the bell and only had to wait a few seconds before a man answered. I explained that I was a friend of Victoria's and was concerned because I hadn't been able to get ahold of her.

The man seemed surprised that Victoria had any friends. He had never seen anyone at her house and had rarely seen *her*. I asked when the last time was. He said he wasn't sure of the day, but it had been early this week. I thanked him and headed back to the car.

"What next?" Rosie asked.

"Back to the hotel. It's been a long day."

She reviewed as I drove.

"We know Victoria hasn't been home for at least three days. So she's obviously somewhere else… but where? And we know she's looking for her baby."

"And probably knows the names on the folder," I said. "And perhaps has already killed two of them."

"Yeah, there's a lot of anger there," Rosie said. "A mother looking for her baby. I can't imagine."

My car phone rang as we were pulling into the parking garage at the hotel. It was Aunt Rose inviting us for dinner tomorrow. Rosie left to get a shower while I chatted for a few minutes. She repeated what Maxine had told me about business and needing another person. As I was walking to the elevator, I thought back to the day I had driven Maxine up to Door County and introduced her to Aunt Rose. That had certainly worked out well for both of them. As I was reaching for the button, I remembered this was the last night of our reservation. I stopped at the front desk and extended it a week, hoping we wouldn't have to use all of that time.

Chapter 17

Friday dawned with a clear sky and a fresh smell in the air. Temperatures in the mid-seventies were predicted. That was the forecast for the whole weekend. We had a leisurely breakfast at the hotel and decided to spend the day trying to turn over some rocks. You never knew what would crawl out.

As we were getting ready to head out the phone rang. It was the Green Bay police... a sergeant Larch. Snark was requesting Rosie's presence as soon as possible. We changed our schedule for the day and headed there first. On the way, we discussed whether I should join her. She left it up to me. I decided I would, and I'd still stick with Iverson's original story but tell him everything else... well, almost. Snark was going to discover the connection somewhere along the way... so why not now? If he was worth anything he probably already suspected. A PI is found unconscious and then a detective from Chicago shows up and leaves a cryptic message. That has to start the wheels turning.

We were escorted to his office. Rosie went in first. He started to stand and then saw me and started to laugh.

"Well that explains a lot." He said hello to Rosie and held a hand out to the chairs in front of his desk. "What's the story today?"

"It's a long story," Rosie said. "And I'd rather not repeat it. You want to have someone take notes?"

He took in a deep breath, sighed, and keyed his intercom. "Marge, will you find me a stenographer, please?" She said she would. An Officer Stillman arrived in two minutes and sat in the corner. He was as big as a house. Not exactly the stereotype for a stenographer.

Rosie talked for the next twenty minutes, starting with Stosh's murder. She told him about the Hanovers in St. Charles and the Freys in Appleton.

He looked skeptical. "And you think this all has something to do with the adoption agency, so your friend here broke in?"

"I didn't—"

He held up a hand. "Yeah, I know. For the moment let's accept that broke in is easier to say than was following someone and the door was open when you got there." He turned back to Rosie.

"It's sure a possibility," she said. "The pieces point in that direction, and there was also a break-in several months ago that wasn't reported."

"And you know that how?"

"A source who'd like to remain unnamed for the moment."

"Uh huh." He looked at me. "And when you broke in you got the names you just told me about?"

"Correct, and one more. There were four names on the folder besides the birth mother. The fourth family is Harold and Claudia Bell here in Green Bay."

"And you're just letting me know this now?"

"We just put it together last night. We called St. Charles and Appleton and you. And here we are."

Snark stood up and walked to the window. He looked out with his arms crossed on his chest. When he turned back his look had changed from skeptical to sad.

"I'm sorry about Lieutenant Powolski. That doesn't cover it, but those are the only words I have." The sad look changed to serious and was aimed at me. "Manning, as much as I'd like to nail you to the wall, I'd have to agree that there is something to your story. It's at least worth looking into. Bullets match?"

"Yup," I said.

"Well that probably ties those two together."

"Probably?" I said.

He shrugged. "Probably. But maybe the gun was stolen after the first murder and used to commit another."

"Who just happen to be people who used the same adoption agency?"

He picked up a pack of Marlboros, tapped the end, and pulled out a cigarette. He stuck it between his lips and continued talking without lighting it.

"Stranger things have happened. I'm saying probably... 99 percent."

"Jesus." I knew he was just giving me crap, but I didn't need any crap. "You heard of Single Mother Outreach?" I asked.

He shook his head, and I explained the letter.

"We'll look into it. You have any reason to believe there's something wrong there?"

"Other than they have a PO box and an answering machine... no. Worth checking."

He stared at me for a few seconds and said, "As busy as you two have been, did you think of checking on Petrace?"

"Yes. We went to her house last night. Three newspapers on the walk, and the neighbor said he hadn't seen her since early in the week."

He hit the intercom again. "Marge, if Dunsley is in, would you have him come in, please?"

"Sure, Chief."

He asked Stillman to get the notes typed up and give them to Dunsley. While we were waiting, he went back over parts of the story, asking a few more questions. A man in plainclothes walked in while Snark was asking again about our unnamed source, and Rosie again was declining any information.

The chief introduced us to Detective Dunsley, who looked like he just got out of bed. He was a big lug of a man with a round face and moppy hair that needed combing. His clothes looked like he had picked them up from where he had dropped them the night before. He wore tan slacks and a brown tie that clashed with a blue sweater that looked like it had been sharing a closet with moths. But what caught my attention the most was his eyes. They were too far apart and appeared to have no desire to focus on whatever he was looking at.

Snark gave him the story in a nutshell. "Get the transcript from Stillman and start looking into this agency. Have a chat with Mrs. Peters. Tell her we're looking into the break-in, and ask if there were any before this one. But first, check on the Bells." He gave Dunsley our contact numbers and told him to keep us in the loop. "Big shot here has a phone in his car."

Dunsley looked at me with disdain and reluctantly said he'd let us know what he found out about the Bells as soon as he knew and would keep us informed about the agency. He said all the right words, but his heart wasn't in it. It sounded like he was just going through the motions because his chief had told him to. And my credibility with the chief wasn't on the high side.

Dunsley left, and Snark asked if we had brought guns.

"Yes, they're cased in the trunk," I said.

"Well, I'd be happy if they stayed there."

"So would I," I said.

On the way to the car I asked Rosie if she had noticed Dunsley's pants.

"What about them?"

"They have cuffs. What's with that?"

She laughed. "That's the latest fashion this year. Where have you been?"

"Not on *my* pants."

"Well, if you're going to flaunt fashion I'll have to decide if I want to be seen in public with you."

"Great... let me know how that turns out."

***

Our first stop was going to be the office of the *Green Bay Press-Gazette*, but it had become our second.

On the way, Rosie said, "Okay, it's 10:40 Friday morning. When do I find out what's going on?"

I laughed. "A little more patience would be a good thing. And I never said you'd find out on Friday... I just said you'd find out."

She sighed.

We started with the lady at the front desk who referred us to someone else who referred us to someone else. It took a half hour, but we finally found a newsman who had been there for thirty-two years. The lady at the front desk said he had a mind like a steel trap, and if anyone knew anything about anything in Green Bay it would be Jack Chesterton. He led us through a maze of desks, cubicles, and file cabinets to his desk in the corner of the large room. A fat cigar was wasting away in a silver ashtray.

"So what can I do for you folks?"

I told him we were investigating a case that had led us to the From Us to You Adoption Agency and asked if he remembered anytime they had been in the news. He, of course, wanted to know what we were investigating. Rosie just smiled at him, and he just smiled back. When they were done smiling at each other he said he knew of them and might be able to help... if he only knew something about why we were asking.

Rosie smiled some more.

"You've been doing this long enough," I said. "We need some information. If we could tell you anything about it we would." I got to be included without having to smile. "But so far, we're not even sure if we're looking in the right spot."

He stopped smiling and stared at Rosie for a few seconds. I couldn't blame him for that... she wasn't hard to stare at. Without looking away from her, he yelled, "Brewer!" A shaggy-haired kid who looked like he was in high school looked around the corner of a cubicle. Chesterton managed to look away from Rosie. "See what you can find on the From Us to You Adoption Agency." The kid moved pretty quickly around the other side of the cubicle and disappeared.

Chesterton smiled some more and then picked up the cigar. After blowing a cloud of smoke straight up in the air, he said, "Suppose I tell *you* what you're investigating."

Rosie extended her right hand toward him, palm up. "Be my guest."

He took another puff, tapped the ash off the end, and put the cigar gently back in the tray. "You've got somebody back in Chicago who adopted a kid. It didn't go well. My guess is there was an upset mother. Whoever you got in Chicago hired a private to look into it. But there must be a little more to it than that because we're sitting here with a Chicago detective. But maybe that somebody has connections that buy a trip by a detective along with the private."

Rosie looked at me and smiled.

"Or maybe the private talked the detective into coming along for the ride because he likes her company." He paused and fingered the cigar and gave us a sly smile. "Can't say as how I'd blame him."

The kid came running up with a folder and said he had found nothing on Single Mother. He disappeared just as quickly as someone else yelled at him from across the room. Chesterton opened the file and picked up the cigar. He handed Rosie a fact sheet on the agency and scanned an article. He handed me the article as he puffed out some more smoke. The article was dated June of 1983, two years ago.

"I remember the article," he said. "We were doing a series on kids... a whole variety of stuff. Backgrounds and information on various companies. What I remember as being odd about the adoption agency was they had what seemed like very few adoptions in eleven years. Less than ten a year if I remember correctly. Hard to make money that way. Most are a lot busier."

I set the article on his desk and asked, "Did anyone raise that point?"

"Yes. That's in the article. A Mrs. Peters said they were in a business where you needed to be extra careful. I wonder if she's still there."

"She is. Yes, they need to be careful, but there's that nasty thing called profit. Employees tend to want to be paid."

"Yes, odd. Maybe you could ask her."

Rosie asked if she could make a copy of the fact sheet.

He called the boy back, and he ran off again.

"So, how close am I?"

Rosie laughed. "Well, it does have to do with an adoption."

He spun the cigar in the tray. "When you can tell me the rest I'd appreciate it. We need profits too."

"No problem," Rosie said. "It's your story."

The boy was back and laid the sheets on the desk. Rosie took one as we stood.

"Thanks for your help," Rosie said. "

"My pleasure. I'll be here." He didn't stand as he wished us luck.

***

When we got in the car, Rosie read the sheet and gave me the facts.

"The company was started in 1972 by a Justine Trainer. It lists her address and the address of the agency… same as now. There's a paragraph giving the company mission statement. Mrs. Cynthia Peters was hired in 1973. Under miscellaneous, it says there had only been fifty-two adoptions since 1972."

"So how do they make money?"

"Good question. Here's another… what next?"

"Lunch." We pulled out of the lot and headed down Maple. "Let me know if something looks good to you."

Rosie saw a diner that she said looked like fun. As I was pulling in, the phone rang. Detective Dunsley gave a very succinct report that he had seen Claudia Bell who was alive and well. I asked if he had spoken to her in person. He hadn't. When I pointed out that I'd feel better if he had actually talked to her face-to-face, he told me how I felt wasn't his priority. When I persisted, he told me to mind my own business and that he had done what his chief had asked him to do. I also wondered how he had become a detective, but I didn't ask that.

I turned off the car and shook my head.

"That went well," said Rosie.

"Yeah, almost ruined my appetite."

As we were making a couple of cheeseburgers disappear, Rosie again asked what the plan was.

I checked my watch. It was almost one thirty. "Well, I'd like to stop in Algoma on the way up to Door County. There's a very cool pierhead light at the river entrance. But I'd also like to stop and see Mrs. Bell."

"What's our excuse for that?"

"Asking directions always works. But we can watch the house for a bit. I'd be happy just seeing her, but I think she needs to be aware of what's going on."

I followed the last bit of cheeseburger with a fry.

***

We found the Bell's house and parked a few houses down and across the street. It was a well-kept ranch on a quiet side street on a hill. It was landscaped with a garden in front of the picture window and flowers along the walk up to the front door. A one-car garage was attached to the south end of the house.

I was ready to go to plan B when the garage door opened and a Buick pulled out with a woman driving. She headed in our direction, and we got a good look at Mrs. Bell. She looked alive to me.

"How do you know that's her and not someone who just killed her?" Rosie asked with a smirk.

"I'm willing to make that assumption."

"Good luck with that."

I knew she wasn't serious. As assumptions go, that was a pretty good one.

***

Algoma was only a little out of the way to Door. It's a small town on the shore of Lake Michigan that had been a part of the trip up to Door County when I was a kid. It had a great hot dog stand.

We had plenty of time to relive some memories and make it to Aunt Rose's in time for dinner.

I turned onto Lake Street and pulled into the parking area next to the beach. From there we could see the red pierhead light at the entrance to the Ahnapee River. We sat at a picnic bench and watched the boats making their way out onto the lake where the sun sparkled off of the waves. After a few minutes, I took Rosie's hand and pulled her up.

"Where are we going?"

"For a walk."

She came along willingly until I turned onto the concrete break-wall on the south side of the harbor. It was about a hundred yards long and angled north toward the light. The wall was conical with a flat top that was about two feet across and was about three feet above the water.

Rosie hesitated. "We're not walking on that, are we?"

"I am," I said with a smile. "You can stay here if you forgot to take your brave pill this morning."

I got a look that I would call unfriendly. "Why?"

"Because it's a tradition. I did this every time we came up here."

"And your folks did it with you?"

"Well, not Mom, and not always Dad."

"No, I didn't think so."

"You have a great view of the light from the end of this wall," I said.

"I can see it from here," she said without much enthusiasm.

A wave rolled up onto the sand.

"Suit yourself."

I let go of her hand, and she took mine again with a look of res-ignation. "If you guarantee this is safe."

"No guarantees in life, my dear."

But she followed as I walked slowly along the wall. The smell of fish got stronger the farther out we got. The wall needed some repair, and we had to step over a few large cracks. But ten minutes later we got to the end on the south side of the river. She admitted that the view of the light was much better, but with the waves slapping against the wall she wanted to head back.

I waited until we were back on firm ground before telling her about my experience in the fog. When I was about ten, I took my walk out onto the breakwall on a warm sunny day. I was about halfway out when the temperature suddenly dropped, and five seconds later the foghorn started to blare. Five seconds after that I was enshrouded in fog and could only see about a foot in front of me. It was a bit unnerving. I remember feeling a bit dizzy and a lot disoriented. But after some deep breaths, I realized if I stayed on the wall and started walking, I'd eventually get back to shore.

But there were two problems. Given the visibility, staying on the wall took some effort. And when the fog rolled in I had been facing at a right angle to the wall path. As hard as I tried, I couldn't remember if I was facing the lake or the harbor inside the wall. But still, I knew if I chose the wrong way I'd just have to turn around. I turned to my right and, a half hour later, arrived back on shore to the welcoming committee of Dad and a very relieved looking Mom.

Rosie hit me on the shoulder with her open hand. "And you didn't tell me about this before we went?"

I smiled. "Would you have gone?"

"Of course not!"

"Well, there you are. Aren't you're glad you did it?"

She gave me a stern, angry look and said with clenched teeth, "Yes... but once is enough."

I put my arm around her waist. "I recall a little incident not far from here where we were both being shot at. And you're giving me crap about this?"

She just shook her head and rolled her eyes.

"Let's go see what's for dinner," I said.

Chapter 18

We drove past Peninsula State Park and the bottom of the bay and turned up the hill of the drive into Aunt Rose's rustic inn in Ephraim. The cat, Amelie, was lying in the sun on the porch railing. As we were walking up the porch steps, Maxine came out to see who had arrived. After hugs, I left her with Rosie and went to find Aunt Rose. At five o'clock, the kitchen was the best bet.

"Are there two spots available for dinner?" I asked from the doorway to the kitchen which was filled with the aroma of a roast in the oven. A cherry pie sat on the counter.

Rose turned with a big smile, set down the wooden spoon she was stirring something with, and put her arms around me.

"You've been away too long, Spencer. I'm glad you're here. I'm so sorry about Stosh. I won't ask how you're holding up. If there's ever anything I can do."

"You already do, Aunt Rose." After my folks died, I had often thought that she was all I had left if Stosh was gone, and vice versa. I knew she realized that too. There were a few other aunts and uncles, but no one I was very close to.

She took my hand. "And how is Rosie taking it?"

"She's trying, but it's certainly hard."

She patted my hand. "Well, I'm glad you two have this time together to support each other."

I was too.

She pushed her chair back and stood. "Dinner isn't going to fix itself. You go say hi to Maxine. You can tell us all about this little adventure of yours at dinner."

An hour later, we were all sitting around the round wooden table in the dining room. Every time I sat at this table I remembered sitting quietly as a kid, waiting patiently for food to be passed and listening to the grown-up conversation. Now *I* had the conversation everyone wanted to hear as Aunt Rose and Maxine wanted to know about Stosh's murderer and why Rosie and I were in Wisconsin.

They listened, enthralled, to our story about the adoption agency and had just as many questions as we did. There were a lot of pieces that didn't fit together yet. And they were both amazed that there had been no progress on Stosh's killer.

As the cherry pie was cut, conversation turned to the inn and the current business problem… it was too good. They were booked up almost solid, and the summer season hadn't yet started. Aunt Rose and I had often discussed the problem of hiring a full-time person versus the high school and college kids she used during the summer. Hiring Maxine had taken no thought; she was replacing someone who had retired. But adding someone else meant a large addition to the payroll.

Rose had decided the extra business would more than cover the extra person, and they had started looking. But the two they had interviewed so far didn't seem serious enough about wanting the job, and neither Rose nor Maxine had felt comfortable with them. As Rose explained, "They just didn't seem like *people* people." And it seemed logical to me that if you're working with people… well...

Rosie gave me a quick glance and joined the conversation. "I'm sure you'll find the right person, Rose."

Aunt Rose shook her head. "I don't know. I'll certainly not find someone as good as Maxine."

Rosie laughed. "Well, maybe Spencer should do your interviewing."

Rose brightened with "Maybe he should!" and looked at me.

"Maybe he has," said Rosie.

With a perplexed look, Rose asked, "What does that mean?"

Rosie shrugged with a smile. "Just woman's intuition. By the way, do you know who bought the cottage next to Spencer on the bay?"

"I had heard it was sold, but I don't know to who. I'm sure it's someone wonderful."

There wasn't a pessimistic bone in Aunt Rose's body. Rosie said she hoped so.

It was after ten when we finally got everything cleaned up and got hugs with lots of thanks for a wonderful dinner.

***

The moon wasn't up yet, so the drive across the peninsula to Moonlight Bay was dark. We didn't pass any cars until we got to Baileys Harbor. It was even darker when I turned onto Highway Q and followed its snaking path through the woods. I looked at Rosie as we turned into the forest, and her eyes were closed. They opened as I pulled into my drive.

She opened her eyes wide and stretched. "Look, Spencer, your neighbor has arrived."

Parked next to the neighboring cottage was a dark-colored Ford sedan. There were no lights on in the cottage.

Rosie opened her door. "I guess we'll find out who these wonderful people are pretty soon," she said.

"I guess we will," I said without much energy.

"Aren't you interested?"

I smiled and shrugged. "Not particularly."

She got out and closed her door quietly. "You're no fun."

I tried to look hurt.

She took my arm and asked what time the moon came up.

"Not 'til after midnight."

"And how do you know that?"

"Man's intuition." When she gave me a perplexed look I explained that the moon is in the same spot forty minutes later every night, so it was pretty easy to predict.

"Well, then I'm going to bed," she said.

"Sounds good to me."

Chapter 19

I was up by six Saturday morning, reading on the deck, when Rosie wandered out at a little after eight.

"Well hi, sleepyhead."

She sat on the deck and put her head in my lap, still half asleep. I put my hand on her shoulder and asked if she was hungry.

"I am, but I don't know why I'm so tired. I got plenty of sleep."

"You just needed to catch up. What do you have a taste for?"

Looking up at me, she said, "Someone else's cooking. Let's go into town. I'll buy."

"No argument here." But she didn't move.

"The bay is so beautiful, Spencer. Sarah would love it here. I feel badly that she has to live in the city."

"Yes, she would."

We listened to the sounds of the birds and the wind in the trees for a few minutes, and then she got dressed and we headed out. I recommended the Sandpiper, just a little south of Baileys Harbor. Located on a golf course, they gave the more famous Al Johnson's on the bay side of the county a run for their money, and it wasn't as crowded. They didn't have goats on the roof, but the food made up for it. We both ordered strawberry crepes.

As we sipped coffee, she shook her head and looked awfully sad. "I don't know if I can face going back to work, Spencer. Walking by

Stosh's office and knowing..." She looked at me with moist eyes, and I took her hand.

"I know, Rosie. It's never easy."

We had some laughs telling Stosh stories until the food arrived and then took a walk through the forest. We didn't get back to the cottage until one, and by then we were hungry again. I suggested brats on the grill.

"Oh crap. I forgot to get buns," I said. "Rosie, would you go next door and see if the neighbor has any?"

"Sure. Gotta meet them sometime."

"And invite them for lunch if they haven't eaten."

"Okay, be right back."

I watched her through the side window, and when she got to the door I followed. She didn't see me behind her as the neighbor opened the door. It took her a few seconds before the words came out.

"Chief Iverson! What are you doing here? Did you buy—?"

Iverson didn't get the chance to answer as a voice from the kitchen yelled, "Hey, what the hell? We got no Schlitz! Iverson, I thought you said you were going to get some Schlitz!" He walked into the front room. "How do you expect—"

That was all he got out as Rosie ran across the room and threw her arms around his neck. I stood in the doorway smiling.

"Rosie, let go! You're getting my shirt wet!"

She wouldn't let go.

"Spencer! Get this woman off of me!"

When she finally let go she ran to me and pushed me hard on the chest. I staggered back, and she hit me again with tears streaming down her face and then ran back to Stosh and put her arms around him again. Iverson just stood there with his arms crossed on his chest and a big smile.

Rosie finally let go and stood with her mouth open, shaking her head. I couldn't tell if she was happy or angry. I don't think she could either.

"Well, somebody better start talking!"

The three of us looked at each other waiting for someone else to start. Finally, Stosh said, "We got no Schlitz."

"That's not exactly what I meant," said Rosie.

I took her hand and led her to the couch as Stosh and Iverson sat on armchairs in front of the picture window.

Rosie looked at Stosh and broke the silence with, "You're not dead." Then she stared at me and said, "But *you're* going to be."

"I'm so sorry, Rosie, but we couldn't tell anybody."

"Who's we? How many knew about this?"

"Just me and the captain and the people at the hospital who obviously needed to know."

"And Iverson."

"Yes, but not at first. I enlisted him when he showed up at the hospital."

She looked at Stosh and started to cry. He went over to her and put his big bear arms around her. The tears fell through her smile. When he let go she wiped her tears on her sleeve and looked perplexed.

"So, Iverson, you bought this cottage?"

He laughed. "On a cop's salary?"

It only took a few seconds for it to hit her. "Spencer?"

I just shrugged.

"Well, I guess you don't have to worry about loud parties."

I laughed.

She turned to Iverson. "Have you filled him in on what's going on here?"

"Nope. I figured I'd leave that up to the two of you. I've mostly been listening to him complain."

"Back to normal," I said.

"Not quite," Stosh said. "I've got a couple new holes."

"What happened at the hospital?" Rosie asked. "Spencer said he couldn't find a pulse."

"There was one, but very faint. But the ticker did stop on the table. They say I was dead for about twenty seconds."

Iverson smiled. "And here you are bitching about beer. Life is amazing."

"Who dreamed up this plan?" Rosie asked.

"I made the suggestion," I said. "But the captain made the decision. Remember, we thought at the time we were dealing with the gang. Seemed like a good idea."

Now Stosh looked puzzled. "At the time? What the hell does that mean? Aren't we dealing with the gang?"

"Maybe," I said, "but maybe not."

"Oh good, that clears it up. You care to explain?"

"Yes, but it'll take some time."

"Time I got plenty of at the moment."

I stood. "Let's start over lunch. Let's go back to my place for some brats."

Everyone agreed.

As we were walking across the drive, Rosie said, "Hey, wait. We forgot about the buns."

"Yes, we did," I said. "Or we could use the ones in the pantry."

She stared at me with her mouth open. "Can I believe *anything* you say?"

"Yes, but you have to figure out what."

"Fine. That'll be fun."

I got the grill going, and everyone settled on the deck. It would be in the sun for another hour or so. I went inside for the brats and Stosh's present. His face lit up when I handed him a six pack of Schlitz with a big red bow.

"Where did you hide that?" Rosie asked.

I laughed. "In the trunk under a blanket."

As I put on the brats the phone rang.

"Would someone watch the meat?"

Iverson volunteered.

It was Detective Springer. "You're a hard guy to find. Took me three tries to get you," he said. "You need an answering machine on that car phone of yours."

I laughed. "That's just what I need. It's too big all by itself."

"Are you staying at the cottage now?"

"Not permanently. We're here for the weekend."

"I heard from Hanover. They also had paid the two thousand down payment, and they also agreed to the monthly payment... three hundred a month."

"Man, I guess people who care about kids are easy marks."

"Assuming that's what's going on, yes."

"Is he still paying?"

"Nope. He stopped paying when Mary was killed."

"Did you tell him about the scam?"

"No. I'd like to be sure before I accuse someone."

"Yeah. But I'd bet my house on it."

"I'd bet your house on it too. Keep me in the loop."

"Will do."

"Coupla more turns," Iverson said as I walked out with potato salad and chips.

We chatted about the beautiful day until the food was on the table.

"So, before I die of suspense," said Stosh.

I wasn't sure how to start. My instructions had been to look in his shoebox after he was dead. Technically, he had been, but now not so much. I took a deep breath.

"It's kinda funny if you think about it." I started in on the brat. "Few things better than a Sheboygan brat."

He wasn't laughing yet.

"It all started with some envelopes I found in the case under your bed."

He almost choked on his brat. After a few coughs, he said, "My case? What the hell!"

I held up my hands to fend off his outburst.

"I told you to open that when I died. Do I look like I'm dead?"

"Well, not so much anymore, but there was that twenty seconds."

"So as soon as you heard I was out you headed for the house. You couldn't wait till I was in the ground?"

Iverson was enjoying the show.

"Of course not. But you have to admit you badly taxed my curiosity with your instructions. I always wondered what was so important in that case."

"Yeah, curiosity and the cat. Everybody has important documents."

"Yes, but not everybody is paying money to an adoption agency for a kid they didn't get."

"That's what this is about?"

"It appears to be. At least it started something that looks pretty suspicious."

I spooned out more salad.

He looked at Rosie and Iverson. "Are you both in on this?"

Rosie answered. "*In on this* isn't exactly the right take, but yes, we're aware of it."

He thought for a few seconds as he ate. "I hope you have more beer. What's suspicious about helping someone out?"

"Nothing, as far as that goes," I answered. "But I just had a feeling and decided I had nothing else to do so I'd look into it."

"You mean nothing else to do like finding out who shot me?"

"The captain assured me he had that under control. Have you been talking to him?"

"Daily. The gang thing seems to be getting nowhere except for the latest theory. Have you heard about the initiation angle?"

A small motorboat entered the mouth of the bay.

"Yes. He told me."

He turned to Rosie. "You took time off?"

She nodded.

I answered. "The captain suggested it. She had time coming, and he thought it would be good for her to get away and help me look into this to take her mind off of things."

He nodded. "You obviously didn't tell her."

"I asked the captain. He wanted as few people as possible to know so that people would react normally. It was a tough decision."

"I bet," Stosh said. "I'm so sorry, Rosie."

"It's okay, Stosh. It was for a good cause."

"So, I hear I had a nice funeral."

Iverson lifted his bottle. "Yeah, the only problem was you didn't show up."

We all lifted our bottles.

"I'll do better next time." He took the last bite of his brat. "So what's this all about?"

"Let's clean up and get comfortable," I said.

Chapter 20

The motorboat docked at the pier of the cottage just west of me, and a man with a fishing pole waved. We moved our chairs into the shade, and I started at the beginning and told Stosh about our plan to pose as parents looking for a baby. We showed him our rings.

He smiled. "So I had to die to get you two married?"

"Seemed like a good plan."

"So how did that go?"

I told him about our interview with Peters and our dislike for her while he opened another Schlitz.

"So the only case you have is a woman you don't like."

"Until I went through their files."

He almost choked again. "Pardon? You did what?"

Iverson was smiling again. "I like your boy, Powolski. Sometimes we have to be a little creative, but we try and keep our officers as close to the center line of the road as possible. Manning isn't even on the road."

Stosh sighed and shook his head. "First of all, he's not my boy. Second, I tell him if I catch him doing something illegal he'll be in the same jail as the rest of them. You condone this?"

"What?" Iverson asked. "I haven't heard anything illegal. Maybe he asked and they let him."

"Yeah, and maybe this year Santa Claus'll come down my chimney."

I pointed out that he didn't have a chimney. The look I got wasn't supportive.

Iverson continued after opening another beer. "But you have to admit he gets things done. I condone *that*. That female detective wouldn't be alive today if it weren't for him."

Stosh took a long drink. "I do admit that. But I can't condone how things happen."

"But you'd like to, wouldn't you?"

Stosh stared at Iverson and didn't answer. He turned back to me. "Okay, so files."

I leaned back and put my feet up on a bench. "There were three file cabinets. I opened a drawer that was marked 'Adopting Family' and found a file with 'Powolski' on the tab. Written on the folder under the tab were three more names of couples from Green Bay, Appleton, and St. Charles. Then there was about an inch of space and another name… Victoria Petrace."

He raised his eyebrows and waited for me to continue. When I didn't, he asked, "So what was in the file?"

I tilted my head, clasped my hands together, and said, "That's where it gets off the road a little bit." He just waited. "Someone hit me on the head, and the next thing I knew I was in a hospital bed and Iverson was sitting there smiling at me."

"A little bit?" he said.

I gave him a pleading look.

He sighed and set his bottle on the table next to his chair as a cardinal landed on the railing and tilted his head at us. "Okay, I may regret this, but give me the whole story."

"We drove to the agency about one in the morning. The plan was to get in and look around."

Stosh held up his hand. "We?"

Rosie squirmed in her chair. "I didn't go anywhere near the place. I was parked down the block."

"Oh, well then that's okay. What's the matter with you two?" He looked at me. "You involved one of my detectives in this? What were you thinking?"

Rosie answered for me. "He was thinking he'd find something about his best friend who had been killed."

He held up his hand. "I get it, but he doesn't have a career to worry about... you do."

"I had a friend killed too."

He just shook his head. Hard to argue with that. He held his hand out, palm up, and I continued.

"I came in through the alley. When I got there the door was unlocked."

"And that, of course, raised all kinds of red flags."

"One, but when I got inside I listened and looked around and found no one."

"Well, evidently you didn't look around enough."

"Evidently."

"How did you get to the hospital room?"

"In an ambulance with a police escort." Before he had a chance to make a comment, I continued. "I obviously wasn't the first person to have entered the building. A neighbor saw the first person and reported it. The police showed up and found me on the floor and assumed I was the person who had been seen entering."

"A good assumption."

"But incorrect."

"Yeah... the other person was long gone?"

"Yup."

"Any description by the neighbor?"

"Pretty vague. No help."

"And you were arrested?"

I smiled. "That's where Iverson comes in."

Rosie spoke up. "I all of a sudden saw red lights... two police cars. I wondered what to do and decided to stay in the car. I figured Spencer was good at taking care of himself, so I drove closer to the building and watched. Ten minutes later the ambulance showed up."

"And you still stayed in the car?" Stosh asked.

"I did."

"Well that was the *first* smart thing you did."

"I followed the ambulance and one of the police cars to the hospital and walked in with the stretcher. They brought him into the ER. I waited for a doctor to come out, flashed my badge, and asked what his status was. He told me he had been hit on the head and was unconscious, but it wasn't serious. While I was thinking of what to do, I remembered Iverson and called, hoping he'd remember me."

Iverson smiled. "Hard to forget someone who lets a prisoner escape."

Rosie looked embarrassed.

"She explained the situation and asked for help," Iverson said. "I got there about six and had a chat with Rosie and then the officers. Manning had regained consciousness but was asleep."

Stosh nodded. "And how did the chat with the officers go?"

"They were waiting to arrest him until they talked to him. I have a weekly breakfast with their boss, Chief Snark. I asked that they get ahold of him. He showed up at eight fifteen." He lifted his bottle and took a drink. "I managed to convince him that the situation was a bit odd. Obviously, someone had entered the building before Manning, and *that* someone had knocked him out. My version of the incident was that Manning had been out for a walk and seen someone breaking into the building. He went in to investigate."

Stosh looked skeptical. "And he bought that?"

"Not for a second," I said.

Iverson glanced at me and then turned back to Stosh. "Of course not, but he had to admit someone else did the breaking… Manning just entered. He didn't file charges, but told me Manning was my responsibility."

Stosh laughed. "Oh, there's something to be happy about. I'd rather be responsible for a rolling grenade."

I had a comment but kept it to myself.

Iverson laughed. "Me too. We had lunch, and these two told me the story."

"Okay." Stosh pointed at me. "So you weren't arrested." He pointed at Rosie. "The cops don't know about you." Then he looked at Iverson. "And you are responsible for my boy."

That was all correct, and no one answered.

"And for all your trouble you have a file folder with names on it. Hardly seems—"

"It doesn't end there," I said.

"I should have known. But before you continue, I'll have another beer."

Now the trouble was going to start. "We're out," I said.

I just got the familiar Stosh look of disgust, and he waved his hand. We'd deal with the beer later.

But now the story got a little tricky. I could tell it to Stosh, but I wasn't sure about how much Iverson would want to know, or not want to know. So I said, "Hey, Iverson… remember in the hospital when I asked you if the cop was in the room?"

"Sure. But I want to hear the story, so the cop just went to the head."

I nodded. "There had to be more, so I went back the next night for another look." No one looked surprised. I looked at Stosh. "The file with your name on it was gone, I assume taken by whoever hit me. But I was interested in the other names. I found a file for the Bells… Green Bay. Their name was on the tab, and it had the same assorted names under the tab, including yours, Stosh. There were the Hanovers in St. Charles and the Freys in Appleton. And under those was the same Victoria Petrace.

"I looked in the drawer marked 'Birth Mother' and found nothing under any of the names. Then I tried the employee drawer, looking for Peters, the lady who interviewed us. It had her work info, address and phone number and hired in 1979. As I was putting her file back I saw the folder behind it… Petrace, Victoria. She had been hired in 1982, and left the company in February. It was noted as 'separated.'"

"Okay," said Stosh. "So Petrace is an employee."

"Well, was… but there's more. She obviously wasn't there when your adoption started but could have taken over your account. Do you recall that name?"

He shook his head. "No. I haven't talked to anyone in a long time."

"You just kept sending checks?"

He took a deep breath, let it out slowly, and looked very sad. I was pretty sure I knew why.

"Yes. I wondered about it and told Francine that it smelled bad and we weren't sending any money. But it was a charitable organization, Single Mother Outreach if I remember correctly, and they said they supported a house for single mothers."

"Did you look into it?" I asked.

"I did. They did own a house, and the outreach was a listed company." He stared out over the bay and quietly said, "I could never say no to Francine. So we sent money."

"Even though I'm betting you suspected it was a scam?"

"Even though. I know it was dumb, but… well, it was worth it to see the joy on Francine's face."

"And after she died?"

Sadness took over his face. "I just did it for her."

Rosie put her arm around his shoulders.

"Why did you never have kids?" I asked. "You both obviously wanted to."

"Francine had a miscarriage. They had to operate, and that was the end of having kids."

Rosie hugged him. "I'm so sorry, Stosh."

"Thanks." He hugged her back. "So where does all this go?"

"We decided to check on the other names on the folder. Carol made some calls and discovered that Mary Hanover in St. Charles had been murdered."

That got Stosh's attention. "Murdered?"

"Two shots in the chest. Same caliber bullet. They live out in horse country. It was dark, and there were no witnesses. Her husband wasn't home. We took a drive and talked to a Detective Springer. There aren't any good suspects. From there we went to Appleton and talked to Chief Werth, who took us out to see the Freys. They are both alive and well but now worried."

Stosh nodded. "Did either of those couples pay?"

"The Hanovers did, but he stopped when his wife was killed. The Freys didn't and eventually asked for their money back."

"What about the people in Green Bay?"

I told him about our chat with Snark and Dunsley. "Dunsley tells us he checked on the Bells. Both are fine."

"How about the payments?"

"That's all we have. Dunsley wasn't even happy about having to do what he did. We'll look into that."

He rubbed his chin with his left hand.

"Tell him about Sarah, Spencer," Rosie said.

"The receptionist is a young girl named Sarah Leek. We like her. The first time we went to the agency there was a couple coming out, and the wife was very upset. We asked Peters about it, and she made up some bull. The next time we were there we asked Sarah if there were any disgruntled mothers. She started to tell us about one and used the name Victoria. But she was cut short."

Stosh stopped rubbing. "Victoria? Same name as the employee?"

"Well, here's where it gets interesting. Same person. We accidentally ran into Sarah a few days later and took her to dinner. She doesn't like Peters either. She's from a farm west of here and isn't happy about the city or the job."

Rosie took over. "She told us Victoria was a birth mother. She gave up the baby but later decided she wanted it back and came into the office very upset."

Stosh looked confused. "They hired a birth mother?"

"Evidently."

"Seems odd. I wonder why."

I shrugged. "Who knows. Maybe she needed a job, and Peters felt sorry for her."

"Maybe something more complicated."

"Maybe.

"So she breaks into the office to look at the files," Stosh said, "and puts you on the floor."

"That's my guess," I said. "But she didn't break in. Snark told us there were no force marks on the door. She still had a key. Peters never changed the locks."

"But she has now," Rosie said.

"Um hmm. So what do we know about this Petrace?"

"She's disappeared," I said. "We stopped at her house last night. There were papers on the walk, and the neighbor said he hadn't seen her since Monday or Tuesday."

Iverson chimed in for the first time. "So Petrace was probably there twice, including the first unreported break-in?"

"Probably," I said.

"Why twice, I wonder."

"No clue. Must not have found what she wanted the first time."

"I wonder when the first time was..." said Stosh. "Before or after I was shot."

"Sarah said it was about six months ago, so that would make it December."

"So let's assume she had my address before I was shot."

I thought for a few seconds and listened to the quiet, interrupted only by the birds. "Seems like a good assumption. And let's add Mary Hanover to that. She was shot in January."

After another minute of birds, Rosie said, "Stosh and Hanover were shot after the first entry. Then there's another entry."

I continued. "Yes. And if we go with the theory that she didn't find everything she needed the first time, maybe she just got the other two names."

"And maybe she didn't," said Iverson.

"Maybe she didn't," I agreed.

"Lots of maybes," said Stosh.

"There always are," I said. I pointed up, and we all watched a hawk glide over the tops of the pines.

Iverson broke the silence as the bird headed out toward the lake. "Let's assume all this is true. Why is she killing people?"

"Let's make that singular," said Stosh.

Iverson laughed. "For this conversation, it's easier for you to be dead. If this is Petrace, then she thinks you are."

"And so far I'm enjoying it, except for the lack of beer."

"You know, there *are* other labels," I replied.

He just glared at me.

Rosie continued. "And if we assume she now has what she needs, then the other two couples are targets."

"Could be," said Iverson. "But back to my question... why?"

The hawk was back. "She wants her baby," I said. "And she's angry. Maybe she's taking a look at the people on the list, but she's looking for her baby. When she doesn't find it, she takes it out on that person."

"That's not very rational," said Iverson.

"Since when is murder rational?" I asked. No one answered.

Stosh was rubbing his chin again. "So the names on the folders weren't just possible parents."

I shook my head. "No, they were *all* parents... for the same baby."

"That's not a baby anymore. She'd be about ten now. But where is she?" Rosie asked.

"Good question." I stood and walked to the railing. "Peters may be the only one who knows."

"I wonder if Peters is in danger?" asked Rosie.

I turned around. "Probably."

"So maybe we should give her a heads up."

"I'll put it on the list of things to do... at the bottom."

"So what next?" asked Stosh.

"Two things," I said. "Paul is coming Sunday. I want him to keep an eye on the agency."

"And somebody needs to talk to the couple in Green Bay," said Iverson.

"Yes, the Bells. That's the second. Maybe we'll go tomorrow. And I'd like to drive by Peters' and Trainer's houses as long as we're out."

"Do you want to have a chat with Trainer?" Rosie asked.

"Maybe at some point, but we need more information first. Let's see what surveillance gets us. But most of all, I'd like to find Petrace. If she's the killer, then she's not done. But who's the next target? The Bells or the Freys?"

"Or Mr. Hanover," said Iverson.

"And where is she?" Rosie asked.

"Are there bulletins out?" asked Stosh.

"Yeah," Iverson said. "Wisconsin and Illinois. And the departments in St. Charles and Green Bay and Appleton and Chicago are all talking. Chief Snark is getting a warrant to search Petrace's house."

"I'd like to be a part of that," I said. "If it even happens."

"I bet you would, but Snark isn't exactly your best friend. I'll fill you in."

I sighed. "Okay, but if Dunsley is the one doing the searching I'm not too confident they'll find anything important."

"We can only hope."

"There's something else," I said. "The house Victoria is living in is the one owned by the agency."

"How do you know that?" Stosh asked.

"Sarah. The odd thing is that Victoria isn't a single mother with a child, and she was fired as an employee."

"Maybe Peters felt sorry for her after she let her go," Rosie said.

"Maybe," I said. "I'd sure like to know what Victoria is thinking."

"We could call our department psychiatrist," said Stosh.

Iverson stood up and stretched. "I have a woman in Sister Bay who consults with us once in while."

"You need psychiatrists in paradise?"

Iverson laughed. "People are people. They carry their problems around with them... doesn't matter where they are. You wanna talk to her?"

"Sure. What's her name?"

"Dr. Long, Lynn. I'll call and give her a heads up."

He gave me her phone number and told me where she was.

"Thanks. We'll see her Monday morning if she's available."

"I'd better get to work," Iverson said. There had been traffic on his hand-held radio, but nothing he needed to respond to. "We've got an undercover operation tonight at Peninsula State Park. We think there are drug deals going on... there've been reports of suspicious activity. The ranger stopped a car that had been reported but didn't find anything."

"So all is not perfect in paradise?" Stosh asked.

Iverson laughed. "Hardly, but our not perfect is a lot better than your not perfect."

"This the first op?"

"No. Third. But my manpower is pretty slim. We've only got one car and two part-time cops who pose as lovers so they have a reason to be there."

I glanced at Rosie. "You want another pair of lovers?"

"Are you volunteering?"

"Rosie?"

She shrugged.

"Well, could sure use the help. And a car with out-of-state plates would be perfect. But I don't know if an old married couple can pull this off."

I smiled. "We'll pretend."

Stosh looked up at the sky and shook his head.

"Okay, I'll call you this afternoon and we'll set it up."

"Sounds good," I said.

We all stood, and Iverson said his goodbyes. He picked up a few things from the cottage and headed out.

As he pulled out, Stosh said, "If you get Rosie hurt I'm coming after you."

"I'll keep that in mind."

He sat back down and asked what we thought about the gang investigation.

"What do *you* think about the gang angle?" asked Rosie.

"A lot less after today. It's certainly possible, but always hard to prove unless we catch them in the act."

"Has the captain said anything about the initiation theory?"

"They're working on it, but no one's talking." He put his hands on the arms of the chair and pushed himself up. "Now if you'll excuse me, I'm pretty tired. I'm not making it through the day without a nap."

"One question first," I said. "Do you remember trying to tell me something when you were lying on the floor? I leaned in close and it sounded like you said *she*."

He shook his head. "I don't remember anything, Spencer."

"Nothing about the person who shot you?"

"Already went over this with the captain. Last thing I remember is the doorbell ringing. But I do remember whupping your butt at gin."

I sighed. "You're right. You don't remember anything."

He stood, and Rosie put her arm around his waist. "I'll walk over with you."

I watched until Stosh had closed the door. It was a moment I'd remember. Rosie stood looking at the closed door for what seemed like ten minutes before she came back. Her hair shone in the sun, a fitting frame for the happy look on her face. She stepped up onto the deck and walked toward me.

"You're not going to hit me again, are you?"

She smiled and put her arms around me. I returned the favor.

The hug was broken by the phone. It was Iverson giving us instructions for the evening. We were to stop at the ranger headquarters at the west entrance to the park and pick up a radio. He asked us to park in the lot next to the lighthouse and do whatever came naturally. He figured we wouldn't have any problem. He asked if I had a camera. I did. Our instructions were to call if we saw anything suspicious and not to try and apprehend. Seemed like an interesting way to spend a Saturday night, and it was certainly a cheap date.

As we were about to hang up he told me to hang on, and I heard his radio crackling. He was back in less than a minute.

"There's a fire. Shipwrecked Brew Pub in Egg Harbor. See you later."

I told Rosie and suggested we head over there. Egg Harbor was one town south of the park, and we could eat somewhere on that side of the peninsula. I told Stosh what we were doing, and we headed out.

Chapter 21

As we made the twenty-minute trip across the peninsula, I told Rosie about the brew pub.

"It was built in the 1880s as a saloon and is one of the oldest buildings in the county. Not long after that, guest rooms and a dining room were added. It's currently an inn and the only microbrewery in the county."

"What a shame, Spencer. I hope everyone got out. I'm assuming the fire departments up here are volunteer."

"For the most part. There are paid full-time positions, but most are paid volunteers… they're paid when they respond. Aunt Rose is good friends with one of the volunteers in Ephraim."

"Does each town have a department?"

"All the bigger ones… Sister Bay, Ephraim, Fish Creek, Egg Harbor, Baileys Harbor, and Sturgeon Bay. There's a joint response if needed."

As we passed a cherry orchard she asked what the population of the county was.

"It's about twenty thousand. But during the summer these towns are wall-to-wall people."

I pointed to a cloud of black smoke above the trees, and as we turned south on 42 we could hear sirens. As we got closer to town, traffic was stopped. Two engines passed the line of cars in the northbound lane. I pulled into a parking lot next to an antique store, and we walked.

I counted engines from six departments and heard more sirens in the distance. Ladder trucks were pouring water on flames coming from second-floor windows and on the neighboring house to the north. As we watched, flames broke through the roof. It was obvious the fire had started on the second floor, and if they could confine it to that they could keep it from becoming an inferno. The wooden frame building was a tinder box. If they couldn't, the neighbor's house would go too. The water damage would make the brewpub a total loss.

The corner building was painted light blue, almost the same shade as my Mustang, with white trim. It was a typical nineteenth century building with a white picket fence that still had a peaceful, quaint charm. But the orange flames, black smoke, and the yellow and red engines certainly intruded on the charm.

We joined the crowd and watched. There were three ambulances parked outside of the engines, but the responders were just standing by. Everyone must have gotten out. Ten minutes later the black smoke had turned to gray and the flames were out. They kept up the water for another twenty minutes, but firefighters had started to recover hoses. I touched Rosie's arm and pointed to Iverson standing next to one of the yellow engines talking with another man. When the man walked away, Iverson saw us and waved us over. We were stopped by a woman wearing an orange safety vest, but after we explained and Iverson waved again, she let us through.

"Hey, Manning… Detective."

I nodded. "Did everyone get out?" I asked.

"Yes. A maid discovered the fire in one of the upstairs rooms. A couch was on fire, and the flames were spreading up the wall. There was only one person in the rooms upstairs, and she and everyone downstairs got out quickly."

"They did a good job containing it," Rosie said.

"They did. We were worried about the building next door. Luckily there's no wind. Let's get away from the trucks." We walked across the street and sat in front of a café.

"That was Chief Bank I was talking to, the police chief in Egg Harbor. He has the guest register. We were trying to talk with guests. There are four rooms upstairs… two of them are a total loss. One of those is registered to V. Petrace."

I didn't hide my surprise. "Really."

"Yes."

"What are the odds there are two V. Petraces?"

"Pretty slim, but not zero. As you two know, this is a pretty good place to disappear. Nobody bothers anybody else, and everyone minds their own business."

"But why would she use her real name?"

"Criminals don't think they'll get caught," said Rosie. "Luckily for us most aren't real bright."

"But some of them have more than their share of luck. As soon as I saw the name I put a car on the highway north of the canal as a roadblock. That's the only road out of here. If she didn't leave too long ago, we'll get her. I'll leave a car there around the clock until we find her elsewhere."

I nodded. "Good. Call me if you do. Have you questioned the manager?" I asked.

"I've been waiting… he's been a little busy. I was just going to do that when I saw you. Let's go."

Iverson walked up to a man talking with the fire chief near the front of the building next to a red engine from Sister Bay. He introduced us to the manager, Jim Wells, and Chief Cascade. "Any idea what started it, Chief?"

"My early guess is electrical. Know more in the next few days."

"Nice job containing it," I said. "Can it be saved?"

"Thanks. With all the water we poured in there, I don't think so."

Cascade put his hand on the manager's shoulder. "Sorry, Jim."

Wells looked devastated. "Yeah, it's awful, but at least no one was hurt. Might have been different had it happened at night."

"Let me know when you have a minute," Iverson said to Wells.

"Any more questions, Chief?" Wells asked Cascade.

"Not at the moment. I'll be in touch."

"Okay. What's on your mind, Chief?" Wells asked.

"We're looking into a murder and another shooting that happened in Illinois. You just became a part of it."

Wells didn't try to hide his look of shock. "I did?"

Iverson laughed. "Well, not you personally, but the pub." He gave Wells the short version of the story and explained about the name in his register. "Do you see Petrace around here? The register shows she checked in on Monday."

"I'm afraid I wouldn't know what she looks like. I deal with very few of the guests directly... usually only when there's a problem. Let me get my desk clerk." He looked around and said he'd be right back. He was back in less than a minute with a girl who looked like she was a teenager and introduced us to Marty.

The fire truck engine started with a loud rumble, and we walked back to give it room.

"Marty, these people are looking for V. Petrace. Our register shows she checked in on Monday. Do you see her?"

Marty looked around. "No."

"Can you tell us anything about her?" I asked. "A description would help."

She shrugged. "I never talked to her, but I know who she is. Pretty short, I'd say a little more than five foot, short brown hair, round face. We could check with the other clerks when they come in."

"Well," said Wells, "they won't be coming in, but I'll give you their names and numbers, Chief."

Marty looked embarrassed.

"Thanks."

I took the register from Iverson. "This shows she has a white Volkswagen. Do you have a parking lot?"

"Yeah, around back. Let's go look. Thanks, Marty. We'll have a meeting tomorrow or Tuesday. I'll let you know."

"Okay, Mr. Wells. I'm so sorry."

"Thanks, Marty."

Her car wasn't in the lot.

"Well, we almost got her," said Rosie.

"Yeah, the almosts are pretty frustrating," said Iverson. "Back to wondering where she is."

Three more trucks left the site.

"I think we can narrow it down to her house and the remaining targets. We need to update the other departments," I said. "Carol will make the calls."

"I'll call Snark," said Iverson. "You get the others."

"Good idea," I said.

***

It took us ten minutes to walk back to the Mustang. I handed Rosie the keys. "You drive… I'll make the phone call."

"You hungry?"

"Yup."

"Where do you want to eat?"

"I can't come up here without going to the Greenwood Supper Club. There are several good places for a steak, but not quite *that* good. Go back the way we came. After about fifteen minutes on EE you'll come to A. Turn left and you'll find it up the road a bit. I'll help you watch for A."

While we were waiting for our steaks, we talked about the plan for Monday over Guinness. The Bells were the only couple we hadn't talked to. Perhaps they'd have some new information.

***

We pulled into the park at dusk, picked up the radio, and headed for the Eagle Bluff lighthouse at the northern tip of the park. I parked where we could see the entrance to the lot and Shore Road in both directions, but we would be pretty well hidden from someone pulling in until they got into the lot. The lighthouse was a small, two-story building made of beige-colored bricks with a steeply pitched, red-shingled roof. The light was only forty-three feet above the ground, but the bluff was over a hundred feet high so the light was well above the water. The sky was clear... a great night for looking at stars, or doing whatever came naturally.

We walked around to the lake side of the lighthouse, and Rosie peered in the windows. As it was dark, there wasn't much to see. But the view out over the water was impressive with islands dotting the bay. The park included eight miles of shoreline on Green Bay. Another couple was reading the information board when we got back to the front, but they didn't look sinister. We said hello as they passed us heading to the lighthouse.

We got in the car, and I mentioned the only disadvantage to my sky-blue Mustang. It was going to be hard to be too friendly with a stick shift between us. But I told her I'd do my best. By ten, three cars had driven past the lighthouse. None had stopped. But at 10:20 one did slow down but kept going. I reported it. The park gates closed at eleven. We had the windows rolled down, listening to the crickets and holding hands. But when Rosie got bit by a mosquito we rolled the windows up. The night air had cooled considerably so that wasn't a bad thing. I started the car and ran the heater for a few minutes.

"Looks like we picked the wrong night," said Rosie.

"Or the wrong spot. There's plenty of other places to meet."

"I wonder how Iverson picked the lighthouse," she said.

"Reverse psychology. He figured the logical spot for someone to have a clandestine meeting would be in an out of the way spot away from visitors. And if someone was figuring that was what he'd be figuring, they'd meet at a popular spot... like the lighthouse."

She turned toward me and laughed. "That's a lot of figuring. I'm figuring Iverson's the only one doing all the figuring."

"Probably, but I'm just following orders, which by the way were to do what comes naturally." I leaned over and kissed her.

As she put her arms around my neck, she said, "The world sure looks different with Stosh still in it."

"It sure does."

"You must have been devastated sitting there in his doorway waiting for help."

"I don't remember much about that, Rosie." I let out a deep breath. "I guess shock takes over. I did what I could and then just had to wait."

She took my hand in both of hers. "That's such a helpless feeling… waiting."

As I agreed, a car pulled into the lot and parked across the lot from us. The timing was perfect. From their car, it would sure look like we were two lovers taking advantage of the empty lot. The headlights went out, and a couple of teenagers got out and walked toward the bluff, disappearing past the lighthouse.

"Is the lighthouse ever open?" Rosie asked.

"Yes, every day during the summer. They've done a nice job of making a museum out of it… lots of period displays."

"Can you get up in the tower?"

"Yup. It's a gorgeous view."

"We should come back."

"Sounds good."

The couple came back at a quarter to eleven and pulled away. Five minutes later so did we. Halfway back to the headquarters we passed a car pulled over on the side of the road. The flashers were on and the hood was up. I stopped alongside the car, a Chevy Impala, for a closer look. There was no one with the car. I jotted down the license number and told Rosie they had probably walked to the headquarters building to get help.

"That's a long walk," she said. "I hope someone picked them up."

"They probably would, but there isn't much traffic this late."

We didn't pass anyone on the way back. I stopped at the headquarters and dropped off the radio. I told him about the car, gave him the license number, and asked if anyone had shown up. They hadn't. The ranger told me it had been a quiet night and said he'd have someone check on the car. I told him I'd call Iverson… maybe we could try again Sunday.

***

We sat on the cottage deck listening to a distant loon.

"There's that sad cry," said Rosie.

"Hence the stories."

We both got bit within seconds of each other and decided it was time to turn in. I hadn't heard from Iverson. Victoria had either left an hour before the fire and driven out before the car was posted, or she was still on the peninsula. If she was, Iverson would eventually get her, but as he said, this was a pretty good place to hide. But you can't hide forever. If she had made it out we were back to square one.

Chapter 22

We drove back to Green Bay just after lunch on Sunday. We had taken Stosh out to a diner on 51, about halfway up to the north tip of the peninsula, and told him about Petrace. He was looking and feeling good. But he wanted to do something… said he was getting stir crazy confined to the cottage.

I laughed. "You have a chance to relax and do nothing in one of the most beautiful spots in Wisconsin, and you're stir crazy?"

He shrugged as he took a bite of eggs. "I miss the sounds of the city."

"Yeah, hard to get to sleep without the gunshots."

He just glared at me.

"Even if you weren't under doctor's orders to do nothing, the plan is to keep out of sight."

"I get it, but it ain't easy. I haven't noticed you doing nothing very often."

"I'm not the one who had two bullets in him."

He ate the last bite, wiped his mouth, and looked disgusted.

"Well, I feel fine, so if there's anything I can do…"

"Okay, but you were the one yesterday who needed a nap."

He didn't respond.

***

We were sitting on the hotel balcony watching the boat traffic on the river when the phone rang at 2:40. It was Paul. He had checked into the room across the hall. I invited him over.

Standing on the balcony admiring the view, he said, "Nice being the boss. I've got a view of the buildings across the street."

"And who's paying for that?" I said with a smile.

"There is that."

We all sat, and Rosie and I told him about the case. On the drive from the cottage we had a discussion about whether or not to tell Paul that Stosh was alive. She said no... I thought it didn't matter, and he might as well know. She won with the caveat that if it mattered I'd tell him. He was watching the boats, but I knew he was listening. He didn't ask any questions until we got to the end. I also knew he'd remember everything I had said. I finished by telling him we'd take a drive to the agency this afternoon so he would know the neighborhood.

"So you have no specific purpose for me watching the office, no one in particular I'm looking for?"

"Correct," I said. "Take pictures of everyone who comes. There's a photo store a block from here. We'll drive by it on the way over there. If you get any pictures, stop and have the film developed on your way back here. Wait for it. If anything happens you think I need to know about, call me." I wrote down my three numbers.

He nodded. "What are you two going to be doing?"

"I want to have a chat with the Bells."

"You don't think your detective friend asked any questions?"

"I don't think my detective friend can tie his own shoes. He's not going to go out of his way to do anything more than what the chief asks. And the chief's not too thrilled about this either."

Paul smiled. "Yes, being found unconscious on the floor of an office that's been broken into can't make a good first impression."

"Nice. Who's paying your salary?"

He laughed. "You do get into some interesting corners. I'd like to follow you around for a year... I could write a book."

"Maybe you'll be unemployed soon, and you'll have a chance to do that."

"What's to do up here on a Sunday night? You guys want to catch a movie?"

"We sort of have plans." I told him about the problem in the park. I had called Iverson and offered our services again. He said he'd always take free help. His officers wouldn't be there... they had a tight budget. I asked if the ranger had told him about the car. He had. It was registered to a Martin Score of Green Bay. They were checking with Mr. Score. A patrol car had driven the road, and the car was gone.

"You want help with that?" Paul asked.

"It'd be hard to look romantic with you in the back seat."

"I wasn't planning on chaperoning."

"That's good to know. Sure. Another car would be good. Let's take a drive over to the agency and then come back for dinner. There's a great brew pub across the river." I called Iverson, got one of the officers, and left a message to call me on my car phone.

***

We took the Mustang and drove Paul to the agency. I told him there would be plenty of room to park on the street. Easy job. Then I changed the plans. We decided to drive up to Peninsula Park before dinner so he could get a feel for it. We pulled out of the park at ten after six and ate in Ephraim.

It was a little after eight when we left the restaurant. I hadn't heard from Iverson, so we made up our own plan. Rosie and I would park again and Paul would roam through the park. It wasn't a great plan, but it was better than nothing. The ranger gave us radios and told us the police weren't going to be there tonight, but he'd be out driving the roads at some point.

The sky had clouded over, and there were overnight thunderstorms in the forecast.

Rosie and I took up our lookout on the seventy-six-foot-tall Eagle Tower overlooking the bay and the Ephraim harbor. We could see six islands over the treetops. The view was spectacular, and it was a popular spot with a view of the road in both directions. The only car that drove by before ten was Paul. At ten minutes after, he called us and reported a suspicious car in the parking area on the west side of the park off of Shore Road. The driver had left the car and, instead of taking the walking path, started to walk toward the water. He was about to the edge of the trees when Paul pulled into the parking area. The man stopped, looked unsure of what to do, turned and walked back to his car, and drove out of the parking area. He turned south on Shore Road, heading toward the ranger station and the west entrance.

I called and asked if the ranger could stop the car, but he was on the other side of the park. Paul followed but lost him as another car coming out of the tennis courts turned in front of Paul. He had the license number, so Iverson could find the owner.

We all met back at the ranger's station at a little before eleven and turned in the radios. The ranger thanked us and said he had reported the car to the police. Paul would drive back to the hotel so he could be at the agency by nine, and we'd stay at the cottage. I told him we'd be back at the hotel in the afternoon and to come to our room when he got back.

I wanted to check on Stosh when we got back, but his lights were out. I thought they would be. Twenty minutes later ours were too.

Chapter 23

We ate breakfast with Stosh on the deck, and I got ahold of Dr. Long as Rosie and Stosh were cleaning up. She had an opening at ten. Her office was just a few blocks north of Al Johnson's restaurant, so I stopped to show Rosie the goats on the thatched roof, a birthday present to Al from a friend. The goats were a county tourist attraction.

Dr. Long was chatting with her receptionist when we got there. Her smile was much better than Peters'. She wore a flowery summer dress and sandals. She was shorter than Rosie, and Rosie was shorter than me. Her office was almost all windows and full of sunlight. With her dress and her smile and the sun, it was a pretty cheery place.

I asked what kind of work she did and if she worked much with the police.

"Mostly individual counseling, but sometimes I work with families. I don't know how much you consider to be *much*, but certainly not as much as you get in Chicago. For one, there are less people up here, and two, they tend to keep their problems to themselves. The schools just started referring cases to me a few years ago."

We explained the situation and asked for her opinion about what might be driving Victoria and what she might be capable of doing. Her opinions weren't comforting.

"Have either of you done any wilderness camping?" she asked.

That took me by surprise. "I have," I said. "I had wilderness training in the army and have been in the back country of several national parks. I've asked Rosie to come several times, but she's turned me down."

"Right," Rosie said with a smile. "My vacations include a soft bed and a hot tub."

We all laughed.

"Why do you ask?" I asked. "Have you?"

She smiled. "I have." She sipped her coffee. "What thoughts would go through your head if you were walking along the trail and all of a sudden a couple of bear cubs came out of the forest fifty feet ahead of you?"

"I'd wonder if my will was in order."

She laughed. "Right. Because where there are cubs there's a mother. And what would she do if she saw you?"

"Well, not entirely sure, but she wouldn't be happy."

"Right again, because her instincts are to protect her cubs, and you are a threat. She's not going to stop to see how friendly you are... she's coming after you."

Rosie squirmed in her chair. "I've never seen a bear in my hot tubs."

"I imagine not," Lynn said. "The point is, the motherly instinct is the same no matter the species. Imagine the state of that bear if she had lost her cubs and was looking for them. Victoria is no different."

I didn't quite agree. "Not entirely the same. Victoria gave up her baby... voluntarily."

"Yes, but the whole adoption process is really fraught with trouble. A mother is giving up a baby because there's a problem—money, drugs, family pressure, the father split, stigma... whatever the reason, it was strong enough to overcome that maternal instinct. But that doesn't go away, and some change their minds."

Rosie was holding her cup in both hands. "Obviously Victoria was one of those. Sarah overheard that argument between Victoria and Peters. She wants her baby back, which raises another point. The baby is now about ten years old... so no longer a baby."

Lynn nodded and picked up a pencil. "Yes, but she may not be thinking that. In her mind, she's trying to find her baby. I'd have to talk to her, but I'd say she's suffering from some psychological disorder."

"And that makes her dangerous?" I asked.

"Hard to say. It could be that she just wants to know her child is okay. Some mothers would be satisfied just knowing that their baby was well taken care of. But she also could be looking for a real baby. She could be stuck at ten years ago. If that's the case, there's no telling what she'll do."

"If they were yelling loud enough for Sarah to hear, I'm guessing she's not just wanting to know her child is okay," I said. "And Peters isn't exactly the kind and caring person that's going to handle that well."

"No, it doesn't sound like it. Doesn't sound like her personality fits the business she's in," Lynn said. "It would be against protocol to tell a mother who adopted her baby, but it certainly should be handled without anger."

"Hard to do if the mother is upset. And even harder if Peters is involved," Rosie said. "We also know someone broke in. I think it's a pretty good assumption that was Victoria looking for information."

Lynn nodded. "I agree. Surprising that she still had a key."

"Peters isn't a good manager," I said. A female cardinal landed on the bush outside the picture window to the left side of the doctor's desk. "It's also surprising to me that she employed a birth mother. Something seems wrong about that... maybe unethical. Would you agree, Doctor?"

"I wouldn't go as far as unethical. But even working with someone you know could be problematic. And someone who worked for you would be even more so. But if there was a close relationship, Mrs. Peters may have wanted to help Victoria."

"My guess is it was all about money," I said.

"I agree. Just suggesting the possibility."

I stood and walked to the window and looked out over a yard with several gardens, a curving path, and two sitting areas that blended into a forested area behind the property. If I ever needed a psychiatrist I was coming back here. But then I had Moonlight Bay. Maybe she'd make house calls.

As I watched a squirrel, I said, "It's obvious Victoria was upset and willing to illegally enter the agency looking for information. So, given her behavior, what do you think she's capable of? Despite what the evidence seems to show, I find it a bit of a stretch to go from looking for her baby to killing someone."

"Hard to say, Spencer. When you're dealing with emotions, especially the emotions of a distraught mother, there are no rules... except that there are no rules. The books and journals only give guidance. If she's unstable, it's very possible that she wants the people involved to suffer as much as she has."

I turned back to her. "So you don't have an opinion?"

She smiled. "I'm not paid to have opinions, but of course I do. They're just usually guided by what I've been taught and experienced. My personal opinions I usually keep to myself."

"Since we're not paying you..." I smiled. So did she. "I'd like your opinions, the personal one and the doctor one."

"They're both the same. Back to the mother bear. If she's lost her cubs she's going to be increasingly upset and angry. Whoever or whatever gets in her way is going to be in trouble. There is no logical thought. She doesn't stop to realize the person coming up the path doesn't have her cubs... she just attacks."

"Sure, but Victoria didn't encounter someone coming up the path. She sought them out and killed in cold blood. It was premeditated."

"Yes, seems to be more of a human thing. We are a violent species."

"So?"

She took a deep breath. "So, she could be capable of anything. Probably all of us could if pushed far enough and under the right conditions. You've notified the other names on the folder?"

"All but one. We're going to see them this morning."

She nodded as I sat. "You need to find her. I assume the police are looking."

"Yes, in two states. Ironically, the last place she was seen was here."

"By here you mean…?"

"You heard about the fire in Egg Harbor?"

"Sure. Up here everyone hears about everything."

"Veronica was registered at the Brew Pub. But she was gone when the fire started."

"Interesting."

"Does that tell you anything?" Rosie asked.

"No, I'm sorry. If I had a crystal ball I could make a lot more money."

"She registered under her own name," I said. "If she killed someone that seems odd."

"You have to think from her viewpoint, Spencer. It's all about trying to find her baby. She doesn't think she's done anything wrong, so why hide? There's only one goal… find her baby... or child."

I thought for a second. "That raises another question. I've thought that if we could find the child and reunite the two Victoria would stop the rampage. But if she's looking for a baby and we showed her a ten-year-old girl, would she believe it was hers?"

"Good question, Spencer."

"Do you have a good answer?"

"I wish I did. The mind can be stranger than you can imagine."

"So she's not trying to hide?" Rosie asked.

She shook her head. "I don't think so."

"Well, there are a lot of people looking, and we can't find her."

"But that's not because she's hiding—you're just not looking in the right spots. Remember, she registered under her own name."

"So she's acting on emotions? There's no logical thought process here?"

"Correct on the emotions. But there is one path that ties her actions together."

"Yes," I said. "The names on the file folder."

"Right. And two of them are dead."

"So the logical place to look for her is where the other two names are."

She raised her hands. "So far that's your only path."

I agreed.

"But a word of warning."

I waited expectantly.

"So far all you have is a good theory. You have no real evidence. It may not be her."

"I've considered that," I said. "We don't know what Peters is doing, but I have a feeling it's not all kosher. And where things aren't kosher, who knows how far not kosher can go."

Lynn smiled. "Interesting way of stating it."

"Yeah," said Rosie. "You give a guy a degree in English and you never know what's going to come out."

My look didn't wipe the smile off her face.

"Thanks for your time, Doctor. Is it okay if we call if there is anything further?"

"Certainly." She jotted a number on a note paper. "Here's my home phone. Call anytime. And I'd appreciate knowing what happens."

"Thanks. We'll let you know."

On the drive back to Green Bay we talked about what Lynn had said. Our only hope was that someone found Victoria before she struck again. One thing on our side—it sure helped knowing where that might be.

We stopped for lunch in Sturgeon Bay and then headed to the Bell's house.

Chapter 24

I t was a little after one when we drove slowly by the Bell's house. The same woman we had seen driving away in the car was working on the flowers along the sidewalk. She had on gloves and wore a wide-brimmed hat. I parked on the street two houses down, and we watched for a few minutes. We had decided that we would both approach her but that Rosie would do the talking. She was the one with the badge. Mrs. Bell didn't look up until we turned into her walk and headed toward the house. She'd probably be wondering who we were and what we wanted. She could rule out Jehova's Witnesses—we weren't dressed well enough. She stopped weeding and stood, the trowel in her hand.

"Mrs. Bell?" Rosie asked.

"Yes," she said hesitantly.

Rosie held out her badge. "I'm Detective Lonnigan with the Chicago police." She didn't introduce me. We had decided to leave me out of it as much as possible unless Mrs. Bell asked who I was. "We're working with the Green Bay police and looking into an incident in Chicago. Your name came up as part of the case."

She looked worried. "I can't imagine. Are you saying I'm in some sort of trouble?"

"Not at all, ma'am. We're looking for some help."

"Well, I'd be glad to help if I can. What's this all about?"

Rosie put her badge back in her pocket. "Can we go inside?"

"Oh, certainly." She led the way to the side door and into the kitchen. "Give me a minute to wash my hands. Please have a seat. She joined us after time at the sink. The worried look was gone, replaced by a stern attitude that reminded me of my high school algebra teacher who never appreciated my humor. And, unfortunately, while she was washing her hands she had time to think.

"Why are the Green Bay police involved in something in Chicago?"

I had found it never went well when the person I was questioning was the one asking the questions. But then I could just sit back and watch... Rosie was the one doing the talking.

"The cases overlap. That led us up here."

She was back on track, at least for a couple of sentences.

"And who is this with you? Can I see his badge?"

It had fallen off the track again, but I wasn't worried. We weren't here because she was a suspect... we were here to help her. I pulled out my wallet and got out my ID card.

"Mr. Manning is a private detective who works with us from time to time. He's the one who discovered this... issue."

She had taken on a stern look with a clenched jaw and narrowed eyes. "And what issue would that be?"

Trying to look relaxed, Rosie covered her left hand with her right on top of the table. "It involves the From Us to You Adoption Agency. We understand you've been working with them."

The stern look got even more stern than my algebra teacher. "And how would you know that? That's supposed to be confidential."

That was a real good question, one that Rosie couldn't really answer except for the standard evasion.

"I can't discuss details of a case. We—"

"So your details are confidential but mine aren't?"

"It's a police matter, Mrs. Bell... or may I call you Claudia?"

It was a nice try.

"You may not. Perhaps I should make a call to the Green Bay police."

"Please do. Ask for Chief Snark. But he'll just tell you the same things we are." Then she tried to make a dent in the Bell wall. "I want to say again that you're not in any trouble… we're here to protect you."

"From what?"

Rosie and I had talked about how to explain the problem and had wondered how to downplay the murders. With only supposition, we were walking a thin line. But Mrs. Bell wasn't giving Rosie much choice.

"Two people have been murdered, and both were trying to adopt a baby from the agency. As a matter of fact, both were in line to adopt the same baby. And there were two others, one being you and Mr. Bell."

That got her attention, and some of the stern look disappeared.

"So you're saying that because two murdered people have something in common with me I need protection?"

When Rosie didn't answer, she continued.

"I would think any two people might have many things in common, like they shop at the same grocery store."

I decided to try and help. "Sure, they might. But these two people were in different states and clients of the agency. In a murder investigation you look into all the angles, many of which turn out to not be relevant. This may be one, but it's better to be aware than not."

Her doorbell rang and she excused herself.

"This is going well, don't you think?" I asked.

Rosie rubbed her forehead. "When she gets back I'll ask about the payments. Hopefully we can get some information before she throws us out."

"Or calls Snark."

"If those are the two choices, I vote for being thrown out."

Mrs. Bell returned without telling us who was at the door. In a friendlier conversation she would have explained that it was the Fuller Brush man. I started before she had a chance to bring up the two choices. I hoped that asking for her help would lighten things up.

"Mrs. Bell, there were four names associated with one adoption. The other three were offered the baby, but then were told the mother had changed her mind, so the adoption fell through. Then the couples were approached by Mrs. Peters saying that the mother was having trouble making ends meet and asked if they'd be willing to donate money for the mother."

I was watching her face while I was talking, expecting her to react if the same thing had happened to her. There was a reaction, but not what I expected. It wasn't surprise, it was a look of anger. If I realized I had been duped, I would have been angry too.

When she didn't say anything, Rosie asked her if the same thing had happened to her.

She was trying to control her emotions and replied, "Yes, exactly the same."

"And doesn't it seem odd to you that the same thing would happen to four different couples with the same baby?"

Her shoulders slumped, and she relaxed a bit.

"I guess it is odd, and it only makes this a lot more complicated."

"What do you mean by *this*, Mrs. Bell?"

"A few years ago we filed a lawsuit against Mrs. Peters and the agency for fraud and a few other things. My husband knows more about it."

"Did you make the payments for the mother?" Rosie asked.

She straightened and the stern look was back, along with anger. "We did, but not by my choice. I thought it was absurd. But my husband was adopted when he was six, and soon after that the husband left and the mother was left with no support. She took care of him as best she could, but they lived a hard life. He said if he could afford to help someone avoid that he would. He felt very strongly about it, and I agreed. But as time went by I got frustrated and angry."

"You were still trying to adopt?" I asked.

"Yes. I wanted to give up, but Harry wanted to keep trying… for the same reason… to give a child a good home."

"You didn't try another agency?"

She clasped her hands together. "We looked into it, but others were much more expensive. From Us was thousands of dollars less. They were all we could afford." She held up her hand. "Don't say it… you get what you pay for. I told Harry that, but he was so hopeful."

"And obviously nothing ever came of the adoptions," Rosie said.

"No, but they kept the carrot dangling. Three separate adoptions fell through at the last minute for various reasons. We couldn't believe our luck was that bad."

"So where does the lawsuit come in?" I asked.

"A couple years ago we got another letter from them asking for money again to help out a mother having trouble, but it was a different mother. At that point even Harry had to agree something funny was going on."

"So what did you do?"

"At first we just asked for our money back, including all the payments we had made for the mother. They said they would refund the fees but not the payments. Harry contacted our lawyer who filed a suit."

"And it's taken two years?"

She nodded and looked frustrated. "Yes, they filed a countersuit that our lawyer says is ridiculous, but the bills keep coming as the lawyers fight it out."

"What's the status?"

"We have another court date in a few months. Our lawyer says we have a good chance of getting our money back, but at this point it's probably a wash with the legal fees. He also says he's about ready to go to the police with the information he's found."

"I'm so sorry you've had to go through this," Rosie said.

She nodded. "One thing I don't understand. If we're in danger, why aren't the Green Bay police talking to me? There's something odd about all of this. I'm going to call them. I don't pay tax dollars to have someone from Chicago telling me I'm in danger."

"That's certainly up to you, Mrs. Peters," Rosie said, "but they're not likely to give you much information."

"They'll give it to my husband!"

She told us it was time for us to leave. We did, and as we were walking to the car we made a bet on how soon we'd hear from Snark. I took under an hour. He wasn't happy with us to start with, but now he'd have a citizen telling him he wasn't doing his job.

As we were driving away, I said, "It's amazing that these couples, and who knows how many more, fell for this."

"Not that amazing, Spencer. You're not looking for a baby. It's a very emotional thing, and they were all pretty desperate. Remember what the doc said about a mother looking for her cub. The same applies to someone looking for a baby."

I turned left at the corner and headed toward downtown. "I was thinking of going back to the doc for some therapy. Maybe I should just listen to you."

With a big smile, she said, "I've been telling you that for years."

"And it wouldn't cost me anything!"

"Oh, it'll cost you. It'll cost you plenty."

***

O n the way back to the hotel we decided to take a detour and drive by the house of Justine Trainer, the owner of the agency. It sat on a hill overlooking the bay, with a long curving drive leading to the front door. Two stories of stone made a strong statement about what money could buy. It was the house of a corporate vice president, not the house of the owner of an adoption agency. Maybe Mr. Trainer was the corporate figure and Justine was providing a public service with the agency. I would have loved to stop and have a chat with Mrs. Trainer. But someone with a house like that would have excellent lawyers, and the ground I was standing on wasn't too firm at the moment. So I did the wise thing… I kept driving.

As I pulled into the garage at the hotel my phone rang. I looked at Rosie and smiled—forty-five minutes.

After my offer of a cheerful greeting, he said, "I got a call from a very irate citizen. I'm sure you know who that was."

That didn't need a response, so I didn't.

"I told you we'd handle this investigation. You have no business making unfounded accusations and disturbing my citizens."

I pulled into a spot and turned off the engine. "Hang on, Chief. I didn't make any accusations. I'm very careful about getting involved with lawyers. I only told her what had happened and suggested some possibilities."

"You think telling someone she's next in line to be murdered and that we're not doing our job is okay?"

"If that's what she said, she's exaggerating things. I never—"

"Butt out, Manning. I see you around this again I'll have you picked up."

"And charged with what?"

"I'll think of something."

It was never good to get into a pissing match with a police chief, but Snark didn't appear to be giving this the attention I thought it should get. I wondered why.

"I'd be happy to butt out. But your detective didn't even talk with Mrs. Bell. That hardly seems—"

"I let my detectives handle things how they think it best, based on the situations. I'll have you know, Detective Dunsley spent twenty minutes this morning with Mrs. Peters. She was very cooperative and appreciative of our concern about the break-ins. She was shocked about the murders and offered to help in any way she could. Dunsley was satisfied with her statements."

"She's a good salesman."

"What does that mean?"

"That means some people might buy what she says. But there are two couples that didn't. They're still alive, and I'd like to keep it that way."

"As would we, Manning, and we're all looking for Petrace. I've told you what will happen if we cross paths again. Perhaps you should get some advice from your detective friend about interfering with an investigation." He hung up and I told Rosie about the conversation.

I stared at the phone and shook my head. "Detective Lonnigan, you have any advice?"

"None that I haven't been giving you for years. And since you haven't been heeding my advice for years, I'll save my breath, except for one thing that I've already said. You're not in Chicago... and Iverson has gone out on your limb as far as he's going to go."

"I don't—"

She held up her hand. "Police departments don't usually appreciate private detectives telling them how to do their job, especially ones from out of town."

"But when they're not doing their job..."

"In your opinion."

"Do you think—?"

"What I think doesn't matter. What you think doesn't matter either. As far as Snark is concerned the only thing that matters is what *he* thinks. But I know from experience that you're going to do what you think regardless. And unfortunately for my logic, what you think has always been right, so it's hard to argue with results. But you can't do much from inside a jail cell."

***

We got settled back at the hotel and then walked to the pub, had a beer on the deck, and enjoyed the beautiful afternoon with blue skies, white clouds, and colorful boats on the river. Rosie bought the beer... she had lost the bet.

We were talking about dinner in our room when Paul arrived a little before six. He set his notebook and a photo folder on the table. I filled him in about our day and the conversation with Snark. He opened his notebook and pulled out four photographs. He had noted the times of arrival and departure. The first was Sarah at five to nine. The second was the mailman at ten fifteen. The third was a woman who got there as the mailman was leaving. She was there for three minutes and didn't get past Sarah. We already knew who the fourth would be, so we weren't surprised. Dunsley got there at ten thirty.

But there *was* something we were surprised about. Snark had said Dunsley had talked with Peters for twenty minutes. Paul's notes showed he had been there for over an hour, and when he left it was with Mrs. Peters. They both got into his car and drove away. He dropped her off two hours later. I told Paul what Snark had said. He just nodded, with little interest. Paul was the best operative in Chicago. His attention to detail and patience had always served me well. But he had no interest in theories or why he was doing what he was doing. He just did it and never questioned what I asked him to do. When I first met him I thought that was strange, but I quickly grew to appreciate his abilities and stopped wondering about the rest.

As he was putting the photos back in the envelope, I asked him to pull out the one of Dunsley. I handed it to Rosie. "Notice anything?" I asked.

She looked confused. "Like what?"

"Like his pants."

She shrugged. "What about them?"

"Same ones he had on when we met him. Same sweater too."

"So? A lot of people have favorite clothes. What about it?"

"Nothing... just noticed."

She handed Paul the photo, and he added it to the others and set the envelope on the table.

***

I bought dinner at the pub, and we talked about the Cubs' chances, the price of coffee, and many other meaningless topics that made the evening go by quickly.

When we got back to the room the red message light was flashing on the phone. There were two messages. The first was from Carol, asking me to call as soon as possible. I called her home phone.

"Hello, Spencer. Chief Werth called about an hour ago. There was a fire. The Frey's garage burned down." He had said to call him at home.

I figured we had found Victoria, at least at that moment in time, and told Rosie we'd head back to Appleton in the morning. I knew who the second message was from.

Chapter 25

Mrs. Werth answered the phone and told me Chief was out in the garage. She said she'd get him. Rosie sat down next to me.

"Hello, Spencer. The plot thickens."

"Looks like it. Any chance this isn't connected?"

"If you mean is there any chance that a person who left a building where she was staying that burned and then the garage of a couple who that person happens to be tied to and may have reason to attack burns, I'd say yes, there's a chance. There's also a chance you did it, but I'd say it's remote."

"Thanks, I appreciate that. I've already got one chief looking for a reason to put me in jail. But as much as I don't believe in coincidences, once in a while they do occur. And we don't know about the pub fire yet. The first guess was electrical."

"Well, let's wait until we have more than a guess."

"What time did it happen?"

"Best we can figure, about two. Someone in town saw the smoke. By the time the trucks got there the garage was totally engulfed. They just concentrated on keeping the flames off of the house."

"No wind?"

"Yes, but away from the house."

"So the house is okay?"

"It is. They got lucky."

"Does the time strike you as odd?" I asked.

"The whole thing strikes me as odd. The fire seems like more of a warning. But if you have already killed someone why send a warning message?"

"No clue," I said. "And I'd think if someone was going to set a fire they'd do it at night when they'd have less of a chance of being seen. And speaking of not being seen, it's pretty amazing she hasn't been. She drove there from Door County, and people are watching."

"There's that luck thing," Chief said. "But you can take country roads from the peninsula to here and hardly go through any towns. She probably knew the Freys work during the day, and given that the only way anyone else can see their house is if they drive by, she could have parked in the driveway and done whatever she wanted without being seen. Even if someone drove by they wouldn't have any reason to be suspicious. I assume Carol will let me know when they get the results of the fire in Door."

"Sure. And you call with yours. But if I were to bet on this, I'd say yours is arson and the one at the pub wasn't. That one just makes no sense to connect it to Victoria. Why draw attention to where she is?"

"We'll know soon. I'll take you up on that bet for a cone at DQ. See ya."

I hung up and turned to Rosie. "You have any questions?"

"No." She was doodling on a notepad. "I think I got it from your side. It'll be interesting to get the results of the arson investigations. One comment on possible motivation, if this was indeed Victoria."

"Please."

"You questioned her starting a fire instead of shooting someone. Let's do some supposing. With Stosh and Mrs. Hanover she had a one-on-one situation. Let's assume she did her homework and knew that Stosh lived alone and that on that particular night Mr. Hanover would be gone, and Mrs. Hanover would be alone. No witnesses. Let's also assume she did her homework with the Freys. They're both teachers, only have one car, and drive to work together. They come home and are together all night. There's no chance for her to get them alone, yet she still needs to do something to hurt them. So, she sets a fire."

She had stopped doodling and was rolling the pencil back and forth on the table top.

"Why just the garage? Why not the house?"

She slowly shook her head. "A good question for Dr. Long. You're way past my pay grade."

"Mine too. Let's head for Appleton after breakfast."

"Okay. What do you want to do about Dunsley? What do you think was up with that?"

"I think I'd rather not know what two sleezy people do over lunch."

Rosie laughed. "Would have been interesting to be a fly on *that* wall."

"I'm thinking probably not."

She made a face. "Yeah, maybe you're right."

"But we'll keep that in our pocket if we need it during a future talk with Snark, like if he finds something to arrest me for."

"I'll do my best to keep that from happening."

"I'd appreciate that."

As we were deciding on a movie to watch, the phone rang. It was Iverson. It was an electrical fire that had started in the room next to Victoria's. Halfway to an ice cream cone. I told him about the fire in Appleton. He could call off his roadblock.

I called Carol and asked her to call Springer and the captain in the morning. I'd tell Werth.

We watched *Raiders of the Lost Ark* and turned in at ten. It had been a long day.

Chapter 26

There wasn't much left of the Frey's garage but ashes, the stubs of studs, asphalt shingles, and charred metal objects that had been in the garage. Part of the roof was still intact, but a good wind would blow it down. We had stopped at the station and were told by Officer Mills that Chief Werth was out at the Frey's place with the fire chief. There was still a lingering smell of smoke in the air when we got out of the car. And as we got closer to the garage we got the smell of wet ashes. Four men, including Werth, were standing on the gravel driveway looking at the remains.

"Morning Spencer… Detective." He introduced us to Chief Warren and two of his team. Werth turned to Warren and said, "You tell him, Chief. I'm not good at accepting defeat."

"Looks like you won an ice cream cone. Look at the burn pattern. The fire started in this front corner." He pointed to his left. "Nothing is left here but ashes. The studs that are still standing are in the rear. The roof in the front two thirds is entirely gone. What's left of the roof is in the rear. The fire started where the destruction is the worst, in that corner where the spread pattern is up from the corner and out to the sides." He pointed again.

"How do you know that, Chief," I asked.

"Follow the path of destruction. If you look from least to worst, you end up back in that corner. And there's nothing in that corner that would have started a fire, like an electrical outlet. I'm betting we'll find gasoline residue on the wood we took from that corner." He shook his head. "This was an old wood garage that went up like kindling."

I nodded. "I wouldn't have minded losing that bet. Either way, what a shame for the Freys. They must be pretty upset."

"That's putting it lightly, Spencer," Werth said. "They're pretty scared. They packed some clothes and moved to the hotel in town. It's right across the street from the station, and they can walk to school."

"Good."

Rosie was looking around the property. "It's so isolated out here. I'm worried about the house."

"Me too," Chief said. "I'm putting a couple of part-time people here until we get this solved. Hard to believe we haven't found this woman."

"Yeah, she's hiding in plain sight. How hard could *that* be?"

Chief Warren asked if Werth needed anything more from him.

"No, Don. I'll call if I need anything for the paperwork. Thanks."

The fire personnel left us standing by the ashes, surrounded by green trees and a beautiful spring day.

"This has left several lives in ruins," Rosie said.

"Yeah," I said. "Just like the mother bear crashing through the forest knocking down everything in her path."

"What bear?" asked Werth.

I told him about the doc's simile.

Rosie turned and looked out toward the road as a semi went by. "Maybe we should be looking for the child."

"That wouldn't hurt, but how would it help? We're certainly not giving her to Victoria. And there's probably only one person who knows where she is, and I'm guessing she's not talking."

"Looks to me like we've got two problems here," said Werth. "We need to find Victoria, and the police have to deal with whatever is going on with Peters. The two are related, but they're two separate cases. Solving one doesn't solve the other."

"I agree," I said. "The first priority is finding Victoria and stopping that threat."

Rosie turned back to us. "How about this? Spencer, you made the comment that she's hiding in plain sight. If her motivation is finding her baby, then everything she is doing is tied to that, and she sees nothing wrong with anything she does."

I picked up her thought. "And if she sees nothing wrong, she isn't trying to hide."

"Right," said Rosie. "And if she isn't trying to hide, at some point she'll go home."

"You people are making some assumptions," said Werth.

I shrugged. "We don't have much else."

"I guess not. Well, you go do what you need to do, and I'll take care of the Freys."

As he was talking, a dark-blue Buick pulled into the drive, and a uniformed officer got out. Werth introduced us to Officer Clemens.

"You out of squad cars?" I asked.

"Yup. This isn't the big city."

We all stood there looking at the ashes, not stating the obvious... we needed to find Victoria.

Chief Werth left, and I told Rosie I needed to make a couple of phone calls.

"Okay," she said. "I'm going to take a look at the cemetery."

"Watch out for the dog," I said.

She smiled.

I called Carol and asked her to pass on the information about the fire. I'd call Iverson. He would call Snark. She didn't have anything new for me. My second call was to Iverson. I caught him just as he was leaving.

"Hey, PI. What corner of my fine state are you in today?"

"Looking at a pile of wet ashes in Appleton, surrounded by all the beauty of nature. This one is arson."

"Yeah, the human touch. Sometimes I think life is just an experiment gone bad."

"Anything new on your drug problem?"

"We got a tip that something is going down tonight, but that's all the caller said."

"Did you get any more on the car that was on the side of the road?"

"Yeah, meant to tell you about that. He ran out of gas."

I thought for a minute as I watched the officer inspect the property and let a theory roll around.

I told Iverson about my theory. "Would you make a call and get me an introduction to the officer in charge at the Coast Guard station in Sturgeon Bay?"

"Sure, that would be Chief Kraft."

"Thanks, we're going to stop there on the way home."

"How's your lieutenant?"

"Fine, but bored. We had breakfast with him this morning. He misses the city. I suggested he just sit on the deck and watch the birds."

Iverson laughed. "I bet that went over big."

"Yeah, he said just walking by the deck into the house is enough deck time. I don't get it."

"Nope, that's why there's apples and oranges. Maybe I can free up time to take him out for lunch."

"I'm sure he'd like that."

The officer was walking toward me. He looked like he was still in high school.

"Gotta go, Chief. Talk to you later." I hung up. "Hello, Officer."

"Hello, sir. Are you going to be here long?"

"Not too long. Why? Do you need something?"

"Chief forgot to give me the key to the house. If you're going to be here for a half hour I can go get it so he doesn't have to come back out here."

"Sure, no problem."

"Thanks."

I walked away from the dank smell and went to find Rosie. As I turned the corner at the front of the house I saw the short, wrought iron fence that surrounded the cemetery. The entrance was through a tall archway with "Appleton Cemetery" written on the arch. The dog wasn't standing watch. Rosie was walking north looking at the markers. I thought of walking up quietly and touching her shoulder but thought, while it would be fun for a moment, the result for me would be painful. So I called her name.

"Look at this, Spencer."

The tiny marker was barely readable, but the date of 1898 showed that Clara Ring had lived less than a year.

"If only these gravestones could talk," said Rosie. "I bet there are some amazing stories."

"Well, if you listen to ghost hunters, they do talk. We could come back at night and see."

"I think not. I'm having enough trouble being here during the day."

We walked down the row.

"I wonder why some are worn more than others," Rosie said.

"It's what they're made from. Marble was popular in the 1800s and early 1900s because it was easy to cut and engrave. But that also makes it easier to weather. Granite holds up much longer."

"So the ones that are in good shape are granite?"

"Or marble and newer. But I think granite is used more today."

We wandered down the rows, commenting on the dates and designs. The peace of the cemetery was only broken by a passing car or the chirp of a bird.

"I didn't see the dog," Rosie said.

"I didn't either, but maybe that's because we weren't looking."

"I *was* looking. He wasn't there."

I laughed. "I don't mean with your eyes. I mean with your spirit."

"What?"

"I've been thinking about it ever since Sarah's story about the owl. From what I've read, to see a ghost you have to want to... your spirit has to be able to connect with the ghost's."

"Right."

I shrugged as I heard the officer's car pull into the gravel drive. I suggested we go, and we walked back to the Mustang. My polite officer was parked at the front of the drive.

"Thank you, sir," he said.

I waved and wished him a good day.

As we pulled away, I told Rosie about my plan for the park, and as long as we were going to be over that way, I suggested we invite ourselves to Aunt Rose's for dinner. She had no problem with either and suggested we pick up Stosh.

"That could be a problem," I said.

"She wouldn't mind setting one more place," she said.

"Yes, but not many of her guests are dead."

Laughing, she said, "I forgot. It'll be a fun surprise."

"Fun? When you found out I don't remember it being so much fun. My chest still hurts."

She smiled. "Don't worry... I won't let Aunt Rose beat you up."

"Okay. I'd better make a list. So far you're protecting me from Aunt Rose and Snark. Speaking of whom, I don't usually recommend walking into the lion's den, but I'm thinking a visit to Chief Snark is in order. And with you there to protect me..."

"I don't recommend it either. Something on your mind?"

"I don't like the time discrepancy with Dunsley. I'd like to get a feel for whether Snark knows about that. Seemed like both he and Dunsley were going out of their way to soft pedal the agency."

"I wouldn't worry about that, Spencer. He's just not happy about out-of-towners showing up on his turf. Be the same in Chicago. One, he's not too happy about someone from Chicago telling him about a problem in his back yard. Two, he can solve his own problems."

"I'm thinking maybe he can't," I said as I made a left turn.

She shrugged. "You don't know what he's doing, and he's not going to share... for the reason I already stated. And getting Dunsley in trouble for whatever he did with Peters isn't going to help."

"Yeah, well, I'm not fond of Dunsley."

"Me either, but that's not going to help find Victoria."

"But shaking some trees might."

"Well, if that's your goal, walking into Snark's office will definitely shake his tree."

I stopped for gas and made two calls. Aunt Rose said she'd be thrilled to see us and our surprise guest. Snark's secretary said he was available at one. Perfect.

Chapter 27

I had no reason to believe that anything I would say or do would get a different reaction out of Snark. But I had never believed in letting sleeping dogs lie. Rosie wasn't happy about it, but she wasn't going to tell me not to and wasn't going to let me go by myself. I had no intention of going without my bodyguard; not that my body needed guarding—but I knew my mouth did. I had no desire to see the inside of Snark's jail, even for a few hours.

We had stopped at the hotel on the way to the station and left a message for Paul to spend some time at Victoria's house this evening and to call me if he had anything important to report from the day's surveillance. After working all day, he could decide how much time to spend. Knowing Paul, it would be more than just a few hours. I told him that there was a gas station, a few stores, and a diner about four blocks away and that a few minutes away from the house wasn't a concern. If she came home while he was gone he'd know as soon as he got back. I gave him Petrace's description.

***

Well, this is a surprise," Snark said, as we were shown into his office. "The fly coming to the spider."

Rosie bumped me slightly with her hip. I got the message.

"We just wanted to let you know what was going on," I said.

He looked surprised. "Well, I do appreciate that." He pointed to the chairs. "Make yourselves comfortable."

I could have felt good about his response, but the condescending tone wasn't hard to catch. Rosie had already told me that Snark wouldn't want or appreciate help from his out-of-town intruders. We had also discussed the information about Dunsley and decided to keep that to ourselves for two reasons. Unless you were sure of who your friends were, keeping some information to yourself wasn't a bad strategy, and sounding like a tattletale to someone who wasn't on your side wasn't a good strategy. But that left us unsure of what exactly to say. I was just doing what I did when I had nothing else to do... shaking the trees to see what fell out.

We sat, but I wasn't comfortable.

He crossed his arms over his chest and said, "So what's going on that you think I don't already know about?"

I could hear Rosie's unsaid warning, but this guy wasn't going to get my goat. "I assume you know that Victoria was staying up in Egg Harbor and that the fire was an accident."

He nodded. "We do have telephones up here... and newspapers too. Every day I get one on my desk."

I wanted to wipe the arrogant smirk off of his face. I would have liked to do that with my fist, but I settled for, "How about the fire in Appleton?"

He just stared at me for about ten seconds, but it seemed like ten minutes. I would have waited the whole ten minutes. The tension was on his side of the desk. I knew he would have liked to make some comment about not keeping track of everything that happens in every little town in Wisconsin... that's what *I* would have said. But I also knew he wasn't stupid... just arrogant. He'd know it was related or I wouldn't have brought it up. And it would be very hard for him to admit there was something I knew that he didn't.

The muscles in his jaw tightened as he forced out the words, "No, but I'm sure you're dying to tell me."

I wondered at what point he'd stop lobbing hand grenades at me... maybe never.

I tossed it back to him. "Only if you want to know. If you don't think we have anything to add to this, then we'd be glad to stop taking up your time."

"If it's pertinent, go ahead."

"The Frey's garage burned yesterday."

"That's a shame." He unfolded his arms. "There were two house fires *here* yesterday. Not unusual."

"Were either of those arson?"

The only response he had to that was, "No."

I nodded. "I didn't think so. This one was... gasoline."

He took a deep breath. "And you think it's related?"

It was a weak attempt at saving some face, but it was all he had. "Don't you?"

"Not necessarily." He looked at Rosie. "The police work a bit differently than you private guys, Mr, Manning. We'd like to have some evidence before we jump to conclusions."

I already knew that was the weak part of my side of the discussion, and Rosie and Stosh had pointed that out to me many times in the past. But the conclusions I jumped to were usually right.

"With everything else that's happened, it seems logical."

"Well, again, there's that proof thing. Any evidence that Petrace was there? Anybody see her?"

"No, no evidence, just—"

"And, despite what seems logical to you, it doesn't fit with *everything else that's happened,* which includes two murders. And there's no evidence those were Petrace either."

I had to admit that my side of the argument wasn't going well, but I wasn't going to admit that to him.

"Let's just assume that Petrace is responsible for the murders. Why switch to arson? Bank robbers keep robbing banks. They don't switch to convenience stores."

I glanced at Rosie long enough to see the fleeting look of "I told you so." Snark wouldn't have noticed it. She *had* pointed out several times to me that my assumptions were probably right, but I had no evidence.

"I think she tried but didn't get the chance. She was able to catch the other two victims alone. The Freys are usually not apart, especially now. And she needed to do something to deal with her anger… so she burned their garage. And she did it in the daytime when she knew they wouldn't be home so she wouldn't be caught."

"Why not burn their house? And if she already killed two people, do it at night so they'd die? Why just a garage?"

"It was a warning. She wants them to suffer, just like she is."

He smiled. "Ah, you're a psychiatrist too. It must be hard keeping all your hats straight."

I somehow managed to stay calm. "No, we talked to a psychiatrist, and she said—"

"A psychiatrist, eh? Well, you seem to have this all wrapped up. All you need is some evidence, even one little scrap. But please… continue."

"Did Detective Dunsley learn anything from Mrs. Peters?"

"Oh, I see. That's how this works. You give me supposition, and I'm supposed to share the facts from our investigation." He stared at me.

"Seems to me it would be better if we all worked together."

"Of course it does. But it's not your investigation. Okay, here's the facts. Mrs. Peters is very upset by all of this. She gave us the history of Petrace as an employee with her agency. She did admit she probably shouldn't have hired Petrace, but she felt sorry for her and wanted to help. Even let her live in the house the agency owns and lets mothers live in if they need help. Not something you know about, eh? Petrace is still living there."

I did know but kept that to myself. I thought I'd find out more if he thought he had the upper hand. If he thought he was throwing strikes he'd probably like to keep it up. So I was willing to bring up another point that I wouldn't win.

"And what about Mrs. Bell?"

"What about Mrs. Bell? What about Mrs. Bell is you're not in jail for interfering with an investigation. That's what about Mrs. Bell!"

I tried to look casual while I crossed my legs. I wanted him to know that his threats about jail didn't bother me. I figured if he had even the slightest reason to put me in jail, he would.

I kept my voice under control when I answered, "The what about Mrs. Bell part I was referring to is the possibility that she also is in danger. And if—"

Snark's face was turning red, and the muscles in his jaw were working overtime.

"And if you interfere with Mrs. Bell again you won't know what hit you," he said in a very controlled voice. "Luckily Mrs. Bell is a strong lady or you would have frightened her to death. I'm not warning you anymore." He turned to Rosie. "Detective, I would think you'd be the voice of reason with Mr, Manning. You know better."

She just looked at him without responding. She had tried the voice of reason approach many times in the past. It had never worked, but she wasn't going to tell Snark that.

Our parting wasn't cordial. When we got into the car I couldn't even remember if Snark had said goodbye.

As I turned into traffic Rosie said, "Let me say it this time—that went well, didn't it?"

"Your sarcasm isn't as good as mine. But it went as good as I could have hoped."

"Pardon? It was a train wreck. You got nothing from him."

"I didn't expect to get anything from him. That would have been a bonus."

"Then I must have missed something. What do you think was good about it?"

"We'll have to wait and see. You can't piss somebody off that much without something happening."

"And what do you think will happen?"

"Time will tell, my dear." After stopping at a red light, I leaned over and kissed her on the cheek.

She just shook her head and let out a long sigh.

Chapter 28

We turned off of highway 42 a little after three. Coast Guard Station Sturgeon Bay, a white building with a burnt-red roof, was on the north side of the ship canal on the Lake Michigan side. A tree-lined dirt road along the canal, with a few homes along the way, led to the station. As we rounded a corner, we came out of the trees and saw the white station next to the canal. As we walked around to the front of the station, the red canal lighthouse came into view. A light drizzle was falling.

"Spencer! What a beautiful lighthouse! Can we walk out there?"

"Wait a minute. You weren't too thrilled about the walk to the Algoma light. This is ten times farther and crosses water."

"But there's not a drop of fog in sight."

"There wasn't in Algoma either."

The light sat on the end of a stone breakwall and was accessed by an elevated iron walkway about ten feet off the ground and marked the entrance to the canal. The last portion of the north wall was separated from the main part by about twenty feet, and the walkway spanned the water. On a windy day it would be a tricky walk.

"We can certainly get closer, but the walkway is closed to the public. We'll walk over there after we're done."

The watchstander said we were expected, and we signed the visitor's log. A petty officer led us to a conference room where the executive officer, a boatswain's mate, first class, BM1, was waiting for us. He introduced himself as Petty Officer Ray Stant and said Chief Adam Kraft would be right with us. He laid out a chart of the Door County waters. He also had a map of the park and the surrounding waters. As he was pointing out the park and the lighthouse, Chief Kraft came in. After introductions, we all sat at a long, wooden table. Chief Kraft started.

"We spoke with Chief Werth this morning, and he brought us up to speed on the drug problem," Chief said. "Your theory is interesting, Mr. Manning. If I'm understanding it correctly, you think the drugs are brought into the park by car and then transferred to a boat by someone from the car."

"Yes, and please call me Spencer. The search of a suspicious car leaving the park turned up nothing. It's possible a search missed the drugs, but if I were delivering drugs I'd feel a lot better about driving a car out that no longer had the drugs in it."

"Agreed, but that's because you're smarter than the average perp."

Rosie laughed. "I tell him over and over that the only reason we catch a lot of these people is because they're dumber than rocks. We caught a bank robber a few months back because he handed the teller a note written on the back of a business card that had his name and address on the front."

Everyone laughed.

"We get the same on the water," said Stant.

Chief leaned toward the chart. "Your theory would require that a boat be able to access the shore. BM1, where do you think the best spot for that would be?"

He stood and explained the shoreline. I already had a good idea of a spot.

"The cliffs on the point present a problem... let's rule that out. So either side of the park, where the land elevation is at water level, are possibilities." He pointed out the two areas. "And there's a lot more of that on the bay side heading down to Fish Creek."

"Since we have limited resources," I said, "I'd vote for the bay side. The harbor side is full of boats and marinas and lots of people.

Easy to get lost in the crowd but lots of witnesses. The bay side might have a passing boat, but it's pretty isolated."

Everyone agreed.

BM1 marked the park map with numbers at five locations on the bay side. We'd use those numbers to identify where they were coming ashore.

"How many boats can you spare for this?" I asked.

Stant responded. "We have two crews. One needs to stay at the station in case of an incident lakeside. We do regular patrols north from the canal up to the park. From there to the north is handled by Station Washington Island, and south of the canal is handled by Station Green Bay. I've already notified the command at both stations, and they'll have a boat in the water on both sides of the park. If there is a boat out there and we miss them, the other two boats will join in."

"Sounds good," I said. "But there's one problem. How do you stop a boat that isn't doing anything wrong?"

Chief smiled. "That's the beauty of the Coast Guard, Spencer. We don't need a reason."

I'm sure I looked confused. "Pardon?"

He laughed. "If a boat moves we can stop it for no reason and board it to do a safety inspection. And whatever we find that looks suspicious is fair game."

I glanced at Rosie. She looked jealous.

"No probable cause?" she asked.

"None. Makes a situation like this easy."

She shook her head. "That's amazing. How do I join?" she asked with a smile.

"BM1 will fix you up before you leave."

"If I wasn't happy where I am, we'd be talking."

"Door's always open. With your police experience, there's a lot of avenues."

"I'll keep that in mind if anyone pisses me off."

I had no idea why she looked at me.

"And you'll be up in the tower?" Chief asked.

"Yes, we—"

I was interrupted by a loud alarm that stopped after five seconds. There was a quick, unspoken communication between Chief Kraft and his executive officer, and Stant left the room.

"Sorry for the interruption," said Kraft. "You were saying about the tower…"

I was surprised that he was so calm… something was obviously going on, and I wondered why he was still here with us. But then I realized that was Stant's job, and if Chief was needed we'd find out soon enough. But I *was* curious about what was going on. I glanced at Rosie who was as calm as the chief and continued.

"From the tower we have a view of some of the roads and all of the water surrounding the park. We'll be able to see boats that are offshore a couple of hundred yards. But if they're closer than that we'll lose them in the tree cover."

"Right, but most boats out in these waters are at least thirty feet and wouldn't be able to get that close. So they'd be sending a raft in for the pickup. You'd just have to look for that launch."

Stant came back in the room. "A twenty-six-foot fishing boat taking on water about a quarter mile into the canal." He had a small hand-held radio that he set down on the table in front of me. "Do you know how to use this?"

"We do," I said.

"Contact us on channel eighty-one." He gave us the boat number.

"Will do."

"What time are you planning on getting there?" Chief asked.

"Around eight," I said.

"I'd recommend seven," said the chief. "It starts to get dark by eight. You need to be in position before that so you can see the boats."

"But even if it's dark, I'll be able to see the lights," I said.

"If they have them on. If I was doing something illegal, I'd turn my running lights off, which would be a good reason to stop them."

I agreed. "Okay, seven it is."

He nodded, and Stant slid the radio to Rosie. "Our boat will stay a bit south of the bay so we don't scare anyone off. Once you have a boat identified we'll be there in five minutes. Do you have binoculars?"

I shook my head. "No."

He nodded at Stant who left the room.

"Being on the water, you have a problem we don't on land," Rosie said. "Assuming all this happens and you stop the boat, what are the chances you'll catch them with the drugs?"

Chief smiled. "Yes, we do. The chances are slim. As soon as they see us they'll throw the drugs overboard."

She raised one hand, palm up. "Then how do we win here?"

He sighed. Stant came back in and handed me a large pair of binoculars.

"Yes, not easy. But depending on where that happens, you'll be watching and can testify that that happened. We'll board the boat and go through every inch of it. I guarantee we'll find something... and perhaps you can give us a location and we'll send a diver down. And hopefully Iverson will be able to apprehend the person in the car."

Rosie sighed. "There is a similarity between land and water... even if they aren't very smart, we need to get lucky most of the time."

Chief agreed. "One other thing... we'll have to watch the weather. There are storms coming in overnight, and the bay will turn choppy. It should stay calm in the time frame we're looking at, but if it comes in early your boat might not be out there."

"Or maybe that'd be the perfect time," I said. "They'd think no one else would be out there either."

"Maybe. It's a guessing game. But most boaters up here are aware of how dangerous that bay can be. It's the tourists who don't know any better who get into trouble."

"Is there a point where you wouldn't have your boat out there?" I asked.

"Yes, it's always a risk when we go out, but we manage the risk. There is a point, but I don't see what's coming in tonight to be a problem."

"Okay, we'll play it by ear."

"Any other questions?"

No one had any.

"Okay, we'll see you tonight," Chief said.

"Thanks, gentlemen. We'll cross our fingers. Would you mind if we wander around the grounds a bit?"

"Not at all. Would you like a tour of the station?"

Rosie perked up. "That'd be great."

He nodded at Stant and everyone stood.

"I'll take you back to the coms room and find someone to show you around," Stant said.

On the way back we passed a female who Stant asked to give us a tour. He told us Seaman Fox knew as much about the station as he did. She seemed excited to do so and spent the next half hour explaining the workings of the station. She was very knowledgeable. At some point I pointed that out and asked why she was still a seaman. Rosie gave me a look that meant I shouldn't have asked.

Fox laughed. "Oh, they've been trying to get me to go to school, and that had been my plan… to make a career of the Coast Guard. But I met 'mister right' and decided to get out and start a family."

"You have to get out to do that?" I asked.

"Not necessarily, but we get reassigned every four years… or less. That's pretty tough on a family."

"I guess. Good luck with that."

We finished the tour and thanked her. The sky had clouded over by the time we got back outside, and we walked toward the lighthouse. When we got to the water, we stood on the rocks, and I took out the binoculars. The red lighthouse was striking against the gray sky.

"Do you have your camera?" Rosie asked.

"No, it's back at the cottage."

"Too bad, this'd make a great photograph."

I handed her the binoculars.

"Too bad that phone of yours doesn't take pictures," she said.

I laughed. "Right… I've got enough trouble making phone calls. If it took pictures, too, it'd be the size of a Buick."

"Yeah, I was just being silly."

It started to drizzle again, and we headed back to the car.

"Spencer, the weather might be a factor."

"Yes, it might." I held the door for her. "But that's not something we can control. We'll go and see what happens."

Before we left I called Aunt Rose. Maxine answered. I told her we had to be out of there by six thirty. She said they'd plan dinner for five thirty.

***

We were back at the cottage by four thirty, and Rosie went over to tell Stosh to get ready for dinner. I had already told him to pack a bag and plan on staying overnight. When we left fifteen minutes later it was obvious he was thrilled to be getting out of the cottage. And he was also thrilled about seeing Aunt Rose. The two of them had always gotten along great. But I warned him about what her reaction might be about seeing a dead person. He thought it would be fun and pointed out it was better to see a live person who you thought was dead than a dead person you thought was alive. I couldn't argue with his reasoning.

On the trip across the peninsula we brought him up to date on the investigation. I knew he was listening, but his only response was, "I'm glad you're pissing off someone besides me for a change."

Rosie thought that was funny. I didn't.

***

We parked in Rose's lot and said hello to two guests who were heading out for dinner. We left Stosh sitting in one of the rockers on the porch and went in to find Rose and Maxine. I told Stosh to look alive. Maxine was setting the table. After hugs she asked where the guest was. I told her she'd see in a minute. She said Rose was in the kitchen.

Aunt Rose was happy to see me, but then she was always happy, so that really had nothing to do with me.

"Hello, my dears. I'm so glad you could come for dinner. But I thought you were bringing a guest. I had Maxine set an extra plate."

"No worries, Aunt Rose. He's relaxing on the porch. Can you come out and meet him?"

"Of course. Just give me a minute to check on the vegetables. I didn't have time to make a roast, so it's just chicken."

No matter what Rose made it was never *just* anything.

"I'm sure it will be wonderful as usual. We'll wait for you on the porch."

Rosie and I were leaning against the railing trying to hold in our excitement when Rose came out.

"I'm sorry to not be dressed to meet your guest, but I'm sure—"

And then she swooned with her eyes and mouth wide open as she saw Stosh smiling in the rocker. I was afraid she was going to faint and took hold of her shoulders. It took a bit for her to find words.

"My Lord, am I seeing a ghost?"

Stosh pushed himself up from the rocker. "My dear Rose, I assure you I'm as real as the rest of you."

He held out his arms, and she started to cry as she put her arms around him. I stood behind Rosie just in case anyone wanted to hit me. Turned out that was the wrong place to stand as Rosie turned around and hit me in the chest.

"Hey! What's that for? You already had your turn."

"That's for Rose. She's too polite to do it."

I laughed.

"I need to sit down," said Rose, and she sat on the bench next to the rockers. Stosh sat next to her and held her hand as Maxine came out to see what all the commotion was.

"Someone needs to explain," said Rose.

I gave her the basics. She took it a lot better than Rosie had. She turned to look at Stosh, still looking amazed.

"This is wonderful. I wish I had known… I'd have made something besides chicken."

We all laughed.

Over dinner we told the whole story, ending with why we had to leave by six thirty. Rose wasn't happy about our getting involved with drug dealers and told me to call when we were on our way home, no matter what time it was. And as long as we had to come back for Stosh, she wanted us to come for breakfast. I knew that not only would she be happy to have us come for breakfast, but if she made plans for us to be there, she thought nothing bad would happen to us. She said God wouldn't interfere with her breakfast. I explained to her that Rosie and I were just the spotters so we wouldn't be in any danger. The Coast Guard and Iverson were handling the dangerous parts. She said she wasn't taking any chances.

When we were leaving, Stosh told me to remember the part about just being the spotters.

Chapter 29

We stopped at the ranger station and picked up radios for each of us and another pair of binoculars. Chief Iverson was already there with three of his officers, and we went over the plan. Iverson and one of his officers would be in unmarked cars near where we thought the exchange would take place on the west side of the park. One officer would stay with the ranger. Rosie and I were the key to putting the plan into operation. We both got our shoulder holsters and guns out of the trunk.

The drizzle had stopped and the sky had cleared, but the forecast was for the rain to return sometime during the night. The temperature was in the sixties, and we had on light jackets. It wasn't a good night for boating or being in the park, so I expected traffic to be light both on the water and in the park. On the drive to the tower on Shore Road we only passed two cars going in the other direction, and the tower was about halfway through the park on the northern point.

The climb up the tower seemed easier than the last time because I was anxious to get to the top. I felt like I was back in the army, getting ready for a night exercise. I was already scanning the waters, and Rosie was only halfway up.

"Well, you won that race, Mr. Blaine," she said, breathing hard.

"If I would have known you were so out of shape I would've requested light duty," I said with a smile.

"Not as young as I used to be. You see anything yet?"

"There are two boats heading south on the bay side, probably heading back to Green Bay. Lots more moving in the harbor. Remember, we're looking for a boat that's not transiting the area."

I checked in with Iverson, who was running Shore Road. His other car was parked just off of Shore Road on the road leading into the cemetery. We could hear everyone, but he would communicate with his other car and the ranger station. At 7:10 I called the Coast Guard on the marine radio. The Sturgeon Bay boat was in position in Egg Harbor doing a normal harbor check. They'd move out into the bay in ten minutes and would communicate with the boats from the other two stations. So the only communications I needed to make were with the main boat and Iverson.

We both had on our shoulder holsters. We weren't supposed to be part of any apprehension if it came to that, but one never knew. I hardly ever carried my Smith and Wesson revolver, but I held to the rule that if there was a chance I'd be shot at I wanted to be able to shoot back. This seemed like it fit that rule.

Only two cars had passed the tower by eight o'clock, and at eight there were no boats near the park. The moon had just cleared the trees. There was only one boat on the bay side, and it was way out by Chambers Island. It was a possible. I'd keep an eye on it and see if it started to move in our direction. At eight thirty it did, and my adrenalin started to kick in. I pointed out the boat to Rosie and asked her to keep an eye on it while I scanned the waters.

There were still no boats on the bay side of the park, but the harbor was busy. I looked to the north and found the Coast Guard boat from Washington Island sitting just north of Horseshoe Island. The boat we were watching would not have been able to see them. I barely made them out in the twilight darkened by clouds and drizzle.

"They're moving pretty slowly," Rosie said.

"They're not going to do anything to attract attention." I turned back to the boat. It was tracking right toward the park. I let the binoculars hang around my neck, called the Coast Guard, and gave them a description of the boat. It was light gray and about thirty-five feet long with outboard engines and an enclosed cabin. It was too big to be able to get very close to shore, so it must have a raft onboard that it would launch when it got close. If it wasn't for the fact that it was coming right at us so we could see the lights, it would be hard to see.

The Coast Guard responded. "Okay, we're moving north up the shoreline. Let us know when it halves that distance to your location. If by chance you get a look at the stern, get us a name."

"Understood."

He called the other two Coast Guard boats and asked if they had copied the conversation. They had.

I called Iverson and filled him in. Three cars had passed his location, and only one had passed the tower. Since we were only concerned with the bay side of the park, cars that passed us heading east weren't suspect. The other two cars had been followed and Iverson knew where they were. Both had pulled into different parking areas off of Shore Road. We'd know which car it was once the boat picked a spot to land.

Fifteen minutes later the boat was still making way slowly and wasn't quite to the halfway point. I could barely make out the boat. The Coast Guard boat to the north hadn't moved. The winds were light but had shifted out of the south, so the front would be over us within the next few hours. It would be a good night not to be on the water.

"Do you think they'll speed up soon, Spencer?" Rosie asked.

"I would. If this is going to happen, it'll be soon."

It was like they were listening to me, as the boat almost immediately sped up and started throwing a wake. I let the Coast Guard and Iverson know as Rosie kept an eye on them. The boat from Sturgeon Bay replied that they were heading toward my location at a faster speed, as did the boat to my north. Iverson told me to update him on their landing location.

As I was putting the police radio down, Rosie said in a worried voice, "I've lost them, Spencer. They turned off their lights."

I brought up my binoculars and said, "Keep scanning where you were last looking. They'll still be heading in the same direction. You may be able to pick up the wake easier than the boat."

She gave me a rough idea of where she had been looking, and I joined the search and found it thirty seconds later. I gave her a direction and a few seonds later she found them.

When they were about a hundred yards offshore they stopped. I told Rosie to keep an eye on them while I looked for the Coast Guard boat. I couldn't find them and hoped nothing had happened. I checked my map and gave Iverson the location. It was offshore of the northerly spot where one of the cars had parked. He started moving toward that lot.

As I was picking up the marine radio, the Coast Guard called and asked for an update.

"He's stopped about a hundred yards offshore of point four on the map. They have their lights out, and there seems to be no activity aboard."

"Okay, they must be getting ready to launch a raft. Let us know when you see something."

"Are you nearby?"

"We're still around the southern point. We don't want to scare them off."

"How quick can you get here?"

"Two minutes. We'll get them."

I hoped so but knew there were ten ways anything could go wrong. But with three boats I was pretty sure we had the bases covered. I was also pretty sure we wouldn't catch them with the evidence… that would go overboard as soon as they saw the Coast Guard boat.

Ten minutes went by without any activity, and I was getting nervous. My adrenalin was telling me to do something, and there was nothing I could do but wait. I was starting to think they had somehow discovered they were being watched. If the exchange wasn't made, Iverson would stop the car, but we wouldn't be able to tie it to the boat.

Iverson called and asked what was going on.

"Still sitting in the same spot. I wonder if they know something's up."

"If they did, they'd be leaving. Keep watching."

The Coast Guard must have had more patience than Iverson... they didn't call.

It was another twelve minutes before a raft finally was lowered into the water, and one man got in and motored toward shore. I let everyone know and asked the Coast Guard if they were heading this way. They said they'd wait until the raft was back onboard the boat.

We lost sight of the raft as it disappeared beneath the tops of the trees and kept our binoculars trained on the spot where we had lost it. I knew it wouldn't take long for the handoff, and it was less than a minute before it reappeared.

"Keep watching, Rosie." I let everyone know it was heading back to the boat. As I scanned for both Coast Guard boats and didn't see either one, I started to get nervous.

"The raft is within fifty yards of the boat, Spencer."

I passed that information, pulled up the binoculars, and watched them pull the raft aboard. I scanned and still saw nothing of the Coast Guard boats and told Rosie I was worried.

"They know what they're doing, Spencer."

The Coast Guard boats were less than a quarter mile away. All of a sudden, two spots in the water lit up like Christmas trees with blue lights. The boat turned west and took off fast. They hadn't gone far when we saw someone throw something off of the stern. Less than thirty seconds later they were intercepted by the Sturgeon Bay boat, and the second boat was there a minute after that. The boat stopped quickly, but it was too dark to see what was happening.

I'd tell them later about the object that had been thrown overboard. Rosie had marked the location on the map along with direction and time from their present location. With that information, they'd be able to make an educated guess as to where to search.

As I was watching the blue lights, I got a frantic call from Iverson.

"Spencer, the car got away! Both of my cars are disabled. He's headed in your direction. It's a light-brown four-door sedan."

I wanted to ask what had happened, but time was critical. The car would be here in less than five minutes. That could wait. Rosie had heard and had already started down the stairs.

"Rosie, stop!" I yelled. The increasing wind was making it hard to hear. I was putting a quick plan together. "Come back!"

She came up the two flights and asked what I had planned.

"I'm guessing he won't be expecting someone waiting in this direction. He'll be looking to be chased, and I don't know if he knows Iverson's cars aren't chasing. I want to try and intercept him, and I need to know when he's coming. You can see some of the road from up here."

She got out the binoculars. "How soon?"

"Less than five minutes. Let me know when you see him." I started down the stairs.

"Be careful, Spencer!" she yelled.

I didn't respond… she wouldn't have heard me.

Chapter 30

I wanted to let Iverson know what we were doing but needed to wait for Rosie's call. I figured the best plan was to casually pull out in front of him and act like a tourist not watching the road and hope he stopped. I tried not to think about my Mustang. Rosie called two and a half minutes later. Those minutes had gone very slowly.

"There's a car coming," Spencer. "Pretty fast. Thirty seconds."

"Got it." I paused for a few seconds and then called Iverson. "I'm going to try and stop him." I put down the radio and watched for lights. Iverson didn't reply.

As he pulled around the curve coming toward the parking lot I started to pull out. He obviously wasn't expecting that, and at the speed he was moving he didn't have much time to react. I had left no room on the road to get around me. He swerved to miss me and ran off the road and into a tree with the right front of his car, blowing the tire. That car wasn't going anywhere.

I pulled onto the shoulder and got out with my gun in one hand and the radio in the other. He got out of his car and also had a gun in his hand… but his wasn't at his side. He raised it in my direction, and I dove and rolled as he fired. It would only have been luck if he had hit me. He turned and ran into the woods.

"Spencer, are you okay?" Rosie was just crossing the road.

"Yup. I'm going after him. Let Iverson know what's going on."

"I'm going with you."

"No, two targets are worse than one, and I don't want to worry about you. Stay here. But get up a little ways in the tower in case he comes back this way. Let me know if you see anything. The keys are in the car. Move it back in the lot. I've got the radio."

I holstered my gun, left a worried Rosie standing by my car, and headed into the woods. The vegetation between trees was pretty thick so at first it was easy to follow his path. I walked slowly, watching the path of broken vegetation and looking ahead. I figured I had several advantages. He probably had no knowledge of the park and was running blindly. And he may not be expecting someone to follow him. It was likely that he thought I was just a bad driver and not someone after him.

After ten minutes I stopped, crouched down, and called Iverson. I told him where I was.

"Okay, Spencer. The ranger and I are heading over to East Shore Road. You're heading toward a marsh. There's an amphitheater about a half mile south of that, and it's not far from where we are on Shore Road. My officers will walk over there and keep a lookout."

"Tell them not to be too anxious with their guns. One of the people out there is me."

"You just told them."

"I've got on a black jacket and a dark blue ball cap. Our guy has no jacket and is wearing a light colored long sleeved shirt. I'll let you know if I get to the amphitheater."

"Right. I'm keeping my people at the amphitheater unless they sight him. We don't need more people wandering around in the woods. Be careful."

I stood and heard nothing, not even a bird. And then I heard a far-off crack of thunder.

By my best guess, he was still moving on a fairly straight path toward the center of the park. Rosie and I had gone over the map several times, and I had a fairly good picture in my memory. If he kept on this path, he'd come upon the marsh, and I was guessing he'd not want to get wet so would go around it. I assumed he had some sense of direction and wouldn't head west toward the road where he thought the police were.

His trail ended at the marsh. I backtracked and found the trail ten yards into the woods. As I came to the eastern side of the marsh his trail straightened and headed south.

The path was still easy to follow… he wasn't taking any time to be careful. Five minutes later I could see an opening in the trees as the vegetation gave way to a small meadow. I stood on the edge and looked, seeing nothing. I picked up a rock and threw it across the meadow as far as I could into the woods and heard it crack against a tree. Nothing. I was hoping he would think someone was ahead of him. I threw another about fifty yards to the left. The sound of its landing was followed by a gunshot. That was two.

I called Rosie again.

"Rosie, he's fired two shots. I'd like to know if he has reloads with him. Go look in his car and see if there are any bullets."

"Okay, give me a minute."

She called back… there was a box of ammunition in the glove compartment. That didn't guarantee he hadn't put a handful in his pocket, but it narrowed the odds. After crashing his car he probably hadn't thought of extra bullets. I clipped the radio on my belt.

If he thought I was on the same side of the meadow as him, I could probably move safely across the clearing, but I didn't want to tempt that 5 percent chance that he wasn't moving and was watching. If he was watching, he'd be able to see me in the moonlight in the clearing.

I could see the eastern edge of the meadow to my left and started moving around it in the cover of the trees. If he was as careless as he had been so far, I'd be able to pick up his trail on the south side of the meadow. An owl hooted somewhere ahead of me, and I thought of Sarah. Maybe she was watching over me. Maybe she'd lead me to the man. Maybe not.

I pushed a branch out of my way and got a face full of water. Five minutes later I was on the south side of the meadow and about where I figured I had thrown the rock. Not many steps later I picked up his trail. The undergrowth was wet and hadn't sprung back where he had walked. I stopped to listen and still heard nothing except continuing thunder claps that were getting louder and closer together. I wasn't very concerned about the lightning, but at some point I was going to get a lot wetter than I already was if the storm hit. The advantage I had was I knew where he had been, and he didn't even know I was there... the noise from the rocks could have been an animal.

I stopped as I thought I saw something ahead move out of the corner of my eye. I watched for a minute and didn't see anything. It could have been something moving in the wind, which was increasing as I could now hear the wind in the trees. It would be nice to get this over with before the storm hit.

A few minutes later I lost his trail. I continued straight for another fifty yards and came to a spot where the trees weren't as thick. In the distance I could see the road. I figured he'd stay away from the road, and I turned to my right and kept walking as quietly as I could. Ten steps later I heard another shot. Something besides me must have spooked him. It's hard to tell sound direction in a forest, but it was definitely coming from somewhere ahead of me. That was three.

I heard a very faint "Was that you, Spencer?" from Iverson.

I stopped and answered. "No, it was our boy. He doesn't know where I am, so something else must have spooked him... maybe a deer."

"Where are you?" asked Iverson.

"South of a clearing on the south side of the marsh."

He was silent for ten seconds. "The ranger says you're about a quarter mile from the amphitheater."

"Are you on the road?"

"Yes, we're moving south along the road where you are. Be careful."

I replied. "His trail got close to the road and then moved back into the woods, so for the moment he's staying away from the road."

"Okay."

As I walked slowly, I asked him to tell me what the amphitheater looked like. I had a vague memory of it from fifteen years ago, but I wanted to be sure. He put the ranger on who described an open-air theater with a semi-circle of tiered stone seats built into a natural small hill. There was about a three foot drop behind the last row of seats. The whole thing was surrounded by trees. Iverson's two officers were positioned behind the seats.

Fifteen minutes later the shrubbery thinned, and I lost the trail, but it didn't matter as I could see a clearing ahead. I notified Iverson and his officers that we were almost at the amphitheater and then veered to my left so as not to come out in the same spot as the man. I went very slowly and quietly and came to the edge of the clearing. The tiered stone seats were ahead of me on the other side a couple hundred feet away. There was no one in the clearing. As I slowly scanned the tree line on my side I saw the man standing in the trees at the edge, about fifty feet to my right and waited for him to make a move. My plan was to wait until he moved out into the clearing and then confront him, but an anxious officer beat me to it.

He stepped out from the trees, his gun raised in his right hand. I took out my gun and waited for him to put some space between himself and the trees. When he was out about twenty feet I started to move out of the trees. I was about to yell at him to stop when one of Iverson's officers jumped out from behind the steps and yelled at him to stop and drop his gun. Before I could respond, he fired and hit her, and she fell. I yelled at him and fired as he turned toward me, hitting him in the hip. He was looking for me and still had his gun raised. I put another bullet into his gun-hand shoulder. He dropped the gun and fell to his knees. As I came up to him he fell over on his left side, writhing in pain. I took his gun and left him there.

As I ran to the officer, I called Iverson. "It's over. We need an ambulance. The man and one of your officers are shot. I got him in the hip and shoulder… he's okay. I don't know about your officer."

"There's one standing by at the ranger station. I'll call for another." Iverson replied. "We'll be there in a few minutes. Which officer?"

"The woman."

The other officer, a man, was with his partner, bending down at her side. She was unconscious and still holding her gun. The other officer was putting pressure on the red spot on her shoulder. I laid the man's gun on the stone seats and bent and checked for a pulse… it was steady but not very strong. I gently took the gun from her hand. She looked to be in her early twenties. The other officer looked a bit older. He looked scared.

"Am I doing the right thing?" he asked.

"Yes, keep up the pressure. What's your name?" The drug runner in the clearing was yelling that he needed an ambulance.

"Dave," he said, looking up at me pleadingly.

"My name is Spencer." I tried to reassure him. "Just keep up the pressure… she'll be okay. What's her name?"

In a nervous voice, he said, "Becky… Rebecca."

I nodded and then looked over at the man.

"Get me an ambulance," he yelled. "I've been shot."

I would have laughed if it hadn't been for Becky. He certainly didn't have to point out he'd been shot. I walked over to him and just looked at him. There was an inch-long scar on his left cheek, and he was glaring at me. He was holding his left hip with his left hand.

"Why are you looking at me? Get an ambulance! Can't you see I've been shot?"

I looked down at him with as much disdain as I could muster. "I knew you were shot as soon as I pulled the trigger." I leaned toward him and said, "You have one advantage at the moment… you're still talking. The officer you shot isn't. And if you say one more word, I'll change that." He just stared at me with wide eyes and more than a little bit of fear.

I saw the flashing lights of the ambulance through the trees. It looked like there were ten of them as the colors were scattered by the wet leaves. Ten seconds later the fire department ambulance pulled into the clearing from the path behind the seats. Iverson pulled in a minute later, followed closely by Rosie. I gave the paramedics a report on the two victims, and they got to work, one of them moving to the man in the clearing. Dave sat down next to Becky and watched. He looked scared and relieved.

Iverson came up. "How is she, Mitchell?"

"One bullet in the shoulder. Her vitals are weak. We need to transport now. I need Ben. Would you go see what the situation is with the other guy?"

Iverson and I ran to the man on the grass, and Iverson told Ben he was needed.

"Okay, Chief. This guy is stable and not much bleeding. Another ambulance should be here soon. They'll give him something for the pain."

I wanted to tell him to skip that part.

A lightning bolt lit up the sky to the west, followed almost immediately by thunder.

"We shouldn't be out here, Chief. The skies are going to open up soon."

The ambulance left with Becky.

"Let's get this guy in the back of the car," said Iverson. He looked down at the man. "You need to walk to the car… we'll help."

"What's this *we* crap?" I asked.

I just got a look. We helped him up and each took an arm as he hobbled to the car, complaining all the way.

"You guys are trying to kill me!" he said.

"I'm fine with leaving you out in the rain and lightning," I said. "Up to you."

He shut up.

An ambulance arrived ten minutes later and took the man in handcuffs. Iverson's other officer rode in the ambulance.

***

Iverson turned to the ranger. "Preston, let's go look at the accident site. I'll ride with Spencer." Rosie drove, and I sat in front.

We were all quiet until we got out to Shore Road, and Rosie turned right.

"I thought you were supposed to be the spotter, Manning," Iverson said.

"Are you complaining?"

"No, but you took a helluva chance."

"What did you expect me to do when you called and said he was coming in our direction... wave as he passed?"

He laughed. "At the time I had no idea."

"To tell you the truth, neither did I."

"I already knew that," said Rosie. "When I saw you pull out in front of that car, I said to myself... that idiot has no clue what he's doing."

Iverson thought that was funny.

"Spencer," Rosie said, "I still don't believe what I saw really happened. You pulled your Mustang in front of that car! I can't believe you did that. What were you thinking?"

I looked at her sheepishly. Looking back on it, I couldn't believe I did it either. "I wasn't thinking," I admitted. "I was just going on adrenalin."

"Do you know how close he came to hitting you?"

"I'd rather not know."

We passed the tennis courts and a few minutes later came to the area where our man had parked and passed Iverson's two cars off to the side of the road. The front of one squad car was in the trees. The other was half stuck in a ditch at the side of the road. I turned in my seat and looked at Iverson. He was looking straight ahead.

"Ahem," I said loudly. He didn't react. "Chief, what the hell happened back there?"

"Nothing I care to talk about at the moment."

"I bet not. But if you ever want to satisfy my curiosity..."

"I don't know how many beers that would take. But I will say one thing... you saved my butt."

"Looks that way," I said with a nod. "That makes us even."

He brightened a bit. "Hadn't considered that. I guess we are."

I turned back to Rosie. "Hear anything from the Coast Guard?"

"Yup, they arrested the men on the boat, so they must have found something. Chief, they said for you to call the station when you got a chance. I told them about the chase in the park."

"Great news!" I said. Iverson was smiling.

Rosie pulled into the tower parking lot, and we walked across the road to the car. Iverson told us we could go. He wanted to take a quick look through the car, and we couldn't help. He radioed for a tow truck.

Multiple lightning flashes lit up the sky. Leaving sounded like a good idea. "Where are you taking it?" I asked.

"To our impound lot."

"You have an impound lot?"

He smiled. "Yeah, the yard behind the station."

"What about your two cars?"

"Busy night for my tow guy. Let's get together in the morning and debrief this. I hate to ask, Spencer, but would you make some notes tonight? Just a rough outline is good, with times as close as you can remember. We'll firm it up in the morning. My office at nine?"

"Sure. But make it ten. We're coming back to Rose's in the morning to get Stosh. I think I'll pick him up and bring him along. He'll enjoy the break from boredom."

We wished him luck, and as we said goodbye the rain came down in buckets. I asked Rosie to drive so I could call Aunt Rose. It was almost midnight, but I knew she'd be up waiting. It was a short call—she didn't need details, those could wait until morning. She just wanted to know we were okay. I told her we'd be there for breakfast at eight.

I was looking forward to being home. I took off my shoes and socks... they were soaked.

Chapter 31

When I woke at six Wednesday morning, early sunlight was a welcome sight. The storm was in full swing as we had run to the cottage at a quarter to one, and I knew it had taken hours to move through. But I was so tired I didn't hear any of it after I fell asleep.

Before we left, I checked in with Paul. There was nothing of importance at the agency. I didn't think we were going to get any more there so I moved him to Petrace's house to do the same thing… take pictures of anyone paying attention to the house and watch for Petrace. I told him I wasn't worried about nonstop coverage and he shouldn't worry about taking lunch. He'd call me if she showed up.

It was a challenge to get to Rose's by eight, but we made it. Rosie fell back to sleep on the way, and I wanted to. But the aroma of bacon and eggs woke us up.

We had a leisurely breakfast with Rose and Maxine and the guests at the large, oval dining room table. After we ate, we helped clean up and sat in the kitchen to tell the story. It'd be the biggest news of the summer. There was some we saved just for Stosh on the ride to the station, such as the two police cars on the side of the road.

When we got to the station, I drove around back to show Stosh the impound lot. There were four cars back there. Two of them were damaged squad cars. He made a comment about the level of crime in Door County. Iverson had coffee waiting for us. We pulled chairs up to his desk, and he turned to Stosh.

"The warden let you out?"

Stosh just stared at him. "Really? A smart-ass remark from a guy whose squad cars are in the impound lot? Nice job with that by the way… you must save a lot of money on expenses."

"There's two other cars back there," I said.

"Yeah, associated with a crime. We're going to auction them at some point."

"Nice little side business," Stosh said.

Iverson turned to me. "The Coast Guard stopped the boat with a cheerful announcement that they wanted to notify them that their running lights weren't on. They then told them as long as they were there they might as well give them a comp safety inspection. After some reticence on the part of the captain, the petty officer insisted and they boarded the boat, which two men did, onto the stern deck. The captain then became very talkative, asking several questions about boating safety.

"After a few minutes one of the men on the Coast Guard boat yelled that there was someone on the bow. He was about to throw something into the water when a petty officer fired into the air and yelled for him to stop. He did. The two crewmen on the stern made their way to the bow and took possession of a metal box. It was filled with baggies of white powder that were sent to the lab in Green Bay."

Iverson stopped and took some coffee.

"The sheriff has the three on the boat in custody. Your man from the park is under arrest and being treated in the hospital. Nice work, Spencer. You came out of it okay?"

"I think my shoes are ruined, but other than that…"

Iverson smiled. "Send me a bill."

"So, if you two are done, back to me," said Stosh. "Still nothing on Petrace?"

"Nothing," Iverson said.

Rosie set her cup on the desk. "That's one lucky woman."

"Well, just about this," I said. "Otherwise not so much." I took a drink. "I wonder… could she be distraught enough to end it? We know she uses a gun."

"Could," Rosie said, "but I'm betting wanting to find her baby will keep her going."

"Well," Iverson said with a sigh, "we'll keep looking. Anybody have any ideas?"

"Anyone watching the house?" Stosh asked.

"I would assume so," said Iverson. "As much as Spencer doesn't like Snark, he's not stupid."

"But I wonder how much attention he's giving to it," I said.

Iverson shrugged. "Gotta have some faith in your fellow peace officers."

"Yeah, you have faith. I'd like something a little more concrete, especially knowing who Snark has on the case."

"Here we go," said Stosh, rolling his eyes. "Like what?"

"Like I told Paul to go watch Petrace's house."

"Not something Snark is going to like," Iverson said.

"Not that I care. You have a law in Wisconsin against parking on the street?"

Iverson just took a deep breath. "I know you don't like Dunsley either, but if he didn't do his job he wouldn't be there."

"Well, maybe not." I told him about the time discrepancy with Dunsley and Peters.

"Hey, what a guy does at lunch is his business."

"As long as it's not with someone involved in a murder case."

Iverson got up and walked to the coffee pot. "More coffee anyone?"

We all declined.

"Your man can't watch the house twenty-four hours."

"You don't know my man. But I'm not a slave driver. I plan on doing some night work."

"Just don't let your night work land you in a jail cell." He pointed at me. "If I were you I'd stay out of her house."

I laughed. "If you were me, I would too."

Rosie shook her head. "I know I didn't have much sleep, but that doesn't make any sense."

Stosh laughed. "Along with most of the other things he does."

"So we'll go back to waiting for her to show up," said Iverson.

"And hoping no one else gets shot," I said.

"What's up for today?" asked Iverson.

"Gonna get Stosh back in solitary and at some point head back to Green Bay and relieve Paul. I'll work on the write-up this afternoon."

"Okay, thanks. If I can get it by the end of the week that'd be good."

***

Stosh complained almost all the way back to the cottage. By the time we pulled into the drive I was glad to be leaving. Rosie and I packed up again and headed back to Green Bay.

Chapter 32

I called Paul and told him I'd relieve him before dinner and take the night shift. Rosie and I had talked about the surveillance and decided it didn't need to be all night. If Victoria wasn't back by one she probably wasn't coming, and if she did come after that, she'd still be there in the morning. I insisted Rosie stay at the hotel and relax in the whirlpool. She insisted that she was coming with. We compromised… she was coming. We had an early dinner and parked in the spot behind Paul at a little after six. The only difference I saw at the house was someone had picked up all but one of the papers and put them in a pile on the stoop.

Paul got in the back seat and basically told us he had nothing to report. The only activity had been the paper boy delivering the paper at seven a.m. I thought of having another chat with the neighbor but decided not to because I didn't want to draw attention to us. Rosie fell asleep at a little after eleven. We had discussed taking shifts, but I had assured her that I was used to this and would have no trouble staying awake until one.

Except for normal neighborhood activity, including the neighbor I had already spoken to coming home at 8:20, the evening was as uneventful as the day had been.

We were back at the hotel before two and asleep ten minutes later.

***

I spent part of Thursday on the phone with Detective Springer and Chief Werth. Springer hadn't talked with Mr. Hanover since the last call about the payments to the agency. Chief Werth told me he checked twice a day on the Freys. They were still at the hotel and very frustrated at not being able to go home. If I was them I would have been frustrated also. But I would have thought the peace of mind would have been worth the inconvenience. I knew that not knowing when this would be over was a major concern.

We spent Thursday night with the same result, except that Rosie stayed awake. That probably had something to do with the nap she got in the afternoon.

Over breakfast Friday we talked about what we could do.

"Sitting and waiting is the worst part of this job," said Rosie.

"Yeah, but it's paid off in the past." I finished my eggs and asked, "Can you think of anything else?"

"No. Everyone who needs to be aware, is. Maybe she's given up." She picked up her orange juice. "Maybe someone will find her body in the weeds one of these days."

"And maybe she's doing something we can't imagine," I said. "The doc said there's probably something wrong with her. Who knows what irrational behavior might come of that?"

She finished her juice. "So all we can do is watch her house."

"Until something else happens."

She shook her head. "I'm running out of patience."

Chapter 33

The wait wasn't long, but it wasn't what we had hoped for. We decided to go back to the cottage Friday morning and check on Stosh. It was a gorgeous morning on the bay. The peace and quiet was only broken by the calls of birds, and a gentle breeze was blowing in off the lake. Stosh was still grumpy. We took him out to lunch to try and cheer him up… food was usually a good cure. It helped a little. He spent the time reminiscing about Francine and the good times. That cheered him up more than the food.

The case didn't come up until the car phone rang on the way back. I was trying to heed Carol's warning about driving and talking and had Stosh answer. I reached over and pressed the button to put it on speaker. It was Iverson.

"Didn't expect to hear your joyful voice," Iverson said.

"Well, sometimes life is full of surprises."

"You alone?"

"Nope. Spencer and Rosie took me out to lunch. We're all listening."

"Hello all… here's another surprise." He gave it a few seconds. "I just got a call from Chief Snark. Mr. Bell just reported his wife missing."

So much for driving and talking. I took the phone from Stosh. "Why are you calling and not Snark?"

"Really? You think he'd call you and admit he was wrong? That's not going to happen."

"How much of the details do you have?"

"As much as he has."

I turned on Ahrens Road and took a cutoff over to County F. "We'll be there in twenty minutes."

"Okay, coffee's on."

As I was putting the phone back in its cradle, I glanced at Stosh and saw the energy back in his face.

***

When we all had coffee, Iverson sat up in his chair and continued. "Mr. Bell had been gone all week on a business trip. He got back into town this morning and got home around ten. Mrs. Bell wasn't home. He thought that a little odd... she was usually home to greet him. But he didn't think more about it until noon."

"When was the last time he talked to her?" Stosh asked.

"He had called around dinner time last night."

"Not at bedtime?" asked Rosie.

"Not last night. Thursday is her bridge night, and she usually doesn't get home until after midnight. She said she'd see him in the morning and would make a special lunch."

"No note?"

"Nope." He took a drink and sat back.

"Did Snark send Dunsley?"

"Dunsley went, but so did Chief Snark."

"That's a lot of attention pretty early for a missing person," said Stosh.

"Yes it is," Iverson admitted. "And it wouldn't have happened if not for Spencer. You now have Snark's attention." He gave me a sideways look. "But don't expect a thank you."

I laughed. "No, I wouldn't think so. What a shame this had to happen to get his attention. What's he doing?"

"Same as any other missing person. There's a bulletin out, and it'll be on the news tonight."

"This is all pretty bizarre," Stosh said. "She's gone from murder to arson to kidnapping. Not your usual profile."

We all agreed.

Rosie sighed. "And we keep following her around as she does all that. We need to get ahead of her."

"That's always the trick, Rosie," Stosh said.

"Perhaps a call to Dr. Long," I suggested.

"Couldn't hurt," Iverson said. He called and talked to the secretary, who said the doctor was in a session but had the next hour free. He told her we'd be there in fifteen minutes.

***

A young woman was leaving the building when we pulled into the lot. She ignored us. Dr. Long was standing at the reception desk when we walked in. She said hello and looked surprised.

"You brought an army. We'll need another chair."

I introduced Stosh, picked up a chair from the reception area, and carried it into her office.

When she was seated behind her desk, she said, "If you're here again I'm guessing it's not with good news."

Iverson told her about the arson and the kidnapping and that we all thought that was odd.

"It is from a logical point of view, but remember we're not dealing with logic here. She's in panic mode looking for her baby and, like that mother bear, is liable to do almost anything when she doesn't find it."

"That's not good for our side," Stosh said.

"No, it's not. She's unpredictable. What's being done?"

I sat up straight and stretched. "The Freys have been moved to a hotel in town, and Mr. Hanover is aware."

"So the only thing you have going for you is you know the players. She's only coming after the names on the folder." She looked at Stosh. "Except for you, Lieutenant... you're already dead."

That should have been funny, but no one laughed. We all knew what she meant... to Victoria, Stosh was still dead.

"What about the lady who runs the agency?" she asked.

"A Detective Dunsley talked to her," I said. "She was upset but of no help."

"Any protection for her?"

"No," said Iverson. "The police aren't in the bodyguard business. But she's just as aware as everyone else. The biggest thing for all these people is just to be aware... don't go out alone, stay home at night. Spencer and Rosie had a talk with Mrs. Bell. The Bells filed a lawsuit against the agency for fraud."

"This just keeps getting crazier," she said.

"She wondered why we were there and not the Green Bay police," I said. "She called them asking why *they* weren't talking to her, which led to my getting a call from Chief Snark telling me to mind my own business or I'd end up in jail."

"Really? Sounds like he's not a part of the team."

Rosie explained that police aren't fond of outside help, especially from a private detective."

Dr. Long sighed. "Not very productive."

"So what do you think, Doc?" Stosh asked.

"Unfortunately, the same thing I thought last time. This is an unpredictable woman acting on emotions. She'll take opportunities as they come and probably isn't making any plans other than to concentrate on the names on the folders. This is obvious, but you need to find her."

"Yes, that'd be the first choice," I said. "But so far, absolutely nothing. Two states are looking and not a clue. The only thing we know is where she's been. We'd like to get ahead of her and be waiting. Any suggestions?"

"I would think Mrs. Peters would be a target, but not because of any logical thinking... just because she's the only one who hasn't been targeted yet. All of the other families have been attacked."

"Do you think she knows she's doing something wrong?" I asked.

"Probably not. Remember the bear… everything is a target until she finds her cub."

"We need to have another talk with Peters," I said. "Maybe Snark will be more helpful now. What do you think, Iverson?"

"Worth a try, but I'm probably the one who should do the talking."

I nodded. "Agreed."

We thanked Dr. Long for her time and headed back to the station where we talked for a few minutes about how to approach Chief Snark. We all agreed that we should continue the surveillance on Victoria's house and step that up to twenty-four hours.

As we were leaving, Iverson asked, "What's all that bear crap?"

I laughed and gave him the short version.

We put the surveillance into effect Friday night with Rosie and me covering until Paul got back at eight. It was a quiet night.

Chapter 34

We continued the surveillance on Saturday. While Rosie and I were having breakfast on the balcony of our room at the hotel, we got a call from Iverson. He had talked to Chief Snark, and Snark was going to have Dunsley have another chat with Peters. I made the comment that, based on the unreported lunch, Dunsley would probably be happy about that.

Rosie and I relieved Paul at seven. He was doing the crossword in one of Victoria's newspapers. He had nothing to report.

A light drizzle started as the sun was setting. Kids who were playing ball in the front yards went in, and I lost my entertainment. At ten, Rosie said she was going to take a nap and to wake her if I got tired.

I finished the crossword, got as comfortable as I could in a bucket seat, and settled in for another night's vigil. I kept myself entertained guessing the make of the next car to go by. I wasn't at all successful, and it didn't occupy enough of my time… it was a quiet street. After guessing wrong at 11:05, my next guess was a Chevy. I was wrong—it was a Volkswagon… a white one, and it turned into Victoria's drive and pulled up to the garage. I woke up Rosie.

She was immediately awake, and I told her Victoria had arrived. At least I was assuming it was Victoria. I didn't get a good look at the driver. We had already discussed what to do if she showed up. I would approach her outside asking for directions, and Rosie would provide cover. We didn't think she would be a threat to us, but there was that mother bear thing.

I crossed the street as Victoria was lifting the garage door. She pulled the car in, and I waited for her to come out at the sidewalk. As she came out I started up the driveway with a smile on my face and a wave. She was immediately defensive.

"Hi, I'm lost… wondering if you can help. I'm looking for—"

Her eyes stopped me as she looked to my right. I knew Rosie was backing me up, but I also knew Rosie wouldn't have let herself be seen. I hoped it wasn't the neighbor. The look of panic on her face let me know she thought she was cornered. The gun she pulled out of her purse confirmed that.

"Whoa, calm down. I told you—"

"I don't care what you told me," she said in a shaky voice. Her hand, with the gun pointed at me, was trembling. "Who the hell are you, and what do you want?"

Trying to stay calm, I said, "I told you—"

"You're a liar! You're after my baby! You—"

"Victoria, listen to me. I just want to help. I want to help you find your baby. I'm on your side."

The gun was trembling. "No one's on my side. You're all against me."

"I'm not. You need a friend… I'm going to help you."

"Why would you help me?" She started to cry.

"Because I know what you're going through. You need to put down the gun and we can talk." Her arm and the gun lowered a few inches. It must have been getting heavy. "Put down the gun, and I'll help you find your baby, Victoria."

Her arm dropped a bit more, but it was still on the target, which was me.

"No one can help me anymore." Her chest heaved as she breathed very quickly. "I killed two people, and one of those was a cop. I have to kill them all!"

"But you don't have to kill me, do you?"

That confused her. "I don't... I don't know. If they catch me I'll go to jail, and then I won't find my baby. I have to kill them first."

"Victoria, you haven't killed anyone. The two people you shot aren't dead."

Her eyebrows scrunched down and she looked confused. "You're lying. The papers said they were dead. I need to kill the rest."

"No, Victoria. Those stories were planted to make you think they were dead so you would stop."

"That's a lie." But her arm kept dropping and was at a forty-five-degree angle down. "Why should I believe you?"

I knew she was breaking, and I wouldn't be shot if the gun went off. With more talk I'd be able to get her to put down the gun. "Because you need a friend, Victoria. I need you to help me with something."

She looked puzzled. "What?"

"I need to know where Mrs. Bell is."

She still looked puzzled.

"Where is she, Victoria?"

"I—"

She was interrupted by a gunshot from behind me, and I watched Victoria fall to the ground. I ran to her and took the gun away and threw it to the side. I looked out toward the street and saw nothing. I couldn't understand why Rosie would have shot... she would have heard my conversation and known I had it under control. I kneeled next to Victoria, who was still breathing. She had been shot in the chest. It seemed like minutes, but it must have only been seconds until Rosie was by my side.

"Why did you shoot?" I asked, not very politely.

"Hang on, Spencer. I didn't. I'll call for an ambulance."

I nodded, not understanding at all. But as she ran toward the street, Detective Dunsley came out from the shadows on the side of the house.

I looked up at him as he walked toward me looking smug. "Dunsley! What the hell!"

"What are you talking about Manning?" he said as he holstered his gun.

"Why did you shoot her? She was ready to put down her gun!"

"I don't know what you're talking about, Manning. I'd think you'd be grateful. I just saved your life."

I was still kneeling and leaned down. "Victoria, an ambulance is coming. Where is Mrs. Bell?" I opened her jacket and put pressure on the red stain on the front of her shirt.

Her eyes opened slightly, and she looked at me pleadingly. Her lips moved, and then she took one last gasp. Her chest heaved and fell as her head rolled to the side. The pressure wasn't going to help. I sat on the ground and stared at her still body.

Rosie came running up. "The ambulance is on its way, Spencer."

My look told her all she needed to know.

"Oh, my God." She turned to Dunsley. "What the hell is the matter with you? Spencer had her talked down."

"She was holding a gun on an unarmed man. I saved his life."

"That's not the way I saw it," she said.

"Well, I don't know how you do things in the big city, but here we take care of the good guys first."

She looked at me, and I just shook my head.

Dunsley started to walk away as we heard faint sirens.

"Hey, Dunsley," I said. "How did you happen to show up here?"

He stopped and turned. "I didn't happen to anything. See that rental house across the street?"

I didn't have to see it... I knew it was there.

"We've had a stakeout here for the last four days. I've been wondering what the hell *you've* been doing here. Come to think of it, if you hadn't been here, we'd have picked her up without any shooting. She'd be alive if it weren't for you. How do you think that'll look in my report, Mr. Bigshot?"

Rosie gave me a look that told me to leave my gun in the holster. I was close to not caring about her look.

The ambulance pulled across the driveway, followed closely by a squad car and then two more. They ran into the garage. It was obvious to them there was nothing to do but remove the body.

Dunsley gestured at two of the patrolmen. "You guys break down the door to the house. Let's go find some evidence."

He turned back to me. "While they're doing that I'll find something to arrest you for." He turned to Rosie. "And you too, Miss Big City Detective."

"Good luck with that, Dunsley. Snark's been trying for weeks," I said.

As he walked away I called out to him. "Hey, Dunsley, you want a suggestion?"

"Don't need any suggestions from you."

"Well let me give you one anyway. You may not have noticed, but the person who lives in the house is lying on the ground here."

"So what?"

"So, I'd be willing to bet she has a key to the house."

He just stared at me for ten seconds and then told one of the officers to find the key. We all watched. The officer went through her purse and pulled out a key chain. He held it up to Dunsley, who nodded toward the house. "Let's take apart the house, then we'll come back here and search the car."

Rosie and I walked back to the Mustang, leaving Dunsley by himself in the garage with egg on his face. Before I got in, I turned to Rosie.

"Did you notice anything about Dunsley?"

"If you mean the pants... yes, same tan pants. But you're wearing the same jeans you had on yesterday, so..."

"Jeans are different than pants, and—"

"I don't see how."

"—and I have several pairs of jeans. I don't wear the same pair all the time."

She shrugged. "Maybe he does also."

"I doubt it. And after looking at how he dresses I doubt they get washed."

She smiled. "It's the cuffs, isn't it? Those are driving you nuts."

"No, it's not the cuffs, but that's not a look I like."

"Well, let that go, Spencer. We've got better things to worry about."

"Yeah, like getting some sleep." We headed for the hotel."

Chapter 35

Paul joined us on the balcony for Sunday morning breakfast. The blue sky was dotted with puffy white clouds slowly drifting eastward. I had called him when we got back and told him to sleep in. He didn't ask any questions... typical Paul. He knew we'd tell him in the morning. As we watched the boats, we told him what had happened.

He poured coffee and asked, "Are you worried about Dunsley?"

I laughed. "Not in the least. I think he should be worried about me."

"Yeah, not exactly protocol. What do you think, Rosie? Could he be nailed for what happened?"

She shrugged as she spread jelly on wheat toast. "He could, but I doubt it. It's not like he shot an innocent bystander... she was wanted in two states for murder. And she was holding a gun. This will be all over the evening papers. The headlines will be all about the Green Bay police catching a murderer. They're not going to spend any time on Dunsley."

"No, probably not." He finished his juice and a last bite of eggs. "Well, I guess I'll head back. Anything else you need from me?"

"Yes," I said. "I think you've earned some paid vacation time. I need you to spend a few days on Moonlight Bay."

"Did you say paid?"

"I did. You interested?"

"Sounds great! You have room in your cottage?"

Rosie laughed.

"Did I miss something?" he asked.

"Yes. You missed him buying the cottage next to him."

The bells on the bridge started to sound.

"That worked out nice."

"But there's one drawback," I said.

"I knew it was too good to be true. What's the drawback?"

"You have a roommate."

"What's her name?"

Rosie almost choked on her coffee. "Dream on."

"I'm still in… as long as I don't have to share a bed. Who's the roommate?"

"You'll see. Let's pack and get out of here."

***

An hour later we were on the road, and I was looking forward to spending the next week doing all the nothing that Stosh was complaining about. We dropped off the rental car, and Rosie called the captain and got permission to take another week off. After a few days, Paul could drive Stosh back to Chicago.

We pulled into my drive at a little after eleven, and Paul parked alongside. Rosie and I dropped our bags on the deck and walked Paul over to meet his roommate. Stosh answered the door, and Paul's jaw dropped. We all met back on my deck fifteen minutes later and, with drinks in hand, told Paul the story. I'd never get tired of telling it.

***

It was Paul's first time in Door County, so we showed him the sights, from the lighthouses to the goats on the roof of Al Johnson's restaurant. But we also did a lot of sitting on the deck. That was something I could do forever. As the sun tracked across the sky, the colors of the water and the shadows through the trees constantly changed. All but one of us enjoyed the sights and sounds of Moon-light Bay.

The only news we had of the case were calls from the captain and Iverson. Green Bay had fired a bullet from Victoria's gun and sent it to Chicago. Snark must have hated that, but the department had the other two bullets. All of the bullets matched—they were all from Victoria's gun. Iverson told me that the search of Victoria's car had turned up another gun, a .38. It had been fired, and hers were the only prints on it. I asked if the house search found the file from the agency. He said nothing of importance had been found. Neither had Mrs. Bell.

Stosh spent most of his deck time napping. We were doing exactly that when my phone rang Thursday afternoon. It was Iverson.

"What are you doing, Spencer?"

"My favorite thing—nothing."

"How would you like to do not nothing?"

I looked out at the bay through the large picture window. "That would depend."

"A hiker found a body."

"Ah, trouble is picking up in paradise. But I've had my share of bodies for a while. Why don't you take care of this one yourself? I don't need a new case."

"That's the trouble... it's not a new case. It's Mrs. Bell."

He let that sink in while I mentally said goodbye to my bay.

"Okay, tell me."

"The call came in twenty minutes ago. A woman hiker found a body in the growth off a path. She saw what looked like a leg sticking out from under the bushes. Not only did it look like a leg... it was. She didn't want to see any more and called us. My officer was there in ten minutes and identified her from her driver's license."

"Where?"

"That's the ironic part of this. Ten minutes from you... the Ridges."

The Ridges was a nature sanctuary with hiking trails that was best known for its many species of orchids. I wondered for a few

seconds about why Victoria had chosen a location so close to me.
And Iverson's ten minutes was an exaggeration… it was more
like five.

"I assume you've notified Snark."

"Yes, he's sending Dunsley. He'll be here in about an hour."

"Well, that'll be fun."

"He won't be happy to see you either, but this *is* his case."

"Unfortunately for Mrs. Bell."

"Play nice, Spencer."

***

I asked Paul if he wanted to join us and got an enthusiastic yes. Rosie got Stosh as I got ready. We took Paul's rental. The back seat of
the Mustang was pretty tight.

There were three police cars and an ambulance in the lot at the
visitor's center. I showed my ID to the officer stationed at the start
of the path, and he told us it was about a ten-minute walk. The day
was warmer than usual, and the air was heavy without a breeze.
The temperature immediately dropped as we entered the forest, and
the change in humidity was noticeable. I told them all about the
orchids, and pointed out several species along the way. There were
thirty-three species in Door County, and twenty-five had been found
in the sanctuary. May and June were the prime growing months.

"This would be a beautiful walk if it weren't for the reason,"
said Rosie.

The afternoon sun was filtering through the trees, and a heavy
smell of plants and pollen was in the air.

After about five minutes a woman passed us walking back to the
parking lot. She looked upset and just nodded at us without saying
hello.

Iverson, two officers, and two paramedics were standing on the
path. He said hello and pointed into the trees. It took me a few seconds to find the foot.

"That's not real obvious," I said. "How did your hiker find that?"

"She was looking for orchids, so was looking at the undergrowth."

"I assume that was her we passed on the trail."

"Yeah, I got all she had, which was very little, and told her Dunsley would be contacting her."

"Mind if I look at the body?"

"Go ahead. But Snark told me not to touch anything until Dunsley got here, so be careful."

I walked to the body and took a minute to look around. Some of the vegetation was broken, but there had been several people walking to the body since it had been put there. The vegetation and undergrowth within a few feet of the path was low to the ground. It got thicker and taller as it led into the pine trees where the body was. There wasn't a path of broken vegetation, so the body had been carried rather than dragged to where it was.

I pushed back the branches that were over her body and looked without touching. She was lying on her back and wearing a white blouse and blue slacks. There were two bullet entrance holes in the white blouse with dried brown patches around the holes. I wanted to move her arm to see if rigor mortis was present, but I didn't have gloves, and I decided to wait for Dunsley before I touched her. As I was looking, a maggot crawled out of her nose.

Chapter 36

Dunsley and his evidence tech and another detective arrived forty minutes later. He gave me a look that told me what he thought of me and then ignored me. He turned to Iverson.

"What's he doing here?" he asked.

"I invited him," said Iverson.

Evidently Dunsley didn't argue with chiefs. He just nodded.

"Who's the rest of these people?"

Iverson introduced Stosh and Paul. He didn't bother shaking hands.

"Has the body been disturbed, Chief?"

"Not since we've been here."

"Where's the lady who found her?"

"Wasn't sure when you'd get here, so I told her she could leave. My officer has a statement, and you can talk to her anytime."

He nodded and looked at his tech. "Let's have a look."

As they walked into the woods, Rosie came over and stood next to me. "You don't need to ask… same pants."

"Really? I hadn't noticed."

"I'm going to keep it to myself that you're fixated on another guy's pants."

I laughed. Stosh and Iverson followed Dunsley into the woods.

The tech took several photos and then Dunsley started clearing branches and undergrowth from the body.

"Jesus!" Dunsley yelled. "There's maggots on her face!"

Rosie, Paul, and I walked closer to get a better look. "You new at this, Dunsley?" I managed not to smile.

He was still trying to ignore me.

Her head was turned with the left side to the ground. Dunsley knelt next to her and rolled her head straight. There were more maggots in and around her left ear and on the ground. He had rolled her head easily, so no rigor mortis, which under normal conditions takes three days or so to leave the body.

Dunsley jumped up. "That's disgusting!"

No one responded.

"Hey Dunsley," I said. "You going to collect the maggots?"

"Why the hell would I want to do that?"

"They're evidence."

He shook his head. "Thanks for inviting him, Chief. He's a big help."

I took that as a no.

"Well, that wraps this up. What a shame," Dunsley said. "At least we got the murderer."

The tech took more photos, and the other detective took notes. They finished a half hour later, and Dunsley walked back to the path and told the paramedics they could take the body. The other detective helped the tech pack up his gear.

I leaned over to Iverson and asked him to keep Dunsley busy for a minute. As the paramedics walked to the body, I followed. I held up a finger and moved in front of them, making them a shield between the body and Dunsley. I kneeled and unbuttoned the top two buttons of Mrs. Bell's blouse. I wanted to see the entry holes. They were closed over and surrounded by the same dark-brown colored dried blood that was on her blouse. I stood, nodded to them, and walked back to the path where Dunsley was talking to Iverson.

Rosie and Paul had moved ten feet to the side where they could watch what I was doing.

"Whenever you're ready, Chief," I said to Iverson.

The five of us left Dunsley and his crew standing on the path. We were quiet until we rounded a few corners and were well out of hearing range.

"What a shame that all this beauty has to be spoiled by humans," I said.

"That man is an idiot," Paul said.

"No argument here," replied Stosh. "And he'll take all of the credit for solving the crime."

"He probably will," I said. "Too bad the crime isn't solved."

"What the hell does that mean?" Stosh asked.

"Victoria didn't do this."

Chapter 37

I refused to talk until we were back on the deck with a beverage of choice. Stosh's wasn't his first choice, but he made do. I had time to think about Mrs. Bell on the way back, and I hadn't changed my mind. The pieces just didn't fit.

"So, please relieve the suspense," Iverson said.

I took a drink. "Victoria killed two people, or at least she thought she did, by walking up to them and pulling the trigger. In Stosh's case, that was a person about a foot taller than her and much bigger. She knew where they were and sought them out. How would she have known Mrs. Bell would be at the sanctuary? That wasn't something that was planned. Even her own husband was surprised she wasn't home to greet him."

Iverson spoke up. "Maybe it was just coincidence. We already know Petrace was up here and was probably familiar with the peninsula. Maybe she came back and happened to run into Bell and then followed her."

"Those maybes might be valid," I said, "except for the fact that Mrs. Bell wasn't killed at the sanctuary."

Even the birds were silent.

"So where was she killed?" Stosh asked.

"No clue. My crystal ball is broken too. But wherever it was it was somewhere else, and she was moved."

"Why do you think that?" asked Iverson.

"I don't think it, I know it."

Rosie came over and gave me a hug.

"What's that for?" I asked.

She smiled. "That's because I know how you know! You're a genius."

"Let's not get crazy here," said Stosh. "I've got enough problems with him. How about one of you lets us in on the secret?"

Rosie looked at me. "Maggots?"

"Maggots."

"Maggots?" asked Stosh. "What the hell are you talking about? What do maggots have to do with anything?"

"Everything," I said. "There were maggots in her nose and ears. They like body fluids and soft tissue."

"Dunsley was right," Stosh said. "That *is* disgusting. But so what?"

"So, there were no maggots on her chest. The wounds had closed, and the blood had dried. If she had been shot at the sanctuary there would have been maggots in the wound, and they would have kept it open. She was shot somewhere else and moved to the sanctuary."

"I've never heard that before," said Iverson. "But it might make sense. How do you know that?"

"Read a book about it... *The Stories Insects Tell*. There's a scientist in Hawaii researching how bodies are affected by bugs and insects. It's pretty fascinating."

"Sounds pretty crazy," Stosh said. "You care to explain?"

Paul was sitting with his eyes closed, listening to every word.

"He has found that certain insects show up at different stages of a decaying body. Flies depend on decaying matter for food. A decaying body is a feast. They're very aggressive and can show up minutes after death if a body is exposed to the elements. They like warm moist areas to lay their eggs, like body orifices. We all saw the maggots on her head. Why weren't there any on the wound?"

With his eyes still closed, Paul said, "Because there weren't any flies where she was shot, like indoors."

"Right. But even indoors the flies would eventually find her. So she must have been somewhere where the flies couldn't get at her."

"Like the trunk of a car," Rosie said.

I raised my bottle to her. "Like the trunk of a car, which would make sense because she had to be moved from wherever she was shot to the sanctuary."

"So why not Petrace?" Iverson asked.

"Two reasons. Because the flies find a body almost immediately and lay their eggs, and then it only takes a day or so for the maggots to hatch. So she had to have been put there within the last three or four days."

"Your logic fell apart, Spencer," said Rosie.

I finished a long drink and shook my head. "No. It's just missing a piece. This is all about the food chain. The maggots feed on the decaying body. Then within another couple of days the second wave arrives to feed on the maggots."

They all looked at me expectantly.

"Beetles. And there weren't any beetles there yet. So Mrs. Bell was moved to the sanctuary sometime after Monday at the earliest. And Victoria was killed Saturday night. She could have shot her, but she sure didn't move her."

"You can tell all that from bugs?" asked Stosh.

"Yup, and a few other things like air temperature and rain and soil content. With those we could narrow it down even more."

"Well then do that," said Stosh.

"Our scientist in Hawaii could—I can't."

A motor started up at my neighbor's dock.

"You said there are two reasons it couldn't be Petrace," Iverson said. "What's the second?"

"She's not big enough. Mrs. Bell was carried, at least part of the way. Someone picked her up and put her into a trunk and then took her out. She's about my height. That would either take someone a lot bigger and stronger than Victoria, or she had help. And she's been a solo act with everything else."

Stosh got up to get another beer. "Anybody want another?"

I was the only taker. When he got back, I said, "And there's a third reason. I asked her where Mrs. Bell was. She had no idea what I was talking about."

"So when was she shot?" Iverson asked.

"Don't know. I can only tell you a timeframe for when she was put there. Dunsley was easily able to move her head, so rigor mortis was gone. It starts within a few hours of death and is full within two or so days. Within four to six days it's gone. So she was killed sometime between Thursday and Sunday. My guess would be Thursday night. Why keep someone alive and give them a chance to escape?"

"So rigor tells us when she was killed, and the bugs tell us when she was moved," Rosie said.

"Exactly."

"So who killed her?" Stosh asked.

"Good question," I said. "Who has a motive?" They were all quiet. "This has all been about a baby. Maybe it still is."

"How sure are you about all of this, Spencer?" Iverson asked.

"About the things I've told you? Positive. There's no doubt that Mrs. Bell was killed somewhere else and moved to the sanctuary and that Victoria couldn't have done that. She shot Mrs. Hanover and Stosh, and she may have shot Mrs. Bell, but I doubt it. It makes more sense that the person who moved her shot her."

"So how do we find that person?"

"Keep shaking the trees. And one of the trees I'd like to shake is your breakfast buddy, Chief."

"He's not going to like that."

"You said you think he's a standup guy, right?"

"Yup."

"You think he'd cover up something?"

He shook his head. "No. He's not happy about outsiders telling him what to do, but he's after the truth as much as we are."

I raised my bottle. "Then let's go shake his tree." I finished off the bottle.

"When do you want to do that?"

"Well, I'd like to talk with Mr. Bell first. I'll do that tomorrow morning. Could you set up a meeting with Snark for the afternoon? There's some pieces missing. Maybe I'll get something from Mr. Bell. If not, I'll just ask questions, one of which will be why Dunsley lied about his time with Peters."

"Sure. I'll give him a call. Should I tell him you're coming?"

I laughed. "Let's keep that a secret until we walk in the door."

"He's not going to be happy with me."

"Welcome to the club. I'll let you know if I get anything from Bell."

***

We all went out for dinner and talked about the case. Rosie, Paul, and I continued that talk as we sat on the deck watching twilight turn into night. Our resident loon was having a conversation with the crickets.

We went over my timeline several times trying to find a flaw. When we couldn't find one, we talked about who could have killed Mrs. Bell and decided that lawsuits tend to ramp things up a bit.

Chapter 38

Rosie and I got to the Bell's house by nine thirty. Mr. Bell was anxious to help. We offered our condolences. He assured us that his wife would not have gone to the sanctuary without telling him. That was a place she loved to visit in the spring, and they had talked about going, but she had assured him she was going to be home for lunch. That was all I was looking for from Mr. Bell. I was satisfied. We spent the next hour just talking… he was glad for the company.

As we were pulling out of the drive, the phone rang. It was Iverson. I parked at the curb.

"We've got a meeting at one," he said. "Have you seen Bell?"

"We just left there. I'm satisfied that there was no way his wife went to the sanctuary willingly."

"Yeah, that seemed likely."

"I just wanted to be sure."

"Right. Here's something else. When I was setting up the meeting, Snark told me they got the ballistics back on the bullets that killed Mrs. Bell. They're a match to Victoria's .38."

I looked at Rosie and smiled.

"Does that help any, Spencer?"

"It's the last piece in the puzzle, Chief. We'll meet you in the parking lot."

I told Rosie about the bullets as we looked for a place to have lunch.

Chapter 39

Chief Snark was glad to see his buddy, but his smile disappeared when Rosie and I walked into his office.

"Blindsided is bad enough... but by a friend?"

"Couldn't be helped," said Iverson. "Would you have agreed if you had known?"

"Probably not." He waved to chairs. "Okay, this better be good."

"I think it is," said Iverson.

An hour later Chief Snark had agreed to a meeting at four. He'd have Mrs. Peters and Detective Dunsley attend.

***

They were already in the conference room when we arrived. We didn't get a warm greeting. Dunsley looked disgusted and said, "Haven't we had enough of you?" To say Mrs. Peters looked surprised was an understatement.

"What are the Blaines doing here?" she asked.

Snark looked at us and made the introductions. "This is Detective Lonnigan with the Chicago police and Mr. Manning, a private detective from Chicago." He pointed at Iverson. "That's Chief Iverson from Door."

I wish I had a picture of Peters' face... I would have hung it in my office. There was no hint of a smile.

Snark nodded at me. "Your show."

I sat next to Dunsley.

"Wait a minute," said Dunsley. "His show? Since when do you let an outsider run things around here? I'm not staying for this." He stood.

"Sit down, Dunsley," said Snark.

He slowly sat with a look of amazement.

"Go ahead, Mr. Manning."

"This all started with Lieutenant Powolski, my friend and Detective Lonnigan's boss, being shot in Chicago. We let it be believed that he had been killed. By chance, I happened upon his history with your agency, Mrs. Peters, and the payments he had been making to support a struggling mother."

"Wait a minute," Peters said. "If that's what this is about, I don't—"

I held up my hand. "Don't worry, that's not what this is about."

The smile was back. "Good, because I assure you that all is—"

I stopped her again. "I don't need any more of your assurances." The smile disappeared.

"As we kept looking into your agency, I discovered the relationship between the Powolskis and the Hanovers and the Freys and the Bells."

She sat straight up in her chair, belligerently. "That's just not true. I don't know how—"

"Mrs. Peters, this will go a lot better if you stop interrupting."

She sat back, but she was fuming.

I continued. "No, you don't know how. I'll tell you. There was a break-in at your office a few weeks ago. Someone was found unconscious on the floor. That was me."

She jumped up. "I want him arrested! He just confessed. Arrest him now!"

Snark didn't move.

"Detective Dunsley, do something!"

Dunsley opened his mouth, but it quickly closed. She sat back down.

"I found a file with all of those names on it, along with Victoria Petrace, and I found an employee file for Victoria. With a little more looking we figured out that Victoria had been an employee and a birth mother… and a birth mother who wanted her baby back." I let that sink in. "You really should change your locks when you fire someone. She was already in your office when I went in. The door was unlocked."

"What was she doing in there?"

"Looking for her baby, just like she was when you had that argument in your office. She found the file with the names and started going after them. When she didn't find her baby she shot them."

"That's just absurd," she said. "Her baby is now ten years old. She wasn't looking for a baby."

"Yes, she was. In her mind, it was still a baby. You need to be more careful in your screening process. We kept looking and discovered that Mrs. Hanover had been murdered. The Frey's garage was burned down last week, and Mrs. Bell was kidnapped and killed. All of the names on the file had been dealt with, two of them killed by Petrace."

Dunsley found his courage. "That's all too bad, but what does it have to do with us? Victoria confessed to the murders and ballistics shows that the bullets match her gun." He smiled. "You can't disagree with that—the test was done in your lab!" He was pretty confident and looking full of himself.

"That's all true, but Victoria didn't kill Mrs. Bell."

"What the hell do you mean? Of course she did."

I slowly shook my head. "No, she didn't."

"How do you know that?"

"Your friendly maggots," I said with a smile. I explained the insect evidence.

He wasn't going to accept my explanation. "That's all a lot of crap. But for the moment, let's assume it's true. Why are we sitting in here? We should be out looking for whoever did that."

"I think we're done looking," I said. "Here's what someone did. They kidnapped Mrs. Bell Thursday night and either killed her then or sometime before Sunday. Then they brought her to the sanctuary and dropped her in the bushes where the hiker found her. Because of the insect evidence, we know she was moved by someone after she was killed, probably the same someone who killed her." I stared at Dunsley. "I think the someone was you."

He laughed and slapped the table with his palm. "That's the most absurd thing I've ever heard. It was Petrace. You probably haven't heard, Manning, but we found a gun in her car. There's a match. The bullets that killed Bell came from her gun."

I shrugged. "I'll give you all that, except she didn't fire the gun."

"You're crazy. Her prints were on it. Chief, are you going to continue with this witch hunt?"

"Let him finish."

"I'll give you that too," I said. "But I think the only time she touched that gun was after she was dead."

"Yeah? How the hell did she do that?"

"She had a little help." I let that hang in the quiet room. "After I suggested that you didn't have to break down the door, the officers went to search the house. You told them when they were done with that to come back and do the car. The paramedics were out in the street. And Rosie and I walked back to my car, leaving you alone with the body. You could easily have put her prints on the gun and planted it in the car. And someone had to get Mrs. Bell in and out of a trunk and carry her into the woods. Victoria couldn't have done that. Even *you* would have trouble… but you could."

He huffed. "What kind of dream world do you live in, Manning? That's all a nice story, but you have no evidence. I don't know how you do things in Chicago, but up here we need evidence."

"When you stood up, I noticed you had a green stain on your pants. Where did you get that?"

"How the hell would I know? Just about anywhere."

"Like the sanctuary?"

"Yeah, like that. When I found those damned maggots… I probably kneeled down in the leaves."

"You probably did. Mind if we check your pant cuffs?"

"What?"

"I'd like to check your cuffs. Lots of interesting things get stuck in there when you're say... out in the woods."

"Yes, I mind. What difference does it make? You know I was out in the woods."

"Humor me."

He laughed. "I'm not going to humor you or anyone else. Why don't you—"

"Then we'll do it the hard way," said Snark. He opened the folder in front of him and held up another envelope. "Search warrant for your person."

"Are you kidding me! What the hell is this?"

Snark started to get up to hand the warrant to Dunsley.

"Okay, okay, what do I care?" He stood.

I asked Chiefs Snark and Iverson to come over and be witnesses. I slowly unfolded his left cuff. There were pieces of dead leaves and lint. The right one had the same and also something that looked like a small twig.

Dunsley was watching intently. "Okay, satisfied? I suppose you're going to tell me you can prove I was at the sanctuary by looking at those. Well, I'll help you out... I was there, and I have you three as witnesses." There was a big smile on his face.

I held up the twig and looked at it closely. "This is very interesting."

No one spoke.

"Dunsley, you didn't notice because Chief Iverson was keeping you busy, but after you walked away from the body I went over and took a close look. There was a dead grasshopper next to Mrs. Bell... looked like it had been squashed when her body was dropped."

He shrugged. "So what?"

"So, I picked it up and saved it. That grasshopper has a missing leg. Looks like we've found it." I handed it to Snark.

Dunsley's mouth dropped open. "This is all about a dead grasshopper? You're insane! I got that when I was looking at the maggots."

I shook my head. "No, that grasshopper died a violent death when the body was dropped. It had been dead several days by the time I picked it up."

"That's the craziest thing I've ever heard," said Dunsley.

It sounded kind of crazy to me too.

I glanced at Chief Snark. He looked skeptical, but let me continue. Dunsley sat back down, looking smug. "If we're done here…"

"Not quite," I said. "The file I saw in your office, Mrs. Peters, is missing. I saw it but I didn't take it."

She looked confused. "Then who did?"

"Victoria. She was the one who knocked me out. She had the file and had the names of all the people who were targeted. But that file wasn't in her house or her car. Or at least it wasn't found by the search team."

"Well, then where is it?"

"Good question. Where is it, Dunsley?"

He laughed again. "Man, you're just not going to come down to earth."

"I think it was either in her house or her car. And now it's in yours, unless you got rid of it, which would have been the wise thing to do."

"Yeah, good luck with that."

"And if we search your house? Are we going to find it?"

He looked worried for just a second, but recovered quickly. "You'd need a warrant."

Snark opened his folder again and held up the next envelope.

Dunsley didn't look worried. He probably *had* gotten rid of it. He waved his hand. "Be my guest. Can we go now?"

"Not quite," I said. "Mrs. Bell was killed anywhere from three to five days before she was dropped in the sanctuary. During that time she had to be somewhere isolated because the wounds had time to close over before the flies found her. Since she had to be transported to the sanctuary, I'm guessing that spot was a trunk… and I don't care how careful someone is, you can't get someone who's been shot in and out of a trunk without leaving trace evidence."

He laughed again. "I suppose you have a warrant for my car too."

Chief pulled out another envelope and handed it to me.

Dunsley waved his hand in the air. "Knock yourselves out." He looked very smug.

"I didn't think you'd be dumb enough to use your own car." I turned to Mrs. Peters. "Which is why this warrant is for *your* car." I handed it to her.

She started to cry. "He blackmailed me. He said he knew something was going on and he wanted in on it. I told him about—"

"Shut up you idiot! They don't have anything!"

"Quiet, Dunsley," said Snark. "Please continue, Mrs. Peters."

She took a handkerchief out of her purse and wiped her eyes. She was sobbing as she continued. "I told him about the trouble the Bells were causing, and I'd cut him in if he'd help. He came up with the plan. He said we could blame it all on Victoria."

Dunsley got up and reached for Peters. I pushed him back down in the chair and took all the air out of him.

Chief Snark looked almost as deflated as Dunsley as he reached for the phone and punched a button. A minute later two officers came into the room. "Gentry, read these two their rights and book them for murder."

Gentry looked confused. "Um, which two, Chief?"

"The woman and Dunsley."

"Dunsley?"

Snark took a deep breath, let it out slowly, and nodded.

On his way out, I said, "You really should change your pants once in a while, Dunsley."

When they were gone, Snark turned to us and said, "I guess an apology is in order."

I smiled. "No need, Chief. Glad to help."

We shook hands and Iverson told me I had earned some time off. I told him I was trying to do that but he kept calling me. He asked when we were leaving, and I refused to answer on the grounds that he might think of something else. We all laughed and said goodbye.

Rosie said she wanted me to take the fastest way back to the cottage, but I had to disappoint her. I had one stop to make.

When we got in the car she asked, "So, where's the grasshopper?"

I started the car. "What grasshopper?"

"That wasn't a grasshopper leg?"

"Yes, I think it was. But I have no idea where the rest of it is."

She shook her head, laughing. "I should have known."

Chapter 40

You coming in?" I asked.

"Sure! Sounds like fun," Rosie said.

We walked across the street, and I held the door for her. Sarah was surprised to see us and greeted us with a smile.

"What are you guys doing here?"

"We're here to take you for a ride," I said.

"That sounds like fun, but Mrs. Peters wouldn't like it. She's not here, but I can't leave before five."

"I don't think she'll mind," I said with a smile.

She laughed. "You don't know her… she'd mind. And I need this job."

"That's the last thing on her mind, Sarah. She's been arrested."

"What? Arrested! What for?"

"Murder."

"You're kidding."

"Nope. So why don't you lock up, and we'll tell you about it on the way."

She agreed and asked where we were going. I told her it was a surprise.

***

We told her the story on the way to Aunt Rose's. The only thing we left out was why we were going to Rose's. As we drove she raved about the scenery, and we were surprised to learn she had never been up here. As I pulled into the drive of the inn, she remarked about how lovely it was.

We found Aunt Rose in the dining room, dusting.

"Spencer, Rosie! I didn't know you were coming. I look awful, and you have company."

We both laughed.

"You look great, Rose," said Rosie.

"And who is this?" Rose asked.

Rosie held out her hand. "This is Sarah Leek, the newest client of the Spencer Manning Employment Agency."

Sarah looked confused.

"Let's go out on the porch and I'll explain," I said.

I did, and Sarah acted like she just was hit with a surprise party.

"What do you think, Sarah?" I asked.

"I don't know what to think."

Aunt Rose stood and said, "Let me show you around, and we'll chat some more."

Rosie and I rocked until Sarah got back and sat next to Rosie.

"Now what do you think?" I asked.

"I think it's wonderful. It pays more than I'm making now! And Aunt Rose is a sweetheart. But it's a long drive from Green Bay, and I don't have a car."

Amelie jumped up in her lap and got comfortable.

"Meet Amelie," I said. "You have her approval."

We all laughed as Sarah stroked Amelie's back.

"How about if the drive was twenty minutes?" I asked.

She laughed. "I'm beginning to think you're a miracle worker, but not even you can do that."

"I can, and I will. I own a cottage on the other side of the peninsula, and I'm looking for a renter."

"I can't believe it," she said. "But I still don't have a car."

"How did you get home on weekends?" Rosie asked.

"I took the bus to Appleton and Dad picked me up."

"Well, I happen to know where there will soon be a couple of cars for sale pretty cheap."

She looked sad and shook her head. "I don't have money to buy a car, Spencer, even if it's cheap. I send every spare dollar home."

"I'll help you out. How much is your rent?"

"Five hundred a month."

"Wow, that works out great! The rent at the cottage is four hundred. I'll buy the car and you can make payments and still be money ahead."

She shook her head, like she was trying to wake from a dream. "Is this all real?"

"It is. Would you like to see the cottage?"

"Sure!"

"Okay, we'll come back here for dinner, and you can meet Maxine."

"Who's Maxine?"

"Let's go. We'll talk while we drive." I found Aunt Rose and invited ourselves to dinner.

"Do you think she'll take the job, Spencer?"

"It's a done deal, Aunt Rose."

She gave me a hug. "I don't know what I'd do without you."

"That goes both ways."

***

Sarah loved the cottage and the bay, and we assured her that the current occupant would be leaving. As we walked back to the car, Rosie warned her about the neighbor.

Please go to *Death's Door* page on Amazon.com
and post a review.

Also, sign up for Spencer news at RickPolad.com.
Click on Contact Us

Acknowledgements

This book would not exist without the help and support of several special people. To my first readers and friends, Mike Polad, Carol Deleskiewicz, Gary Lindberg, Ellen Tullar Purviance, and John Zelman. Thanks for your edits and input. Any remaining errors are the property of the author. And, as before, to all my friends and readers who have asked for more Spencer, my undying thanks.

About the Author

Rick Polad worked as a geologist, taught Earth Science and Astronomy at a junior college for twenty-nine years, and volunteered with the Coast Guard Auxiliary on Lake Michigan. Rick edited the English version of Living With Nuclei, the memoirs of Japanese physicist, Motoharu Kimura, and currently works as chief editor for his publisher, Calumet Editions. Rick also worked at Fermilab, the country's highest energy particle accelerator, and currently volunteers at Microtrace, one of the world's premier forensic chemistry labs. You can find more information on the Spencer Manning mysteries at rickpolad.com.

www.ingramcontent.com/pod-product-compliance
Lightning Source LLC
Chambersburg PA
CBHW022012010726
47494CB00003B/1000